CABALIFORNIANS

PJ TOWER

CABALIFORNIANS

Paperback ISBN: 979-8-8229-3818-2
eBook ISBN: 979-8-8229-3819-9

TABLE OF CONTENTS

0

PROLOGUE

I am going to have to try to kill someone for the second time in my life. It's not entirely my fault, just the way this life has been. I apologize in advance for being me, but it's no longer a course I travel alone. I wish there were a different way, but the tides move of their own accord, and I have been dragged back to the depths, drowning in the unknown.

In return, this life wasn't ready for me. It wasn't ready for the fortitude I was bringing with me. It wasn't ready for me to pay in blood, then jump up and start screaming for more—the spirit of a Viking, adrift with a heart for war.

As I write this, I am certainly going to lose my job in this when and where; no doubt it won't be long. The job was supposed to be a dream come true but has since turned into a living nightmare. My family and I currently occupy space in California, where my money is everyone's money, so I need to work twice as hard to have half as much. The empire no doubt has gained the West.

A previous eighteen-year career, just a short while ago, was peaking, the cabal taking an ample share. Despite that, goals had been reached.

Unfortunately, the relentless pursuit of a deeply examined life brought about much personal turmoil, yet answers were coming. The demons that lived within were being forced to the light. My past brought a raging storm, then death, addiction, and sickness brought the hurricane ashore.

Life spiraled out of control; the harder I fought, the faster it spun. The storm continued to grow, and in short order, I found myself shipwrecked and brutally beaten against the rocky shore of the Pacific.

Thus a face-down life began, day after day, week after week. Then month after month. Only undeserved grace kept me breathing.

I was stranded on an island of despair, the horizon never changing or yielding the secrets of tomorrow to the hidden eye of hope. I was cast away by life, left to face my jinn, mara, and self alone.

I have lived on the fringe of insanity for too many years now and fear I can no longer hang on. It claimed my childhood, stained my adolescence, and holds my life in chains. I either have to let go and welcome the abyss of madness or claw my way out, despite the journey beyond. This island of many minds can no longer be; I am splitting in two.

The following pages tell of addiction, despair, and darkness; of loss and where all my trouble began, a place where worlds collide and grow of their own volition. These pages detail the first time I set out to take a life and when one was lost because of me, hard times from a hard life—a heavy heart for a young boy in the world as it was, enduring things there shouldn't be firsts of, much less seconds. Unfortunately, the soil I was grown in was watered often with my own blood and tears, bringing much discomfort from bones of truth—not a gospel account, but certainly a tumultuous beginning of a boy's life.

Yet who really knows? Reality is unquestionably thin these days.

J-

1

UNDER THE MOUNTAIN

The sweat ran down my back as I pedaled across the river bridge, knowing work was only minutes away. It was 6:28 a.m. on a Friday morning in February, and it was cold—in the mid-twenties. There was no snow, but the wind chill from the river was biting; it brought teeth, giving the weather callous, harsh life. To keep it at bay, I pushed myself and kept my legs pumping until I hit the bridge. It was a cold and painful seven miles, and I needed to stop and stand, breathing deep, despite the frigid temperature. I pulled the brakes and dismounted, leaning my bike against the rail, and looked out at the water, stretching my back against the barrier and shaking the muscles in my legs loose. Daybreak had yet to come, but the sky was growing lighter. Mist rose off the river, adding a dramatic effect to the sparse plant life and leafless oak trees along the bank: life on hold.

The pedal down the bike trail was a kick start to the life I was chasing, and the street urchin that survived from childhood was never going to let go of his love for two wheels. I knew enough to not let opportunity pass me by, barely-but I was trying to seize it and hang on as best as I could.

"Opportunities don't come often, and if dey do, you haf ta jump right in. Adapt quick, midstride, change direction. God don't have time for you to be messin' around when he giving you something to do. Das' what repent mean. You gonna change direction in life a few times, little missus; you hear me? God gonna bless you afta you listen sho' enough." My old memaw bustled with enthusiasm.

I could still hear the sound of the archaic woman's voice telling all the young hens in our family how to walk a righteous path from her tiny kitchen table with a plate of applesauce cake for each. If I were a smarter lad, I would have known the tiny table at Memaw's was intentional, to keep everyone close, leaned in and huddled together as the old sage imparted her wisdom. I hung around hoping for table scraps after eating my crumbs and heard many of her ideas as a youngling. She was a devout woman of faith and raised all her children and younglings to follow in her footsteps. Her astute teachings often fell by the wayside, and many only listened to her briefly. Yet I heard her stern but kind and soothing voice in my head often as of late.

The truth, though, was that she wasn't my memaw, and I wasn't one of her hens.

"Hard work ain't the only thing you gonna haf to do in this life. When the Lord come calling, you best answer da door. He ain't gonna wait fa eva on you, chile. You set your stuff down, and you RUN, girl!"

I heard the old woman's thick and happy laugh as she counseled her brood, her hens bristling and guffawing at her ageless and loving guidance.

I, on the other hand, stood by the kitchen doorway, eyes bulging and ears burning, with not a single idea of what any of it actually meant yet. I was a bastard child of her late husband and his alley cat, my real mother, who died of a heroin overdose when I was five. I stayed in the family house with memaw and her hens until my aunt Jo and most recent beau snatched me up a few years later.

The biting weather and my burning thighs pulled me back to the present. I was lucky to still be breathing and knew it, but even the smallest shred of gratitude was difficult to hang on to at times. My most recent attempt at sobriety was turning a hearty ten days old. I made it to work, daily at that, since starting the new job back in January, and I was no longer drinking until I dropped. At least not yet—it was cycling down at the moment, but the roller coaster was always moving. I was going to the gym on a regular basis, riding my bicycle to work a few times a week, and I thought I had finally turned a corner on the road to recovery. A new chapter, it seemed, might be finally dawning—one less of quiet despair and dysfunction.

Or so I thought.

The day dragged on, eventually ending the same way it started: sober, confused, and cold. Later that evening, my quartet was heading to Disney on Ice at the newly constructed arena downtown. The invitees had a suite, and they were kind enough to extend the courtesy to our family. I wanted to join in but felt hesitant; there was a tug of emotion from thoughts not yet developed. Some call it intuition. My wife took a hard stance, demanding it would be rude if I did not attend; thus we loaded up the car and hit the road despite my internal warnings.

We arrived at the arena and found an exclusive entrance for suite holders. The line was short, and we passed through security quickly, then were ushered to a private elevator. The suite door was open, and smiling faces waited with open arms as they welcomed us in. The facility was only a year old, and the suite itself was top notch. It whistled of a better life with more expensive habits. There was a refrigerator stocked with water bottles, a bar top in the middle of the room with stools around it, and two large wall-mounted flat screens above the balcony seating. Everything glistened brightly, still favoring the look of an untarnished building. Directly in the front of the entry door was stadium seating with large comfortable leather chairs overlooking the arena. The kids were bouncing off the walls with excitement, as expected, but my suspicious nature was aroused. Our host greeted us, and introductions were made.

She was involved in mental health locally, and her employer gave use of the suite.

The alarm bells broke the silence in my thoughts, and the foreboding I felt earlier materialized; the oncoming semi cut loose in my mind, shattering the quiet winter night with a thundering air horn. No doubt I was in the middle of the road and about to be run down. Like a deer frozen in the headlights, I began to panic as the terror welled.

My skin started to crawl while my mind began winding up the scenario. I helped the kids settle in and offered to buy the adults some beverages as a measure of gratitude. The escape hatch opened, offering relief, as I took orders, then walked away. I needed space and something to drink.

How easily the fight was lost. The previous years were filled with similar attempts to break the cycle. None lasted.

I had to get out of the suite and have a look around, regardless. The other family and hostess were certainly harmless to my wife and children.

It was only me the Cabalifornians wanted.

The destructive march of thoughts began unfolding, trapping me in yet another nightmare. I could feel heat stir as anger began to climb. I kept up my smile as I picked up two twenty-four-ounce beers from the nearest vendor. The first was gone in seconds. What did they want? And why? That latter was always the one that hung me. Why? A crossroads of a question in life. One line of thinking would lead a way out of the fog to peace, freedom, and indifference. The other led down a road filled with self-pity, anger, resentment, and war. Thoughts and memories of different lives were slowly cracking the hard, clear surface of the present.

I pitched the empty cup and started in on the second beer, following the darker path opening in my mind.

The drink would keep my crawling nerves from melting down, but the thoughts began to twist my mind askew. Hypervigilance was at the tip of the iceberg, but I was well below the surface now. My mind was spinning and bent, my body headed for lockdown, and the intense feelings were swallowing me whole from the inside out. It was the howling fantods of dis-ease.

I chugged the rest of my second beer and went for a trifecta, scanning the crowds and walking slowly, on the lookout for my would-be persecutors. I made eye contact with a large tattooed man sporting a tank top and leaning against one of the coliseum's ornate pillars. He held my gaze far too long, watching my every move. No question they were out there. Was he one of them?

He stared back in discord, grunted, then looked in the other direction. I turned and headed into the crowd. Once I moved through the mass of bodies a fair distance, I found my own pillar and slid around the backside, mostly out of sight.

I watched the man from afar. He was casually leaning back, hands in pockets, and continued watching the crowd, then looked back in the opposite direction. His shoulders lifted up and settled back down as he sighed. A phone appeared in his hand, and he seemed to lose interest in his whereabouts and other people altogether.

I polished off what was left in my third cup and flipped it into a nearby waste bin, then went back to watching my man. I was shocked to see a young woman with her arms wrapped around him. She seemed to be talking quickly and with some animation. I slid closer—she was apologizing.

I turned and slipped into the nearest drink line, collected beverages for the suite, a fourth for myself, and headed back upstairs. The destructive fugue-like state of psychosis began to slowly loosen its grip. The alcohol lubricated the gears of my mind before they could overheat. I was restless and on alert, but my mind was finally starting to slow down. I went back to the suite and sat down with my children after distributing the drinks and tried to watch the show but couldn't shake the thoughts of the cabal.

Somebody knew. I could feel it, and my instincts were uncanny throughout the years of my life. Borderline clairvoyant uncanny. A stir of guilt welled slightly and measured into my heart a small cup of feeling. As I sat with my family, there was little doubt that my past was finally coming back to haunt me, and the Cabalifornians, real or imagined, were the group of humans that were hunting me down for it on the surface of my life.

Later that night, I felt relief flood my body, and my broken mind let the nightmare go as we made our way home after three-plus hours of spinning away in chaos. I was exhausted from the mental marathon and standing on a razor's edge of reality. Did my enemy have a face and a heartbeat or was I creating my own hell to live in?

Well into the wee hours of the morning, sleep finally came. My past and all the feelings that came with it were waiting on the other side of the darkness, haunting me.

2

BLOODY KNUCKLES

I was standing in my new third-grade classroom. Attendance had just been taken, and the bag of wrinkles leading the procession of heres and raised hands just kept squawking. The old crow was pecking at me. I needed to take my seat but only half listened from miles away. I watched the rain bounce off the weathered, rusty red pole that was in terrible need of a sanding and a fresh coat of paint—the flag bearer of the playground, the crusader, the standard Americana. I watched as it was slowly pummeled, one massive raindrop at a time. Portland was not a place of happiness and joy. Good mind had been evicted from residence in this land of sorrow and gray skies. Anxiety welled as I watched another raindrop collide violently with the pole. Then another drop crashed hard, and the feelings slid out, quietly, all on their own at first.

"No." A barely audible whisper, it was meant to put a halt to the feelings creeping up on me. It was meant to stop the rain. It was meant to defy where this life was heading.

"Excuse me, young man. Young man! Take your seat!" The gas bag tittered from her queendom of sterility and bleach. She was the lone voice of authority and experience, and defiance was most certainly not on her agenda today. All the kids turned and stared. I heard the shifting of chairs and could feel the multitude of eyes on my back. The anxiety shot through me as the sky broke and punished the flagpole in a gusting blast.

"NO!" I screamed and hit the window with both hands.

My fervor seemed to bring about a torrent sheet of rain that completely broke my will. A seed of depression sunk deep into the bowels of my soul. In another world, hushed silence ensued as gasps spoke directly to the type of authoritarian I was newly enslaved to for a handful of hours each day. I heard the sharp and angry click of heels grow louder as she crossed the room, then felt the painful tug at my ear as she escorted me out of her classroom.

On the walk down to the principal's office, the darkness within stirred again. The little beastie growing inside of me had something to shed his water on and care for as the depression spouted. The two would live together from now on. My Isaac and Ishmael.

Despite the day and any misgivings, I frequented a small deli on the way home from school. I usually managed to find a couple bucks here and there, often from Dick's wallet, and it only seemed fair to help myself.

If I didn't, who would?

The shop had a delicious selection of handmade chocolates that would temporarily cure my feelings about life.

"LOOK OUT! MOVE!" a panic-filled voice yelled, echoing off the sides of the buildings. He came flying in and sent his bike sideways to avoid impact as my brain finally engaged, and I skirted out of the way in the nick of time, jumping back into the doorway of the deli. The rear tire caught on a crack in the sidewalk as he slid the back end around, braking hard. The rider was thrown from the bike, crashing and skidding along the pavement as I watched in awe.

I will never forget the look on his face—pure bewilderment, like looking in a mirror, with my face reflecting the same. His backpack hit the ground and the boxed contents shot out, littering the pavement. They looked like little boxes of cologne and perfume. The kid came to a stop in a heap and lay still as stone for a minute. Suddenly, he jumped up with heavy road rash on one forearm and blood seeping from it. He shot a stream of curses my way under his breath and limped at first, then scrambled to pick up his bounty. He wasted no time once on his feet. I broke from my trance and began gathering up his stray goods. He snatched a blue box that read "Coolwater" from my hand, shoved it in his pack, looked me square in the face, and smiled.

Then I reeled away in shock.

He leaned in, staring at me curiously. Then he crept a little closer for a better look. I was kneeling down, reaching for the remaining smelly contents but stopped and stared back. I was too mesmerized and afraid to do anything but watch. I could smell an apple Jolly Rancher on his breath, the cologne on his clothes, and the sweat on his body. He reached a hand out to my face and pinched one of my cheeks. His gloved hand held it firmly between forefinger and thumb. He gave a slight tug, made an expression that was both questioning and understanding, then let me go. He was bruised and had a fat lip with a scab on it. The wounds looked fresh, only a few days old.

"Good luck, kid; you're gonna need it." And with that he stood up and went for his bike.

I stared slack jawed and watched the boy ride away, legs pumping hard, moving as fast as he came in. I picked myself up and began to take my own inventory. After another minute of watching his tracks, wondering what had just happened, I dusted myself off and looked around. I wasn't who he thought I was and had never met the kid before today. A glint of sunlight bounced back at me: treasure missed in the chaos, but it wasn't a box, and it certainly wasn't a bottle of cologne. My fingers fit into the four distinct loops. It was ribbed on the outside and made of some type of metal. It was heavy and seemed powerful.

Brass knuckles.

It felt as if someone had whispered it into my ear. I panicked as fear shot through my body. I whipped my head in one direction, then another, and spun around to see who could have been so close. The hair on the back of my neck stood up, and goosebumps riddled my flesh as I surveyed the street but didn't see a single person. I hustled across the street and leaned against the building, trying to calm my nerves. I could feel the weight pulsing in my hand. The knuckles were stained and dirty. I looked closer and picked off what may have been paint with a fingernail. Thinking better of it, I shoved the weapon into my pocket and looked around again. I flipped my hood up and moved quickly toward home, afraid that someone was watching.

After several blocks, once I felt safe again, I slowed down, pulled my bounty from my pocket, and examined it closely. Inscribed on the flat part, the side that sat in the hand and flat against the palm, were the words *praeparet bellum.* I had no idea what they meant, but the road I was born to walk as a boy had now taken me by the hand. I played with my new treasure the rest of the way home. A smile crept across my face as hope began circling my thoughts, asking for a dance.

Richard Ventosa owned a cable installation business. He was an independent contractor and claimed to be a successful businessman. We lived in a house the size of a Cracker Jack box. He had a couple of trucks that barely ran and a coke habit he couldn't afford, and he drank enough daily to choke a horse. When a week went south for him at the casino, he would come home and take it out on my aunt Jo or myself. My cousin always seemed to skirt away right before the madness began. The conflict would blow through the door like a gale and leave quietly in the dark of the night.

I was a young lad, a voracious reader, no stranger to violence, and like an animal backed into a corner, there was no chance I was going down without a fight.

Gnashing teeth, venom, and rage, I had a fury that unleashed a small dose of my own hell into this world. I was wild and knew nothing of cowardice, wielding courage by the pound.

One time Dick got me pretty good, though, and it took the fight out of me for several weeks. I couldn't move fast enough to stop it from happening—an amazingly cheap and cowardly shot, all things considered. Nobody saw it coming, which was the new normal. Out of the blue, he would just snap. Unfortunately for him, it sparked a rage that inspired the years of war that would follow.

He ripped me off the top bunk, pulling me from the bed, and slammed me face down on the floor—no stopping or slowing the momentum. In fact, he propelled me along quite handily. I did an exceptional job of holding the floor right where it was, first with my chest, then my face. He knocked the wind out of me and cracked some ribs, smashed my nose, and damn near broke my neck. As if that wasn't enough, he stepped on the back of my head to grind my face into the floor to make a point. It was his knee-jerk reaction over something meaningless and trivial.

Then he chuckled and walked off. "Better luck next time."

I desperately missed memaw and her applesauce cake.

I am going to kill that motherf.... someday. It was the first time I had a thought like that, and I remember it as clear as day. I lay there, silently pleading for help, choking on my own blood, wondering if I would ever be able to move my head again. It felt like I'd been hit by a car and left to die.

The inferno of revenge began as a single pious, hateful flame. It had to be quenched with blood—with his blood. A sacrifice. The limp, lifeless body set ablaze.

I was struggling against the tide, the power of the ocean, in the convoluted dream of my youth, to stop it from sucking me back out to sea in a rush of feelings. I saw a spirit, a faceless no man, standing by with a life preserver, watching quietly as I was engulfed by long-buried feelings.

To war, to death, 'til only one is left!

My head popped through the surface of the water just in time to see the no man throw the life preserver my way. Thoughts and feelings assaulted me no less violently than the sea of despair I was drowning in as I relived some of the hard times of my youth. I was pulled back under, my hand slipping from the edge of the float he had thrown my way, back into the dream world of yesteryear.

The growing feelings were clamoring constantly and creating conflict. The abyss of death, the black dog of depression, was seeping through my skin. It made me feel empty and cold, loosening my skin from my bones, making sure it never fit right. Violence fertilized it all.

The depression, anger, and chaos—different worlds growing of their own volition, spawned from the darker seasons of life.

I knew I would have to kill Dick at some point. It wasn't exactly a plan formed in my young mind back then, just something I knew. It made me feel horrible and happy. I would laugh in glee and cry in horror when the moment struck just right.

I imagined the drugs were shredding his paychecks and knew that had something to do with the arguments he and my auntie had over money, but I wasn't totally sure. Despite that, he seemed to be a man of cash. His wallet was always flush, and I didn't mind helping myself. He was a junkie, that much I gathered.

Don't take too much, or he will know, I warned myself once again, as I saw my child-sized hand slip into a man's wallet.

Back in the thinning real world, where I lived in flesh and blood, life dragged on in timeless misery.

The no man carried on nightly, painting pictures in my dreams of the past, real and imagined, most every night. He was pulling me deeper into long-buried feelings, weaving stories, situations, and thoughts together of my doppelgängers and me. The Cabalifornians continued to haunt life in the real world but never showed a face to go with the story. What little relief I found was in the dreams of my past.

3

A MAGNUM MISS

The mirror rippled in a liquid, wavelike motion, then became still again. I leaned in for a closer look and blew hot breath on the glass. It fogged up. I ran a finger through the moisture buildup and examined the streak; it was solid glass. I stepped back and looked again. I knew what I touched but didn't hesitate to step back and blow on it again. I reached to touch it a second time but hesitated slightly. My hand stalled, then made the shape of a gun pointing directly at the small foggy patch. Instead of swiping this time, I stuck the tip of my index finger directly into the glass. I could feel the resistance, the glass, and then I felt it give way. I pushed my hand in slowly. I stopped at the second joint on my pointer finger. The missing tip of my finger felt cold. I pulled my hand back, and the liquid substance moved with it, then my finger slid out. I pulled it clear with a slight pop. The liquid mirror resumed a solid, flat, and crystal-clear reflective surface.

I steeled my nerves, took a breath, and pushed my finger, then my whole hand into it, expecting the glass to break, but it never did. I felt the resistance, felt it give way, then felt the pop into through liquid. My hand cleared, and I could feel space on the other side of the mirror. It was some kind of door after all!

I pulled my arm back quickly and held my hand up to my face. It was clean—no evidence of space or time travel. I inspected it closely again and held it directly up to my nose and inhaled deeply. I could smell my alpine gel body wash. I wiggled my fingers—not a trace of anything but me. I stepped closer to the newly found door and stopped. Thoughts were rushing through my head, none of which were going to stop me. I took a deep breath, held it, then stepped forward, pushing through the mirror. I lifted my arms, shielding my head and face, and crossed over to the other side.

I was standing on solid ground, both eyes still closed. I let the breath out and inhaled; instantly I was assaulted by the acrid smell of burning electrical. My eyes popped open as the scent wafted in. The new world had a red hue and was smoky. I could vaguely see the flickering light of a TV screen across the room.

There was a distinct, familiar feel.

I walked through worlds nonetheless, maybe time too.

I continued surveying with haunting comfort, and slowly the truth unfolded in my mind. The boy from my dreams led me here. This time it was no longer from the corners of my mind. I was in his world.

A sigh ran through my body, and I shuddered slightly from the chill of heavy disappointment and understanding. I was dreaming once again.

The haze began to clear up slightly, and the burning smell faded. I could see the TV, and a few feet in front of it, sat a man in a recliner. The small table next to the chair held a bowl of chips, a few beer cans, and a remote control. A dozen feet behind the man was the kitchen, and to the left of that, a dining room table. Movement on the man's backside caught my eye.

It was the boy. The boy I was in my youth, but not me all the same. If a keystone world existed, this wasn't it. It felt so close but so wrong, so dirty and vile. I could sense the layers to the other boy, like an onion. He wasn't just one boy, he was many. This was the world we all had to pass through. A nexus for all of us. A point in time we travelled through to get where we were going and when we passed through, we all did it together. He was one of many and many made of one.

He stood a few feet behind the man and off to the side, almost hidden in a hallway. All of a sudden, he leaped in the air and caught a flying object. He landed without a sound. The silence was eerie and uncomfortable. I saw the boy turn sideways, preparing to throw the object back to whoever was catching it at the end of the hall. He half turned sideways, and his mouth moved, but the words never landed on my ears. The tiny football took flight again. I saw the man in the chair say something back. His mouth stopped moving, and his head turned slightly to watch the boy with venom in his eyes. He spoke again, and I watched his mouth closely, but to no avail; the words fell silent once again. Then I saw the man get up and move his chair back.

He lined it up directly with the hallway and the boy. I could see the man's mouth move some more and sensed the boy had said something else as well. My contempt became rage as I knew there was only one outcome of the man moving his chair.

The air filled again with a haze, the vapor of a dream. My reality, fantasy, and the unknown were all here, broadcasting, warning, wanting, and fearing. It was lucid, real, and a circus of smoke and mirrors trapping us all. I could feel the presence of the dream keeper and knew he was showing me the onion boy and that was why I was here. The light vapor swirled, and everything went dark.

The boy of many layers, Onions, was halfway in the living room, and another kid was at the end of the hall with a wall behind him and bedroom doors on both sides. Down at our end of the hall was a closet and a bathroom door. They were throwing a vinyl, cotton-stuffed ball back and forth. The boy said something I am sure he shouldn't have. It provoked a reaction. I wanted to move in and call the game off, but the boy held his ground. The dream keeper would not relent to my protest. I could hear the cacophony of a crowded room in the distance, an echo chamber of the many layers of his mind. All of us seemed to be in protest together.

The tension was growing by the second. Explosive. Violent. Toxic. The man was looking for a reason to fight. Filled with ire, contempt, and anger, he would find it no doubt.

This where and when was ruled by something darker. Something bent, broken, and estranged.

The next throw came in hot, fast and low; maybe the man hit the onion boy in the back of the knees so his legs would buckle, or maybe the pass was aimed at his head. Either way, with his chair in position and the ball in flight, it glided through fingertips to hit him directly in the face.

Onions took a quick shot to the temple from an elbow; maybe it was intentional, likely just his good luck, but he was out of the fight before we even realized the man moved. The other kid, like a cunning gazelle, ran right into the corner of a bedroom at the end of the hall. The miscreant jumped the gazelle like fellow and began choking the life out of him.

Onions followed suit as a late arrival and jumped on the attacker's back, trying to put his own puny choke on him. It happened in blinks, and then time stood still. He bit down and tore into the flesh on his neck.

Like a savage. Like a vampire. Like a desperate boy trying to stop someone from killing his only kin.

Time came rushing back in. Onions was lying on the floor with blood on his face, and the other was lying on his bed, still breathing.

The man stood in the bathroom, sponging off a minor wound on his neck. He was satisfied with the outcome, his hunger for violence sated for now.

We paid in carnage, fear, and chaos. He would pay the same. Then he would burn for his sins.

Time spun on.

Onions and I were watching quietly from his bedroom doorway as the man unloaded a .357 magnum and gave the cylinder a spin. It was a six shooter, a revolver. It was silver with a wooden handle and looked huge in his malevolent hand. The gun was oiled, polished, and clean. It glistened brightly, reloaded with six heavy rounds of thunder and mortality. We watched greedily from the distance, peeking through the crack in the doorway. The thoughts spun through our shared mind like the bullets through the cylinder. I was no longer watching from the outside but from the inside this time. I was the onion boy or at least had access to all the mechanisms of his mind. I could even hear the internal clicking come to a slow as an idea buried deep in the back of the boy's brain became locked and loaded. It was a huckleberry, no doubt. The man may have been drunk already, but he was certainly not going to stop drinking. I pushed the idea closer to the surface of the boy's mind and sensed him struggling to grasp it. There was something else too, among the many others in the recess of his mind. Watching. Feeling. Waiting. We were all one, sharing the same body and mind, though I could step away at any moment and wake from someone else's nightmare. I could feel his emotions and see his mind. The poor child was broken, like a splintered popsicle stick snapped in half. He was young but not naïve; the emotions were raw and consuming, the sadness a vast ocean that carried on for fathoms. He was me after all but still not me just the same. All our realities were being forged together.

I may have been able to pull myself out of sleep, but I had a strong desire to be a part of the boy living in the flames, he wasn't of the keystone world, but lived at the center of spider's web nonetheless. I watched his thoughts like a passing car on the road. He was afraid all the time but knew nothing of cowardice.

I could wait until he goes to the bathroom and just shoot him. No way—if it doesn't work, he will kill me for sure or worse.

Or worse?! Does it really get worse? This isn't living; it's dying. I wonder if the police will throw me in jail.

I gently tugged at the original thought, slowly trying to reel the boy in.

I can't just shoot him…but…what if he accidentally shot himself?

The boy was hooked now. I backed up, giving the idea room to land. Once the thoughts were out of the water completely, the boy didn't hesitate. Fearless, no doubt, we were cut from the same cloth.

We watched the deadbeat put the gun down on the coffee table and drain what was left of his beer.

We went to the fridge and grabbed another. Had to be careful here; he was unpredictable, and the wrong move could have us fighting for the boy's life in no time.

We quickstepped to the coffee table and set it down.

"Need another one?" the boy asked and walked off before he could say anything. The man grunted something, but we weren't looking for a heart to heart. We headed back to the bedroom and began digging through the stack of comics.

It was all in the attitude, bub. Once the claws came out, there was no holding back.

After several minutes, we dropped the comics and went back to the fridge, grabbed another can, and dropped it off on the way by without another word. We went outside in search of answers. The porch light was pale and flickered. The gravel outside the open garage door glistened with the raindrops. We walked out and looked around, just catching the moonlight tucked behind a cloud. The boy thanked a God that he didn't know then sped back to his waiting treasures.

We sighed heavily and pulled out another stack of comics. Deliveries were made on cue, and the boy continued to think heavily of the coming actions.

I wondered if Onions would have the stones in the end, or if I would have to impose my will. The boy took another step further down the hall, and his resolve became steadfast. He was certainly of my ilk, born in the land of nightmares and reality.

Another few steps, quiet as a mouse. The snoring cut the silence like a buzz saw. There was certainly no longer any need to creep; it only felt right. I stepped away, watching Onions from the outside. We were connected through time and space. He was emotionless—void and vacant of feeling. He stopped and stood in silence, head cocked to one side, listening for any sounds of potential intrusion. There were none. He stepped around the chair and stared at the weapon. It gleamed of death and destruction. He reached down and picked it up with a bandana between his hand and the grip. He was almost crying now, tears of joy the only proof of emotion. This part of his life would soon be over. It was a good plan, easy to execute and almost foolproof. He would call 911. He would cry. He would wait. He would cry some more and then just be a boy again, free of the devil and the chaos that had consumed his life up to now.

The stale stench of alcohol, cigarettes, and Old Spice assaulted the boy's resolve as he leaned in close. He had to get the right hand up and in position just under the chin. It put him in a precarious position, leaning over the man and holding the gun. Very gently he set the gun on the man's chest, praying that he was out cold. He waited, watching the man closely. Any hint of him waking up and he was going to the floor as fast as possible, then crawling away like his life depended on it—because it certainly would.

I turned back to watch time unfold. The boy picked up the limp right hand and laid it carefully on the top of the gun. Gently he moved the bottom four fingers around to grip the handle, the pointer sitting loosely on the trigger guard.

I looked down at my own hand and saw it growing more transparent and panicked. I sent a thought at Onions, like a spear.

HURRY UP!

I felt the world around me growing tighter and shrinking, like I was going to pop out of existence.

HURRY, BOY, HURRY!

Another thought spear launched, and I saw the boy fumble and almost drop the gun. It was in both of his hands now with the man's sandwiched in between. He wasn't moving fast enough. I knew he had to finish the job while I was here. If the boy didn't kill him now, he might not kill him at all. Worse yet, if he didn't kill him now, then the man might kill him instead. My fate was tied to this boy of many minds—how or why I didn't know, but I wasn't willing to wait and find out.

It was just a dream!

I knew different.

Time was pressing and threatening. I gathered all my energy and shot into Onions, meaning to finish the terrible task myself.

I hit violent bloodlust like a raging river and went careening through the boy's mind, like I was dropped off a waterfall. I was pinned to the side of his mind, unable to move. I felt something timeless and powerful surge through the boy's body and saw the hulking figure raging like an inferno across the darkness. This wasn't a projection of Onion's mind. It was suffering come to life. It was angry, it was violent, and now it was in control. The beast was a layer in the boy's mind and it was alive. I watched in horror as the man began to wake up, and the gun started to move.

Deafening thunder shook the room as the hammer dropped on the hand canon…

I shot upright terrified, sitting in my bed, safe and sound. I quickly pulled my blankets up around me, then touched my face. I rubbed my eyes and face, making sure I was still human and just myself after all. I let out relieved sigh after several minutes and sat quietly staring out the window, listening to the soft snoring sounds from throughout the house. All were safe and sound.

4

THE REPUBLIC

The bus slowly rolled to a stop. I could see the outline of my grandfather through the foggy window, standing at the top of our driveway waiting for us. I grabbed my backpack as the bus stopped and the doors opened, then shuffled along the isle and stepped down into a shockingly cold world blanketed by white.

"Hi, guys," Grandpa said, still with a big smile. The weather showed the breath of life hanging in front him with every rise and fall of his chest. He wasn't a big man, maybe five foot eight and 160 lbs. He had on thick hiking boots and blue jeans, a brown marshmallow jacket, brown leather gloves, and a green stocking cap. His blues eyes were gleaming. Even without the blustery glow, his eyes were striking. Intimidating, fierce intelligence simmered just below the surface. He was kind and loving, but his voice and eyes could draw a hard hand without lifting a finger. His presence alone always brought about a measure of respect, and his piercing hawklike gaze commanded it.

He was standing there smiling with one clenched fist and the other hand in his coat pocket. I looked at the clenched hand and saw a thin rope. It was attached to a runner sled at the other end. It was complete with a steering column and steel rails for skis.

"Hi, Gramps," we said in unison as the bus pulled away.

We took in a few icy breaths as our feet crunched in the snow, then waited to hear the plan. The chill began creeping down my neck, looking for my bones.

We crashed into the snowbanks propelled off the icy drive, repeatedly. Maximum speed was achieved several times before we shot off the edge of the road into the pillows of snow beyond. It was always followed by demands that a new pilot captain the ship to see if it could be done better.

Time sped back up, moving fast, bounding recklessly toward his destiny. Mornings bled into evening. Days were just a blink. The tracks ran for miles and miles, it seemed, but the old mine was out there, under the mountain, waiting for the boy.

"Your mom is on the phone, Paulie," Gram said, handing the receiver out to me as I came around the corner in the kitchen.

"Hi, Mom," I said.

I wonder why she called.

"Hey, Bud, how are you today?" she asked.

"Fine, just reading a book. What's up?" I said, eager to get back to my cookies and swords. I was deep into a fantasy about dark elves.

"I just wanted to let you know we will be up next week," she said.

"We?" I said, and my heart dropped. I knew what she meant.

"Your auntie is coming with me to help us move and see your grandparents." Relief flooded my body.

"GREAT! That's awesome, Mom; can't wait to see you!" I was excited, but knowing he wasn't coming popped the pressure on some bottled-up emotions.

I was up a tree not far from the driveway when I heard the tires roll off the highway onto the gravel and begin heading down the road. I sat with one leg wrapped around a limb and the other standing on a branch below so both hands were free to work the bow. I nocked an arrow, leaned out a little, and aimed at a squirrel on the ground. I had set a few snare traps along the forest floor hoping for a rabbit and was watching quietly from above, but the squirrel was the only animal found. I was moving slowly and intentionally. I drew back and sighted in the big gray squirrel as he was picking at a pinecone. I waited until the bottom of my breath, then released the string and let the arrow fly.

A slight miscalculation sent the arrow pinging off a big branch just a few feet in front of me. The backlash whipped me across the face in a blink, and I slipped. My bow dropped out of my hand as I grasped for purchase, and then it clattered down through the tree.

Good thing my leg was wrapped around the tree branch, or I would have been bouncing back and forth all the way down like a pin ball.

I tried to catch my breath as I clung to the tree, waiting for my heart to slow down.

The rumbling grew louder, and the noise from the driveway brought me back to the outside world. It sounded like a few cars. I carefully began my descent and could taste a bloody lip.

Stupid squirrel.

I grabbed my bow and pulled it from the bush. I touched my bloody lip and looked at my fingers. The smear was bright red and tasted salty. I could feel a lump in the middle of my bottom lip as I gently ran my fingers across it, then sucked on it gingerly.

Gonna be a good one. Been a while.

I let my feet carry me home and relived a memory.

I came around the last corner, and the parking area next to the house came into view. I could see the front of a U-Haul and our silver Subaru. My grandmother stood down by the car, hugging her girls. They all looked happy. I was just about to step out of the tree line when I heard the screen door close on the front porch.

Gramps must be out front smoking his pipe. I could almost smell it.

The women were all laughing now and moving toward the house. I couldn't help but to watch the excitement for a minute. My mom and aunt were headed in, probably competing for the bathroom. My grandma turned back to the woods and cupped her hands to her mouth to give me a holler. She stopped when she saw me and instead of yelling waved me in. I went to wave back, then stopped. My grampa was coming around the corner from the front porch followed by another man. He was laughing.

I waited.

The world around me slowed to a crawl. I heard the exhale of breath and my heart beating in my ears. My vision intensified, and I zeroed in, forgetting everything else around me.

It was him, but it wasn't. He had lost weight, a lot of weight. He was laughing a lot and patting my grandfather on the shoulder. I took a step backward, concealing myself further in the tree line. I could feel eyes on me and knew my grandmother was watching. She saw my reaction.

I kept watching as the man, and my grandfather joined my grandmother. She turned away so they wouldn't look my way.

I stumbled back a few more steps, unable to take my eyes off him. He gave my grandmother a hug. She looked one more time over his shoulder but didn't let her eyes linger long. We made eye contact, then they went inside.

I turned and stormed back into the woods.

I picked up my bow and quiver, then slowly worked my way deeper into the trees.

I walked on for what felt like hours.

The squirrels were chattering away, letting the forest know a stranger was about.

No kidding, you little jerks.

I saw one sitting on a branch not too far away, his belly heaving in and out rapidly with the intruder alert. I pulled an arrow, knocked it, and let fire. I missed. I repeated the process and missed again. The anger was building. I stood there, arrow after arrow, letting them fly. After the third arrow hit close enough, the squirrel leapt away, but the chittering kept up. I was furious—no choice but to let the anger slip through my hands, losing control.

"AAAAAAGGGHHHHHH!" I screamed at the squirrel.

I grabbed my bow with both hands and ran at the tree with a full-hearted battle cry. The bow swung like a baseball bat. I danced around the tree in a half circle to keep up with the momentum after contact. The madness engulfed me quickly. I cut my hand on a broken piece of my bow but couldn't feel the pain. The sight of my own blood enraged me more. I dropped the broken bits of bow and ran on.

The sun fell over the mountains in the west. Rising like a conquering king in the east, night came on rapidly. The temperature dropped what must have been fifteen degrees once my forest was beyond the sun's long reach. I knew I had to go back but wanted desperately not to. I only had a T-shirt on and had chill bumps the size of peas. I was shivering in cold sweat and still hadn't quite mastered my fear of the dark. Besides, the porch light would have been on by now, and the grandparents didn't tolerate excuses. It wasn't quite summer, and the days were longer, but we were buried far enough north that the cold lingered for months.

I crossed the railroad tracks and could finally see the glow of the porch light. I knew the trail from here, so I picked up the pace. I was probably going to be late as it was.

"Hey buu…" My mom's voice trailed off as soon as she set sight on me.

"WHAT HAPPENED?" She hadn't seen me in a month, so her voice had tolerance, love, and borderline irritation.

"Good grief, Paul, did you get into a fight with a mountain lion?" My grandpa said as he took a puff of his pipe. They were all sitting around the table staring at me. I had tried the back door first, but it was locked. I knew it would be.

I looked down at my hands. There was dried blood on both. My shirt was even worse. A plain white tee doesn't do much to hide blood. I tried to hide myself but there was nowhere to go. They all stared at me, eyes wide and watching.

"I was climbing a tree and slipped," I said with all honesty. I sounded funny. My fat lip was interfering with my story. They all just stared at me, waiting for me to elaborate. I knew my rights, though, and closed my mouth instead.

"Well, let's get you cleaned up, then," my mom said as she came toward me for a hug, with a rag in her hand. She leaned in, and I leaned back. I wasn't really in the mood for hugs.

She grabbed me anyway. Guess she missed the memo my sour mood delivered.

My brother just kept staring at me. His eyes had a lost look of wonder; his mouth was agape in confusion. Sitting next to him were my grandmother and Auntie. Nobody else was in the room.

My grandmother had an interested look on her face. We made eye contact, and she smiled at me in love and understanding, even some amusement. She kept quiet, though. My mom, on the other hand, hadn't stopped talking since I walked in. She ushered me into the bathroom and began wiping me off, clucking the entire time. I caught a look at myself in the bathroom mirror and was a little shocked.

I looked like I had been in a scrum. My shirt was bloody and had a few snags and a tear on my right sleeve.

My face was even worse. The fat lip was a bleeder, and there was blood ringing my lips. I had a small cut on the bridge of my nose and a little more blood smeared and dried inside my nostrils. My face was streaked with dirt and blood.

My fingers must have been bloody.

I had a few small pine needles in my hair. My jeans were dirty and bloody on the thighs.

"Helloooo? Earth to Paul. You in there?" my mom asked, staring at my twin in the mirror.

"Uh huh," I said, staring back.

She turned me toward her and began wiping off my face, looking for the outlet of all the blood. She caught my lip with her thumb and pulled it down gently, with the touch of a mother.

"Is that it?" she asked. I held up both hands. She inspected my left palm before she began wiping. It wasn't the first time she had seen me bloody. She moved on to the right, seemingly satisfied with her work. It had a healthy slice across the palm.

"Oh. That really doesn't look good," she said, concern deep in her voice. She was different too.

My grandmother was at the door. I could hear my grandpa and aunt talking in the other room. The TV was still on. I imagined Bryan lying on the floor watching. My mom asked for something to clean my cut up with.

"It's under the cabinet; the Band-Aids should be next to it. Did your bow make it out alive?" my grandmother asked. She knew but wasn't going to make a point of it in front of my mom.

"It hit the tree and broke," I said not wanting to lie. My mom had a rag with rubbing alcohol on it. I was basically immune to the sting of it. At first it was like punishment for being a bleeder. Like all pain, after enough of it, you become numb. The gash wasn't really what was on my mind. I was straining to hear any other voice that didn't belong. It's like he wasn't here. Vanished.

My mom peeled off my shirt off to look for more damage.

"You really need to start being more careful. You are constantly bleeding, son. What are the girls going to think?" She sighed loudly and smiled at me. She turned on the shower.

"In ya go," she said and handed me the rag. She closed the door, then opened it almost immediately.

"I missed you and love you so much," she said and leaned in to stroke my head before closing the door for good. I locked it and stared at the mirror. I had a few scrapes on my face beneath the dirt. I looked at my hand again and wiggled my fingers. Not too much pain. For being a bleeder, I always thought I had mutant-like healing powers.

I climbed out of my clothes and into the shower.

The table was set and dinner ready. It smelled delicious, and I needed food like plants needed sunshine. My grandmother had made fried tater cubes; they were a staple in our house, and I could eat them by the pound. Along with the taters, green beans, pork chops, and salt rounded out the menu.

"So, Paul, what happened?" my grandpa asked, loading up his plate. I stared down for a minute, editing my thoughts.

"Well, Gramps, I set my snares and climbed up a tree to watch. I had my bow and was sittin' on a branch, watchin' this big gray squirrel. I decided to take a shot, and next thing I know, I am fallin' out of the tree and bleedin' all over the place. I must have cut my hand on a branch," I said, telling a three-quarter truth. I learned to not make up stories: weave the truth throughout. My grandpa nodded. My mom sat by listening intently, watching me. Both her hands were wrapped around a steaming mug of coffee.

"Time to eat, Bryan," my mom said. I could hear him get up and turn off the TV.

"Did wittle Paulie fall out of a twee?" he said, mocking me as he came around the corner into the dining room. He was already twice the outdoorsman I would ever be. It all came naturally to him.

"So, Ma, what's the plan?" my brother said in a chipper tone. "Hopefully our house isn't in town?" The only thing he really cared about was being in the outdoors. I didn't blame him.

My mom's eyes lit up like she had been waiting for the question.

"Well, guys, I found the absolutely perfect place," she said, then waited, adding some suspense and watching our faces closely, panning between my brother and me.

"We are moving to the other end of the lake. It's not quite on the lake, BUT it is on five acres, has a pond, and is surrounded by national forest." She stopped talking and watched. She got the reaction she wanted from my brother as an ear-to-ear grin spread across his face. My own face was wrought with skepticism.

"REALLY?" he asked in disbelief. His face flashed quickly from a smile to questioning wonder, like maybe she was pulling his leg.

"Yes, really. It's a two-bedroom, one-bath, has a barn and a pasture, and it comes with a surprise," she said, looking at me. My foray into the forest was forgotten. Her demeanor was much too confident to not be telling the truth. The news of a real victory was being delivered.

"WHAT IS IT?" my brother asked, shoveling another scoop of fried taters into his mouth and chewing quickly.

"I'm not telling," she said, smiling slyly, "but you are going to love it."

"What are we waiting for?" said the sloth as half-chewed taters fell out of his mouth.

"Bryan," Grandpa said sternly. One word was all it took. My brother sat back, closed his mouth, and chewed his food quietly. Grandpa had some strict house rules, and table manners were high on the list. I leaned back in my chair, waiting for mom to drop the bad news. Good news always had a catch.

"Four on the floor, Paul," Gramps said and put his hand on the back of my chair, pushing the front two legs back down gently. I complied.

Obviously, my mom and grandparents had already talked. My grandparents didn't have any questions and were not saying much. My grandmother was acting oblivious, but I could tell she already knew what my mom was up to.

I decided to ask.

"Where is our stuff?" I said, sitting on the bottom of my nerves.

My hand was burning a little, and my plate was clean after two helpings of everything, especially taters, extra salt, and ketchup.

"In the U-Haul at the new house. A friend followed us here, then dropped it off. He is heading back to Portland." Her nostrils flared just slightly at the end.

The world had just been made right. My chin quivered as the pent up emotions flooded my body in relief. The dam almost broke, but I kept the tears in check.

"One more thing, guys," my mom said. Here it was: the bomb was about to be dropped; I could feel it.

"Your hunter's ed classes start in a couple of months. Grandma has agreed to take you out next fall for your first hunt. Lord knows I am useless when it comes to that kind of stuff, but your grandparents think you're both ready," she said. My brother couldn't contain himself anymore. At least his plate was empty.

He jumped up and ran around the house whooping like an Indian. He had been waiting for this and had asked my mom every time she called. I forgot about any bad news and joined in the celebration. Hunting aside, I couldn't wait to have my own gun.

5

HEAT

I sat in the lobby of a local shrink waiting my turn. The cork in the bottle kept my emotions from spilling out, but the pressure began to drive up the temperature, and my flesh was writhing against it. Frustration, discomfort, irritation, and anger were all boiling just under the surface.

The no man was crippling me now. I slept a few hours each night but never rested. The insomnia from my youth had returned, and those few precious hours of sleep were under attack from the supernatural, from the ghosts of my childhood and the gate keeper I called the no man. The events were vivid, clear, and lucid. All the while the no man was pulling me through it, stretching me, asking something from me, but what he wanted always dissolved away in the mist of dreams. Which, as of late, had shifted to a boy I never was and his family. It was like watching somebody else's life through a fishbowl, except I was him in the dreams. The confusion was blinding as the wellspring of my mind began pouring out one character, thought and idea after another.

The door to the office opened, making my invitation clear.

"Joseph, you can come in now," the voice in the office said.

I rubbed my face and stood up, distant and weak. The irregular heartbeat, the lack of sleep, and the chaos in my head made me question if I was going to drop dead right then and there. I took a deep breath and closed my eyes. I wasn't sure if I was cursed or if this was hell, but it certainly felt like both. Memaw's voice cut through the fog.

"When Jesus set you free, chile, he set you free indeed." Her happy laugh followed and condemned my broken mind even more. I walked into the office and gently shut the door behind me, hoping if nothing else I would find some peace after spilling more of my childhood tears and fears to the empathetic heart. I picked up where I left off with the head doctor last. Jumping back into middle school from the life I thought was my own.

Middle school was in full swing. The four of us continued, and the monster Dick helped create inside of me finally blossomed. My protector, my war dog, called Jamis, came alive and would fight for my life as required. Any scent of conflict, and I could hear the beast bellowing for war. Once he arrested the controls, it was a fearless and full-throttle battle, my body an instrument of war, my mind a passenger pushed aside.

Over the last year or so, our chaotic life had briefly settled, and it seemed like it might mellow out, but just when I began to feel some comfort, I came home with a black eye. If I just wasn't me…I have imagined a different life many times, softer and more poetic, quieter, and void of the venom.

Dick decided to intervene, his naturally atrocious, fatherly instincts driving him on. He found out who was responsible for my bruised face and somehow got ahold of the father. The two came to the most levelheaded decision: make the boys fight it out.

My knuckle-dragging pseudo father figure arranged for fisticuffs with the other kid, at his house, in his front yard. I didn't like the other kid much but liked the plan even less. My stomach rolled, and I almost threw up. A poke in the chest reminded me that I had better win.

This was a cold fight, no heat or emotion beforehand. I didn't want to go, but my choices were limited.

I was resigned to my fate and slowly walked out to the truck. My chances of winning the fight were slim, but with no fire and knowing I couldn't throw the first punch, the odds became nil. The resolve to never strike first was wearing thin. Being honorable in this world was starting to feel trivial and meaningless, like upstanding character traits were only for those from the silver-spoon life. It ate at me.

I stood facing my opponent while the real enemy stood smugly behind me. The thought crossed my mind to turn around and kick him in the biscuits. I raised my head and looked at the boy standing across from me. It was evident I wasn't nearly as scared as he. The butterflies in my stomach fluttered despite my thinking, and I wasn't convinced I could continue to hold my lunch down.

I felt a hand land in between my shoulders, and words of quiet encouragement fell to my ear: "Kick his ass."

Then I was propelled forward.

The other boy still looked like he was going to wet himself. With self-imposed rules to abide by, I couldn't hit him first, and I knew it, so I went for a leg instead.

The other boy cried out and stumbled forward as he was given his own hand of motivation. We collided and tangled up, then hit the ground. I couldn't bring myself to hit him yet, but I could keep him from hitting me. I snaked up his back and pinned one of his arms to the ground and trapped the other arm between us. He didn't struggle much and latched on to one of my wrists. We held each other down, no blood being drawn. After a minute of this his father was having none of it.

"You stand up and punch that little sucker in the mouth!" he yelled; I dragged the boy back down as he tried to get more upright. I wanted to cry and knew the waterworks were coming. It was the way.

I felt a tear sliding down my cheek. The boy struggled against my takedown, but I was convinced that if I kept him down, he would have no choice but to eventually yield. Once again, I was wrong.

I felt rough hands grab me and pull me off my rival. I was spun abruptly and slapped hard across the face.

"I will give you something to cry about," Dick growled between clenched teeth. A second, hard slap, and I was shoved again back across the yard and directly into my opponent's waiting fist.

The savage inside broke his chains and was set free. Jamis roared for blood and chaos, filling my world red as relief flooded my body.

A few minutes later, the world came back into focus. The boy's father was trying to pull me from his son. My nose was bleeding, my knuckles were bloody, and I was in the middle of a war, one arm pumping wildly and connecting solidly with my opponent's face, the other hand on the boy's throat. I was mounted over him on my knees, and he was on the ground beneath me.

The man shoved me off his son. I snarled and tried to kick him in the face for his efforts. Snot, venom, and blood flew from my mouth. He backed away, pulling his son from the fray. Dick grabbed the belt at my waist and tried to pull me away too, so I spun and swung wildly before whipping back around to the boy on the ground. A second later, a heavy kick to my ribs brought my attention back to reality and forced me to turn away.

I scrambled to my feet and squared to the man, Dick, my nemesis and bane. My ribs and nose were burning, but the time had finally come.

Hate flooded my face, and he stepped back in hesitation.-

I was consumed with visions of war, fire, and his head on a pike. I was prepared to dance around the pyre naked, painted in his blood while the limp, headless body burned, and the dead eyes watched the flames eat the rest of him one inch at a time.

Jamis unleashed booming thunder within my head.

"TOOO WAAAR!"

The priest in me begged forgiveness and prayed for absolution, then thanked God for delivering my adversary to the battleground.

Dick told me to stand down or get hurt, but his voice was filled with more question than confidence, and his eyes flickered in uncertainty. I spat a stream of blood at him and smiled through the tears and pain. He knew I was going to kill him. Today. Tomorrow. His time on earth was almost up.

I took a step toward him.

Then I heard the dull thud of a flat shovel hit bone, and it reverberated through my skull. I never felt anything except darkness settling in while my legs gave way.

As I faded, I heard a voice and a laugh: "That'll slow him down."

I came to on my side, in the bed of the truck, with the sound of the GMC rumbling down the road. My nose ached, and I had a growing knot on the back of my head. The daylight was too much for my eyes; I tried to squint, but it caused too much pain. I could feel the dried blood around my swollen and tender nose.

Next time he was going to die. Next time, I would use a weapon of my own. I tried to smile at the thought, but a low moan escaped instead; the sound of my own voice surprised me. I shut my mouth and my eyes, wondering, not for the last time, which one of us would die first.

The fights, the fireworks, and the misery most of all were leading me by the hand. God had a task for this rough-and-tumble childhood, and I wasn't going to get out of it. From the very first bloody nose to now, I was being molded and prepared for combat.-

A friend later asked, "Why don't you just kill him and get it over with?" The sun rays cast through the treetops and made her smile glow. I looked away, afraid she would see the shame I hid behind my eyes. I took another drink of my beer.

"By fire," I said resolutely. Oh, how badly I wanted him to burn.

We shared many secrets, but it was an idea that was never spoken of again. It had been incubating in my mind for years, where I kept it safe and warm, but I was starting to crack. Subconsciously, my mind was running laps day and night, biting into the details.

Dig a hole. You know where.

Later that summer, I was up at 3:00 a.m. I crept through the house gathering all my stuff for another round of throwing hay bales back and forth. I could hear my cousin snoring away as I passed by his room. I made it to the top of the stairs and listened for my aunt. She was also cutting thunder with a chainsaw.

I peeked into the enemy's camp and caught a glint of blued steel in the moonlight. It aroused a darkness within.

I could hold out for the final battle or give in to the feelings and just sneak in and end it all now. Quiet as a mouse and deadly as a mamba. The struggle was all too real. The day ahead became a question, along with my future. I knew the gun was loaded, and he was sleeping off his latest drunk. Slide it out of the holster on the bedpost, cock the hammer, and pull the trigger; that's all it would take. A second or two, then no more. The beast inside raging for war hushed as it realized there would be no fight. All those years of torture and violence would be blown away in the hot, acrid smoke of gunpowder and lead.

Guilt took the driver's seat. Using a gun was for the hand of a coward. There was no justice in it. An eye for an eye wasn't a bullet fired from a gun.

I heard a story on the news of a girl who was kidnapped, raped, tortured, then left to die. She came back from the dead and pursued her captor—hunted him down, tortured him, sodomized him, then hung him with the ropes he had used to tie her down. That was an eye for an eye. That was vengeance with the weight of suffering behind it.

From deep within, a new voice broke through to the surface of my thoughts. I felt Jamis whisper the intruder's name in shock, then recede back into the shadows of my mindscape.

Jaka was a different creature altogether, and I could feel it. He was violent and full of bloodlust like Jamis, but his intelligence was darker, more devious. He was even tempered. He was a planner, a thinker, a manipulator.

Kill him now, and your life is over. Wait for the fight, boy. Kill him with your own two hands. Then take him up to the woods, throw his body in, and dance around the pyre.

I was angry, but I knew I couldn't use a gun, it would never be the way in this life. It was for the weak and cowardly, and I was anything but that.

Witnesses, fingerprints, daybreak, blood in the house. Are you sure you're not the dumb one, or shall I keep going?

The voice of condemnation laughed at me from inside my own head. We both knew the answer. I felt Jamis move farther back into the shadows, then vanish as he was apt to do. He wanted the fight more than he wanted a limp body, but his dislike for the newest occupant of my thoughts was raw and distinct. I cried silently against the two usurpers imprisoned in my mind.

Listen, boy, you will get your chance. I come bearing gifts.

The next picture to slide through my head was my hand slipping a pint of whiskey into a golf bag. I saw an ice chest full of beer in the back of Dick's truck, next to his golf bag. A fire raged brilliantly as I chanted, dancing around it naked, face painted in blood, head on a pike in my hand.

Then my mind went quiet. Once again, I was alone with my thoughts, and they were dark and powerful indeed. Lust was a weapon to be used sparingly, greed the catalyst in an elixir of hate. Jaka and his ideas were calculated and deadly.

I gathered my stuff and quietly shut the door behind me. I let out my breath and sat down on the step just outside the door. I was visibly shaking as I put my boots on. I had to walk down to my comrades a few blocks away, where today's farmer planned to pick us up.

Jaka rattled me. He was a denizen from a different plane—a malevolent, cold-hearted butcher. There was no valor or integrity in him. His ideas scared me because I knew the plan would work, and when I realized that it would soon be truth, it scared me even more. I thought about a time when I was younger and tried to feed Dick enough alcohol to shoot himself, but in the end the plan failed. I am sure the bullet is still lodged in the wall of that house.

I heard Jaka laugh again in the depths.

Try and try again...

I shivered and let the cold thoughts float away into the predawn gloom.

I knew how it sounded as the last few words fell out of my mouth. The omission of Jaka and Jamis to the counselor left me feeling dirty. I hadn't told the entire truth, and it nagged at me. I told her of the violence, or most of it, at least. I was being fed parts of the story by the no man and other parts by my own memory. I wasn't sure if Jaka, Jamis, or the plan were real in my youth or if the no man was painting them into the soured memories and visions. The world my imagination created and the world I stepped in were becoming one and the same. I was no longer convinced, as I walked out to my car, that I wouldn't simply melt into the ground, or disappear entirely.

My experience with hallucinogenics and LSD were minor but left a track of distinct footprints in my mind. Memaw's God and her astute teachings left the same. Experiences of both and more were wound together tightly. I shut the door of the truck and put my face against the steering wheel. I heard Memaw again as I recalled tripping through my youth.

"Believe to receive. Das what you gonna do. You gonna believe, den shore enough you gonna receive. God, he ain't gonna waste no time on dem people dat can't believe. He gave us all a mustard seed, but we gotta water it if its gonna grow."

I saw myself walking through the grocery store, my mind enhanced and overloaded with LSD. The sparkling, fresh waxed floor was a liquid wave. I believed to receive some mind-altering substances.

"Don't melt into the floor!" I cried as I approached my friend, reaching out to steady him. The other group of teenagers nearby laughed and watched my friend and I as we navigated our way through the liquid-like floor maze to the checkout stand. Our excessive inebriation was obvious to even the untrained eye.

I began drifting into slumber as the warmth of the sunshine and the rhythm of my breath gave me a slight respite from the land of blood and bone, thoughts fading away. The no man arrived on cue, determined to show me what I was missing, once again tugging and pulling me into his world.

I spent the next several weeks bucking bales, eating, sleeping, partying, and ignoring all the wicked thoughts. The farmer's wife made us eat everything she put on the table. They had to be feeding us more food than the hay was worth.

I had work until school started in September. It was only the middle of July, but the school year felt fast approaching.

Fifteen was coming, though, and so was the whitewater. Life was a roaring river now; it was no longer timid and trickling, nor was it deep, slow-moving muddy water. The rushing current swept up everything in its path. I had few choices if any at all.

It was homecoming. My fifteenth birthday passed without incident.

My date and I arrived at the dance, but it wasn't long before another suitor was demanding to talk to her privately. She kept me at bay and wanted to hear him out. He was angry, and I didn't understand. By the time I got it, my date was crying and caught in the middle. The other boy kept his distance but started yelling at me. We'd had a handful run-ins previously, but he was never a threat.

The girl begged for me to stay calm. I owed her a debt and kept quiet, but I twitched and writhed under the pressure of holding back. The other boy was no threat to me. His cousin and friends were a different story, but they never showed up. The boy continued yelling in his rage and stormed out the door in fury, his frustration aimed entirely at me.

I yelled after him that if he wasn't careful, he might end up dead in a ditch. Meaningless, angry, empty words.

He died in a car accident just a few short hours later.

The psychologist shifted in her chair, and I could feel the weight of her looking at me. I'd managed to crawl through another week and was back in the head doctor's office spilling more of the details from my younger years: The weight of the guilt I carried from that night. The weight of loss and the fallout that came after.

We sat in silence. The moment was forever memorialized in my memory and laden heavy with years of guilt. The feelings wouldn't absolve just because they were spoken out loud: the conflict, the argument, and then the accident. The latter, in my mind, was always a product of the former despite the facts. It framed my guilt and had a hand in shaping what was left of my adolescent youth. It became a chasm that no bridge could span. I lived on one side and the rest of humanity on the other.

All I felt was cold. And empty. It was the first time I ever spoke of the guilt and shame I carried from that night. Without the alcohol, the Band-Aid that covered all my childhood scars, the twenty-five-year-old wound was festering, raw and infected. The no man was magnifying the most painful parts of my life. Against my will and against my wishes and without the alcohol, I was going to have to face them head on.

6

IGNITION

Life took a sharp and drastic turn into darkness after that. I was isolated, cast out, and disliked by others but most of all by myself. I was willingly expelled from the remaining social circles except for a small crowd of vagabonds, and I started to isolate. Then I began to drown myself in alcohol.

Our tormentor had earned the taste of his own blood, by my hand. He was going to pay, and before this life was over, I would have my revenge. It was all I had left.

Heartbroken and alone, the emptiness of it all consumed what was left of me. It would extend to consume what was left of Dick Ventosa as well.

The insanity of the depression contorted my soul and bent my feelings. Thoughts of my own end began creeping in. I could see death winking at me in my dreams when I did manage to sleep, courting me, inviting me in. It followed me around, all the while feeding me ideas and thoughts that weren't mine, trying to steal the last shred of hope that my broken heart was clinging to.

Killing Dick. It would be my retribution on this world and on this life. It was the final flickering, fickle flame of hope.

No doubt, other townsfolk knew of the violence but turned a blind eye. Even those who took an oath to protect and serve had an iron hand in shaping my future, if they would have only stepped in. But it wasn't their business; my aunt wasn't one of theirs, and neither was I.

Time was fleeting, and I could feel the clock starting to expire, ticking away the minutes each day. I had one last chance before the snow would fly; the last golf tournament of the year was looming heavy in my mind. The golf course would close until spring after that, too long to risk it. Winter was his heavy-drinking season, and as the years passed, it only worsened. We were lucky to live through the previous winter, and I knew it was our last. *He dies, or one of us dies first.*

The seasons changed the world over, and fall had a majesty, a feeling of royalty, and all that was grown in spring and thrived in the summer was in the final throes of life before embracing the long, dark, cold sleep of winter, especially in the North. Graves were dug in the fall when the ground was wet and soft. The spade of the shovel would sink deep, and the earth moved without protest. Bodies were buried and forgotten over the span of the dark skies, snowfall, and frigid, lifeless temperatures. The earth reclaimed its bounty, and the gates of hell would open wide to welcome home one who belonged.

I looked in the mirror in my room as the thoughts spun endlessly. I had grown much since the first real test of manhood. I was almost six feet tall. I would have wrestled at 168 pounds. There wasn't an inch of fat on my body. I had been in countless conflicts since my days with memaw and her hens. God himself had been preparing me for this battle for as long as I could remember. He created the dogs of war that lived in my mind and unearthed a demon that lived in my heart. The darkness of it all pulled at my broken soul like a magnet drawing me ever closer to a well of hopelessness, yet I was still breathing. The whisper on the wind of Valhalla kept my heart beating.

I stopped, looking in the mirror, and fell back onto my bed. I had no doubt I was big enough now. The battlefield was mine to prepare, and the plans unfolded in my mind: From the alcohol to the trove of weapons, if needed. If I could get away to get one. If he drank all the alcohol. If he came home. If he wasn't coked out of his gourd, and if he didn't kill me first.

If, if, if.

Turns out the plan had a few flaws after all. Maybe I should just dump gas on him while he slept and let him burn. Alive.

The dark heart relished the thought but put it away quickly.

Premeditated, boy. That's called murder, and it will cost what's left of your pathetic life. Jaka was as smug as he sounded. An image of my hand, the whiskey, and the golf bag flashed again through my mind. Then my thoughts were flooded with pictures: A bat leaning near the front door. A knife in the kitchen drawer. A loaded gun in the bedroom.

Better move that so he doesn't get to it first.

The pictures cycled through all the rooms in the house. If it went the way I wanted, though, the fight would stay in the living room or end in the carport outside. Jamis wasn't going to give in to using fire or anything else. He was here for the work that had to be done, and it was going to be done by his hands.

I slipped on the key to Jamis and knew in my heart that he would need nothing more. Once unleashed with a weapon of such brutality, the fight would end in a bloodbath, and quickly at that: the brass knuckles from the boy with the bicycle. I slid my fingers in and out of the loops and ran my other hand over the outside ridges. I lifted the weapon flat in my palm, feeling the weight of it in my hand, heavy and comforting. I looked closely at it and noticed divots and imperfections in the brass. I wondered how many others had felt the personal touch of the knuckles.

The cocaine-fueled, hate driven monster should not be underestimated, and there was no doubt I was going to have to take at least one shot if not more. I assumed if the savage inside were loosed, it wouldn't matter how many shots I took.

What else could possibly go wrong? My mind tripped up on the first and most obvious detail. It could be me that dies. That was a possibility to be sure; so be it. I shrugged off the thought without much feeling. It wasn't quite suicide, but if I was going to die, I wasn't upset by the thought of it. Seemed like it might be a relief after all. I sure as hell wouldn't be going alone, and that much I was certain of.

I dropped the self-pity and let my thoughts skip on. My kin. It would be late Saturday night by the time Dick came home. If my cousin wasn't gone, he would stay downstairs. It didn't matter much either way. If he heard the psycho and I headed for our final showdown, he wouldn't stick around to see who won.

My auntie. My thinking stopped and hung there. She was going to be the wildcard, the unknown. How to keep her out of the way, how to keep her safe, and how to keep her alive? Aunt Jo was a staple in my life. We were a family and managed to stay together through the hardship, but her decision-making often put us in bad situations. Yet we were all still here, and we were all still breathing. She knew what I was, though: the product of a preacher and a junkie, born to walk a road of fire and fury.

Drug her.

Jaka was cold as ice. I ignored the thought at first.

She could have left him behind a few years back, but she didn't. Maybe I should just drug her for the hell of it. I mean, for her own safety. The gears in my mind spun endlessly the rest of the night. I finally dozed off at 4:00 a.m., after crying myself to sleep while wishing for a different life.

The missing seasons of a child.

Sleep had become a dream. It was like a cold I couldn't catch or a God I couldn't see. I knew it was out there, somewhere, but like the rest of the world, it wanted nothing to do with me. The insomnia would come crashing into my life like waves on a beach. I would get strung out on being awake; life would become vapid and meaningless. Three days to go but no end in sight. When sleep finally did come, I ceased to exist in the world, and dreams became my reality.

Darkness swept in and carried me away, surrounding me and dropping me in the middle of a desert, vast, flat, and empty. In the distance, I saw a glow of light coming up from the ground on the horizon. It didn't flicker like a fire but held constant in the face of darkness, calling to me. It felt pure and full of hope, so I walked on. For weeks the arid landscape passed, never changing. Like a movie reel playing in a loop, from days to nights or nights to days. It was always dark, my hope but a dot of light on the horizon. So I walked on, for what seemed like miles, until I finally stood over the radiance as it poured forth from a hole in the earth. At the bottom of a seemingly endless well was a massive beast, trapped in a cage. His prison looked old and frail, yet it still held the monster fast. He tipped his head back and made eye contact. His blazing blue eyes burned brightly.

He bellowed with rage, then shook the cage with fury. I stared at the key to the bindings, then jumped into the well, knowing his time for freedom had come.

I woke up back in the bedroom of my youth.

I opened my eyes and stared at the ceiling. The alarm clock continued to chip away at my sanity. I reached over, fumbled with it, and shut it off.

Six thirty-three a.m. Two and a half hours of sleep. The bloody fangs as Jamis cut his rage loose stood tall in my mind. I wouldn't need anything else.

Ah, ah, boy. Take no chances.

I could hear the smirk in Jaka's voice. He didn't seem to care for the battle warden or his brutality.

Yet it seemed they shared a common goal.

After another lifeless day at school, I arrived home to a cold and empty house, dropped my backpack, then set about my tasks. I was ready for the end, whatever it may be. I wanted it over: my soul was restless and agitated.

First the whiskey. I went out to the storage area in the carport, unlocked it, and opened the door. I pulled out his golf bag and slipped the bottle into the smaller upper pocket after I removed an empty. Right size, right brand, right golf bag. I zipped it up and put everything away. I thought twice, unzipped it, and reached back in for the bottle. I twisted the top and took a long pull, then put everything back into place. It burned all the way down, reminding me for the moment that I was still alive.

Next, I went through the small storage area collecting a few seemingly innocent items. I locked it and went back inside, trophies in hand. I put the bat right by the front door just like the picture in my mind. Everyone used the door coming in from the carport as well, so there was no harm in leaving it out in the open. It looked natural leaning against the wall, like it was left there from the previously ruined baseball season. My breath caught as I realized exactly what I was doing; the tears welled and began to drip out. The whiskey burned in my throat still but wasn't having the desired numbing effect. It was an instant and carnal reaction. I was going to take a man's life, or he was going to take mine. One way or the other, someone was going to die in this house in just a few days. I sucked the tears back in as I had no other choice. The fight was coming regardless of what I wanted. Either I planned and prepared for it, or I let him kill one of us. I stopped holding back and let the tears flow.

I went back downstairs and thought about doing homework. It was a fruitless effort. I couldn't focus, nor did I want to. I went outside and grabbed my bicycle instead. I rode all over town, stopped by a payphone to call my aunt at work and let her know I would be home late, then hit the road again.

Later that night, completely exhausted, I snuck in through the downstairs door and pushed my bike into the laundry room. I could hear my cousin snoring and felt relief at the sound of his nocturnal habits. Our rooms were right next to each other's, but we rarely saw each other or spoke anymore. He kept his distance, and I tried to keep mine. I dove headlong into every situation we ever got into, yet at the end of it all, I was alone. It didn't matter in any case. He wasn't meant to live the kind of life I was. It was for me and me alone.

Jesus was back. He sat quietly across the table from me. To his left was a magician, a soothsayer, a silver-tongued denizen who was everything I could never be: a vampire man sitting still as stone, but his eyes watched my every move, knowing my every thought. I had never seen Jaka before, but this was certainly him. One green eye blazed while the other lid hung halfway over his pupil and remained limp. His jet black hair was slicked back. He was well groomed with jewels on one hand, a cane and a top hat sat across the table in front of him. We made eye contact, and he smiled. Then his face fell flat.

TO WAR, TO DEATH, 'TIL ONLY ONE IS LEFT!

The chorus floated through my mind, and Jaka smiled again, then clacked his vicious maw together. Behind him a theater screen was showing a screenplay of the soundless ritual that had played in my head dozens of times. The pyre was built up, the inferno raging. Life dripped from the pike, the savage carrying it painted in crimson, circling and chanting in a dance of death.

I can give you a better life, boy. Follow me, and I will.

Jaka waved his fingers across the table and dismissed the Christ.

I woke up coughing and gasping for air, choked by thoughts of Jaka. His voice hung in my mind, like a festering sliver in my skin, infecting me.

Whatever was going to happen was my fate, and I was resigned to it.

Friday had finally come. School offered the drab emptiness I had become accustomed to. My familiar.

7

RELIEF

I was no longer sure where I came from, if Memaw and Aunt Jo were mine or if I was simply schizophrenic as the creations of my mind began leaking into every area of my life. The dream boy, Paul, and his family were back as the battle for my attention between him and the no man continued. As in my youth, the insomnia came with a benefit of death like sleep when it did come. I was fully immersed in my dreams and that became my reality.

My mom turned on her blinker and slowed the car down. It looked like we were taking a right onto a dirt driveway.

"Are we there?" I asked.

"Sure are. You're going to have catch the bus from here," she said. I looked around and saw a bench inside what looked like a three-sided shed. There were some mailboxes next to it.

"What's that shed for?" I asked.

"It is probably for the winter when kids like you have to wait for the bus," she said. I knew she was right. There was a church behind it and a small community of houses across the way. We started down our dirt road and passed a small farm. A few minutes later, we crossed through a gate that was open. There was a private property sign up on the gate.

"We are here; this is us," Mom said. I was excited. The driveway was lined with pines and spruce. There was forest on both sides, but the trees were sparse. You could see through the forest, which wasn't typical of this part of the world. Brush was thick around here, making it hard to see more than thirty yards most of the time. I could see reeds and cattails through the trees. A few minutes later, we rounded a corner and saw the house. It was a single-wide mobile home. It sat perched on the top of a small knoll, and the driveway took us directly to the barn, then swung a hard left, and uphill another hundred yards was the trailer.

We pulled around the back of the house, and there sat the U-Haul. The back door was still closed and locked.

My brother and I could not have picked a more perfect place.

This will do for sure.

The barn had a carport on one side; the other side was a closed in and big enough for a few cars at least. The carport was closer to the house, and I could see into it from the porch. There was a large blue tarp covering something up.

"Hey, Mom—" I started but was cut off by car doors shutting behind us.

"Wow, Jamie. This is great," my auntie said, nodding in approval. She and my grandparents were walking toward us. The trailer sat on a bluff.

Fifty yards or so behind the parking area was a fence, and then it dropped off. It was a mostly vertical slope for a few hundred yards down, then flattened out into pastureland. I could see the entire valley in that direction. To the right the pasture merged with the forest, then began climbing again. There was a powerline road that followed beneath the power poles, cutting a distinct path through the forest. The rest of the property was hemmed in by trees. We were invisible to all our neighbors, who at the best were three quarters of a mile away. I couldn't believe it. It was paradise.

"I thought it would be perfect for the boys. The trailer has been here since the '70's, and it has some damage, but we didn't move here to sit in the house. Right, boys?" she said with a big smile. She was right, but it all felt like a dream. I wasn't sure what was real and what wasn't.

"The pasture on the other side of the drop isn't ours," she said, pointing to the fence the edge of the parking area. The U-Haul was in between the house and the drop. She turned a little farther right, and her finger followed the fence line that went down a hill, declining away slowly. In the distance where the pasture met the forest at the bottom of the hill, another fence met ours.

"You see that corner down there where the two fences meet? That fence marks the back of our property." The fence hugged the tree line around the back of the pond and disappeared into the forest, then popped back out and ran right into the gate at the barn. "With the chunk the house sits on, it is just about five acres." She pointed to the same fence behind the pond. "Back there is national forest," she said with a little pride. "We should have this little corner of the earth to ourselves for a few years at least."

"That's it," said my brother loudly as he set the last box in the kitchen. It was a small U-Haul and didn't take long. My mom and auntie were in my mom's bedroom; the elders had already left. Our bedroom was all put together, and our stuff was moved in. Our bikes were outside next to the porch.

I could hear giggling coming from the back room.

That didn't take long.

My mom poked her head into the doorway of our bedroom a few seconds later.

"Hey, tiger—what's say we go for a walk?" Her eyes were bloodshot, and she had a huge smile on her face, then laughed loudly at her own joke.

"I want to show you something," she said with a serious face and gave me the "let's roll" finger twirl.

"*Let's all go outside!*" she said cheerfully. The world was turning sideways. My mom was happy and bouncing along. She went out the front door and down the steps, then danced along like there was a song playing in her head. My auntie was giggling and dancing along too. My brother looked at me and scowled as I headed for the door; he couldn't help but follow.

I joined in the dancing. We finally had something to celebrate, after all.

We all went single file down through the front yard and out toward the barn. Mom led the way with her dancing, giggling troop behind her. My auntie, of diminutive stature and sprite-like spirit, twirled and laughed, then pulled me into her circle of joy. We spun around and around.

Bryan was too stoic to ever participate in such silliness unless he started it. I flipped him the bird behind my auntie's back and carried on.

My mom stood holding the edge of the tarp. Three sides of the carport were open with just a roof overhead, the fourth side the red exterior sidewall of the barn. The tarp was large and covered almost the entire parking area.

"ONE..." She counted loudly and feigned suspense. "TWO..." She held her hand over her heart and acted is if she couldn't take it anymore. Then suddenly, she dispensed with the theatrics and with both hands ripped the tarp off the surprise. In an instant she was ten feet away with the tarp at her feet.

"Three," she said in a whisper. And that was all we heard. The crickets stopped, the wind didn't blow, and not a noise was heard except deafening silence exploding in my ears.

It was a four-wheeler and a motorcycle. There were new helmets on each one.

"Holy shit," Bryan said. His jaw dropped, then more silence. He just looked back at the machines in silence. I looked at my mom, then back at the bike. I looked at my brother, then back at the bike.

I looked at my mom, walked over, and touched her shoulder, then grabbed the other one and squeezed them. I let go and turned around, walked back over next to my brother, and stared.

My auntie howled at that and did exactly the same thing, then came and stood in line with us and stared. My mom stayed quiet, just smiling and enjoying the victory, watching us closely. She howled with laughter when the sprite in my aunt teased with mimicry.

The bike was orangeish red; it had a blue seat with the letters XR on it in white. It said Honda on the gas tank and had an emblem of a single gold wing. The helmet was hanging on the handlebars. There was no doubt in my mind whose was whose.

"I get the four-wheeler," Bryan said and pushed me out of the way as he ran over to it. He grabbed the helmet off the handlebars and jumped on. I went over to the bike and inspected it. It had scratches and dings all over the place, one of the emblems was missing from the gas tank, and the grips had seen better days.

I twisted the throttle and let go; it snapped back into place. It seemed fiery and tough. I thought it was a little scary. A picture of a reddish-orange dragon unleashing death popped into my head. It was Smaug, from *The Hobbit*. I was living in a fantasy. The idea, no doubt, wasn't new. The surreal moment, the motorcycle, the dancing. I had lights in front of my eyes. I exhaled in a whoosh, letting my breathing resume.

"So? What do you guys think?" Mom asked.

"It's amazing," I started to say.

Bryan cut me off. "It's the best present ever, Mom. Is it really mine? Like we get to keep them, right? They are ours? Can I take it hunting? See these things on the front? They are gun racks…I can't believe this. Can I ride it right now? How do you start it? Does it have reverse? PJ, get in front and push…" He was excited and talking fast.

Our grandparents' neighbor had some old four wheelers. Earlier that year we had to help them clear brush and move firewood and chase down some missing cows. Our reward was a weekend of riding. By the end of the weekend, I was pretty good.

"Your grandpa fixed them up, so they both run well and everything works. They were part of the deal for the house. It took some doing, but I thought you guys would love them. Paulie, I can teach you how to ride if you want. The pasture should be a great place to learn. I'm sure it won't take you long," said Mom.

"Can I go right now, Mom? Can I?" Bryan would beg if he had to.

"Go put your hiking boots on. Jeans and a sweatshirt too. There are two pairs of leather gloves in the U-Haul," she said. He was off in a flash and running toward the house.

I was testing the weight to see if I could hold the bike up. It wasn't too heavy until I imagined it lying on the ground. I climbed on board. I was a little short for it still. I could touch on one side or the other but not quite both at the same time. I could imagine flying along through the woods. I tried to roll it forward. It wouldn't move. I remembered the clutch and pulled it in, and the bike rolled forward unexpectedly. I managed to keep my balance and let it roll a little toward the road. The barn was inclined to the road, so I had a nice little runway to coast down. It wasn't too steep, so I felt pretty safe. I even managed to get both feet on the pegs. I let the clutch out to stop the bike at the bottom, and the engine roared to life.

"MOM!" I yelled in panic.

"BALANCE!" she yelled back at me, running to catch up. The momentum of the bike rolling down the hill and popping the clutch while it was in gear had brought the beast to life.

It threw me back in the saddle just enough to twist the throttle a little more. I was moving even faster now. The thumper beneath me growled loudly.

"JAMIE!" my auntie yelled, running toward us. I was hanging on for dear life. Mom was too late; I was rolling down the driveway, too consumed by fear to tip the thing over.

After a full minute of rolling along without carnage, I realized I was riding a motorcycle. I let off the throttle a little, and it slowed down. I gave the throttle a small twist, and the engine revved and lurched forward, causing it to spin even more as the weight of my body slid back on the motorcycle, putting all the pressure on my hands and catching me off guard again.

The front end tried to pull hard one way, and it took everything I had to keep the bike upright. The fence posts next to the driveway were whizzing by.

I'M GONNA DIE!

I was in full panic. I glanced quickly at the controls and tried to steel my nerves. I knew the front brake was on one side and the clutch on the other, but all the excitement kept logic at bay. *WHICH IS WHICH?!* My heart was going to beat its way through my chest. I wasn't sure I could hang on much longer. I climbed a small rise in the driveway. The highway was looming.

Fortunately, I had great balance, but at the moment that was all I had. The panic swelled and choked out any sensible thought. All I had to do was…

Somehow, I managed to keep the bike going forward. I glanced down again. I regained my footing and shifted my weight so I could let off the throttle. The bike slowed down. I had five hundred yards to figure out how to get off.

I didn't know how to stop. I didn't know how to shift, but I could keep the bike upright if it kept moving. I pulled back on the throttle again, only this time I prepared for the lurch. I hung on with my left hand so I could control the throttle with my right. My feet and legs were locked to the bike. I was getting the hang of it.

The fear was melting away. I was stuck between bewilderment and excitement. As long as I could more or less go straight and not stop, I would be fine. I looked at the highway again. The fear crept back in. Our driveway merged into the right lane. *Not much of a turn; I can make it.* I had to keep moving until I could figure out how to turn around. I heard an engine behind me.

"PULL IN THE CLUTCH!" I heard mom yelling from the four-wheeler.

"PULL IN THE CLUTCH AND STEP..." The wind carried her voice and the rest of the instructions away. I could hear her yelling but couldn't make out the words. There was a logging truck up on the highway somewhere, his Jake Brakes filling the rest of the void, buffeting loudly.

I kept moving forward, eating up the real estate; it was all downhill from here. I tapped the lever on the right, and the front end of the bike dived hard to the right. I almost lost it again, but my determination not to die kept me upright.

WAS THAT THE BRAKE? WRONG LEVER. I grabbed the other lever and pulled it in quickly.

The log truck air brakes were pumping away; the highway had a steep hill before our driveway. Gravity was carrying the fully loaded truck downhill. Another fifty yards and the trucker would have to let the brakes rest.

The bike started moving faster. *Too fast. Way too fast.* I had just crested the hill when I pulled in the clutch. The motor died down to a hum. The driveway was far steeper than I realized, and the bike was gaining momentum every turn of the tire. So was the truck. Our impending destiny cemented our fate.

I could use the brakes, but last time it almost killed me. I was going too fast to jump with no helmet. I steeled my nerves.

Make the turn onto the highway.

I was flying now. Our roller coaster of a driveway was dropping me down the final, steep descent, and I had no choice but to cross the trucker's path.

The log truck released the Jakes and was running full tilt out of the corner.

It was too late to change course. I couldn't stop the bike in time even if I knew how.

Icy terror gripped my throat. I tried to scream but couldn't. The timing was all wrong; the truck was going too fast. Time stopped, and I blinked.

The front tire hit the highway. I could see the whites of the trucker's eyes. His mouth was open in a silent yell. He clutched the steering wheel with both hands, his knuckles white with a grip of panic. I could see his coffee cup steaming next to his right hand. It read HAVE A NICE DAY in bright orange letters. I could smell the hot brakes and the diesel engine only a few feet away…

I blinked again. Time came back to life.

Mom's scream woke the devil, and he opened his sleepy eyes once again to find Republic, Washington.

Paul's familiar world twisted and spun away as the no man pulled once again, tugging me back into the world, back into the past, that I walked through.

I was Paul. Wasn't I? Or was he me? I thrashed around in my bed as I struggled to grasp who was who or where I came from. I kicked off the sweat soaked sheet and tried to sit up to make sense of the last scene, but the groggy and deep feeling of sleep sucked me back into what remained of the violent life I left behind those many years ago. The no man was relentless.

8

CHAOS

I heard the rumble of the green-and-white GMC from downstairs. Aunt Jo was home, which was out of my control. I didn't have the heart to drug her and couldn't exactly kick her out of her own house. She was upstairs, waiting for Dick to get home from the golf course. I could only hope for the best, but I was prepared for the worst. It came on hauntingly fast. I heard the screen door shut, and as expected, the arguing started a few minutes later.

I sat on the edge of my bed staring at the brass knuckles, wondering why my life had turned out like this. I thought of all the fights, all the people, and all the problems. I thought about the time I ran away, the loss of Little League, and the loss of my childhood. I thought of how different it could have all gone if Dick would have just been aborted as a baby, how different my life may have turned out. None of that mattered in the end; the river of emotions had finally run dry.

I sighed, wishing I could be anybody but me, then I slid the brass knuckles into my pocket and headed for the stairs. I didn't bother praying or reaching out to God. The man Jesus was dismissed in my last dream by the soulless magician without a care. I stood and listened. I took a deep breath and held it. I could hear the argument escalating. I let the breath out in another sigh, my emotes were cold and lifeless. Not a fire burning in sight, I poked and prodded around for Jamis but felt only emptiness. I curled my hand around the knuckles, then heard the yelling escalate. That was my cue.

I was up the stairs in a blink. The door at the top was closed. I stopped, held my breath one last time, and leaned my head against the door. Kill or be killed: this was the path I was destined to walk.

To war, to death, 'til only one is left.

The chant floated through my mind. I could taste blood in the air. Every scent, every drop of fear, every trickle of chaos, every hint of anger assaulted me. My finely tuned and hardened body was ready, like a sword's honed edge of purpose, to cut a man down.

The doorknob felt small in my hand. I could feel the cords of muscle in my body pull tight. The summer of bucking bales built rock in my shoulders and arms. I knew what I was walking into and let all the fear slip away. Redemption was at hand.

I opened the door and pushed through. I went right and rounded into the living room. It was empty. The bay windows glistened with light. The TV was off, but all the lights in the room were on. To my left was the door to the carport. The kitchen was behind me and lit up as well. All of my senses were peaking. The light in the room was calling to me.

Suddenly the house fell silent.

The calm before the storm.

Then the cussing and the rising voices from the next room brought me back to my purpose.

I reached down into my sock and pulled out the mouthpiece. I slid it into my mouth and worked it around until it was comfortable.

The arguing escalated and was coming my way. I saw Jo moving quickly toward the kitchen with the dead man savagely pursuing her. Neither even noticed I was there. I slid my hand into my pocket. Then time vanished, leaving us to find our places.

I slipped around the corner into the kitchen, unsure of what I would find. I caught sight of the bat and the front door but kept my eyes moving.

His hands were wrapped around her throat. Her face was turning blue as she struggled to breathe, struggled to stand. He had her pinned against the counter with the sink and window behind her. He was putting all of his weight and anger into it, pushing her backward and down, trying to kill her. His keys began to slip from her hand and fell to the floor. The life in her eyes was rapidly burning out. He was breathing hard and straining, his jaw clenched tightly, his face drawn back in hate and anger.

TOOO WAAAARRRR!

The sound of violence rang loudly through the house as time slipped back in slowly, then stopped for the last time, immortalizing the moment. I gripped the knuckles and felt my hands on him, shoving him hard enough to get him to turn and release his grip. The cocaine fueled him as he spun toward me, eyes widening and blazing with hellfire at the sight of me. Spit and slobber dropped from his mouth in his renewed vigor and hatred. His extra-large right hand landed cleanly just below my eye socket.

Calculated. Expected. Worth the risk.

Red blossoms rained down inside my head from the blow. Time came rushing back in.

Darkness. Then light.

No need to hold back anymore, Jamis was unleashed. The knuckles were in my right hand and my arm began pumping like a piston back and forth. Blood sprayed from his nose and mouth and splattered across the kitchen. I pushed the woman out of the kitchen, out of harm's way, and stepped back in, watching him bleed. I slowed down and took it in. I wanted to see him in pain, I wanted to watch him suffer. I hit him twice more with the speed of a jackhammer. He was acutely aware of what just happened, acutely aware that the fight for his own life had just begun.

Darkness. Then light.

I stepped back and watched the blood cover his shirt, running profusely from his mouth and nose. His eyes were wild in shock and fear, lolling about in his head trying to find purchase in reality. He sucked wind through a cavity loaded with blood, trying hard to breathe, coughing and choking. Suddenly, he spat the life-giving liquid onto the floor. He steadied himself and spat again. He lifted his head slowly to finally make eye contact and saw the full wrath of Jamis, the war dog built for his demise.

I stared back with contempt and hatred of my own. I let the knuckles slide from my hand and fall to the floor, knowing they had fulfilled their purpose as I was about to fulfill mine. I pulled the mouthpiece out and let it drop.

"To war, to death, 'til only one is left." It came out in a taunting tone just above a whisper. There wasn't a trickle of my own voice in the timeless anthem. Except this was no battle. It was atonement, finality, the end.

I let go and unloaded what I had left. Blood by the ounce covered the kitchen and the floor. I stepped back again and watched as his eyes spun in his head. He could barely stand and put up a hand to let me know he was defeated. I spit my own mouthful of blood at his face and slapped him hard enough to knock out a tooth.

"Now, I will give you something to cry about."

His time had come. No doubt he had seen me in this nightmare before. I waited until he recognized who I was, who he made. The years of violence that forced a boy to become a man, and now that man was going to end his life.

His defenses were weak and crippled. His pathetic attempt to slow me took the beating to the floor. I mounted him and his death march began.

His grave was dug.

The pyre was built.

I was prepared to put his head on a pike.

His slick wet hair was in my left hand. Every breath was one step closer to his end as I put everything I had into my right hand. In the distance, a far-off land, I could hear a woman crying and a boy screaming.

His face was mangled and beaten. He needed to cough but couldn't. I leaned in, kneeling on the dying man.

Not in this life. Never again.

I moved in closer to watch the fire burn out as he drowned on his own blood—victory over this life, over him, and over my destiny within reach.

Suddenly, I was pulled from behind.

Through the bloodlust and rage, I knew the woman who had raised me and there she was once again in the middle of something she couldn't possibly understand.

I should have drugged her.

She was crying and begging me to stop. She pushed me toward the door. Told me to run. Told me to leave. She begged me to go. I was consumed with violence and anger. She pushed me away again, protecting him.

"NO!" I roared in defiance. Appeal denied.

My own face was bloody and bruised. My eyes ran wild with hate and adrenaline. Blood dripped from my mouth. I stepped back toward my prey. He coughed in spasmodic fits and curled into a fetal position.

I watched intently with pure venom in my heart, praying for his death. Jo shook in terror and backed up a step but held her position between us with a hand out and eyes wide, begging for it to stop. After all these years, all the pain and all the suffering, here she was fighting for his life, pleading for it, crying me off. The blood. The tears. The confusion. I saved her life, and now she was on her knees for his.

"Run. Just go."

With shaking hands and a mother's broken heart, she whispered her prayer.

I turned and walked out into the rain, furious that he was still breathing.

9

SACRIFICE

I ran out my frustration and anger. I ran until I was exhausted. Then I ran some more. Eventually, I made it to a friend's house and was invited in. The boy in me couldn't hold back, and my story spilled out like a flood. In the chaos, I forgot about my own face and how I must look, even after much of the blood had been washed away by the rain. I was cleansed, baptized even, by the tears of the sky as those above wept at what was to come. The swelling and bruises were very much evident. My friend's mother was a bartender and no stranger to men and their evil; one look at my face and she knew. I was given dry clothes and a towel. My friend's sister, an angel I shared many secrets with, held my hand and my broken heart.

Then my old baseball coach showed up, in his police cruiser, on official business. He wanted to arrest me. Dick was in the hospital, alive but in bad shape. My own flesh and blood had taken him there, and upon arrival the police were notified. My Little League coach was on duty that night, the same one that did not ferry Dick to jail for domestic violence a few years back. The same one that never asked what happened the next day at baseball practice. The one that knew but pretended to know different, and here he was standing before us, telling an angel and her mother that he needed to speak with me.

I was calm, my reservoir of emotes depleted, and I knew exactly what I had to do now; I saw the truth at the bottom of the empty well. I needed a body to burn, a head on a pike, and a pyre to dance around naked, my body painted in blood. I wasn't done yet; this was only the beginning of Dick's end. I would see the terror in his eyes before the light burned out. Tonight.

I stepped around the door of the mobile home and stood face to face with the police officer. The wind blew in gusts and torrents, blasting the metal side of the mobile home, then whipping back in the other direction. A storm was coming, the first of winter.

I raised a hand against the weather and said, "Bill."

The light flickered, and the wind howled, so I kept my head low.

"Hey, Joe," he said with a sad smile. "We were called to the hospital earlier tonight. They said they had a man come in who took a pretty serious beating. He was barely breathing when his wife brought him through the door. I imagine you know the story better than I do, though. Want to tell me what happened?"

I stared blankly at him, then looked to the ground, my hand still shielding my face from the weather. There was no need for a response; I assumed my right to remain silent.

"Can I come in?" he asked my den mother politely and raised a hand toward the weather and the soaking he was taking. I looked at her, knowing that cops, like vampires, should not be invited in, but contrary to my belief, she nodded at both of us. He came in and shut the weather out behind him. He stood, dripping rainwater onto the small entryway carpet. He was not a big nor particularly intimidating man and was slightly shorter than I was. Yet his badge gave him a few extra inches and the posture of a man intent on his business.

"They want to press charges," he said, getting directly to the point. That was all my den mother needed to hear. She had no love for the law nor stupidity of men. She also was well endowed with the attitude of a honey badger. All I heard through the commotion was "they." My mind turned over the loose ends. The brass knuckles and the mouth guard were still lying on the kitchen floor, as far as I knew.

I didn't care much about what he said, except for the "they." More trouble headed my way. I was a delinquent anyway. A juvenile detention center seemed a very likely course for my future at this point. Why not finish what I started? I listened to my friend's mother protecting me like one of her own.

"Look at his face, William! Are you blind? Do you not realize he is just a kid? Had you done your job in the first place, this kind of shit wouldn't happen in this town." She didn't hold back, and her tone said she thought he was a moron and that he was personally responsible for my face.

In a way, she wasn't wrong. She reached over, cupped my jaw, and gently turned my face into the light, "Look. Look at his face."

I had a whopper of a black eye. The eyeball itself was blood red, and the eyelid hung fat and swollen, barely open. The entire socket was seven shades of purple, black, and blue and heavily swollen. A greenish-red hue ran down that side of my face. My upper lip was fat and split. No doubt I looked far better than Dick, though, and almost laughed out loud when the thought crossed my mind. I had been down long enough, and my mind was finally relaxing. I had won the battle; now it was time to win the war.

"He was drunk. He was going to kill her. I pushed him away, and he hit me." The gospel truth of that night. "Look at the marks on her neck where he was choking her. I don't remember what happened after he hit me." Not a total lie. The fact that he lived through it was unfortunate.

Officer Bill knew I was telling the truth.

He may have wanted to press, but the honey badger was ready for a fight, so he smiled a sad smile and let it go. He left with a written statement and an apology. Most people would say Dick deserved it and move on. He did, but I sure as hell wasn't moving on, not yet and maybe never.

I was heading back home, then to the hospital.

Time to finish it.

I thought about the time I got slammed face first off the top bunk, when all the violence in my life started.

"Better luck next time," he had said. Clear as day, the picture flashed through my mind. I wasn't finished; I couldn't be. Kill or be killed. It had become all too common in this life.

The rain eased, and the streets reflected a thousand tiny gleaming spotlights as the headlights from the car brought each drop to life.

All eyes on me, watching every move I made.

It was surreal. I was in a euphoric state, watching the lights warm the road, then leave it dark, cold, and empty, as we had found it. We were just across town, and it wouldn't take long to get home. The tires rolled along, hissing against the wet pavement. I stayed quiet for the duration of the ride. Once we were close, I asked her to pull over so I could go in through the basement door. I gave my driver a hug and thanked her for the ride. She said she would be around if I needed anything else. Just call. A quick kiss on the cheek, and she let me go. I watched as she drove away.

I turned to the house and saw the empty carport, and the loneliness of it all hit me in the stomach. I shook it off and headed for the door. Once inside, I bee-lined for my room. I grabbed a duffel and loaded up some clothes and a few other things from my room. I found a raggedy brown jacket, some gloves, and an old stocking cap. I jetted upstairs and went searching for the evidence; they lay on the carpet just outside of the kitchen. I let out a sigh of relief and picked the knuckles up, the mouthpiece as well. I caught sight of the kitchen and was drawn in; blood was splattered all over the place. It was wiped across the floor, on the cabinets, the countertops and across the broken table. Hand streaks smeared across the oven door; dried drops hung on the ceiling. It looked like someone had been murdered and bled dry.

Almost. A smile crept across my face, knowing it wasn't mine for the first and last time.

I broke my trance and went to the closet, grabbed his revolver, shoved it in my bag, and started digging through drawers, looking for Dick's hiding spot. Then it dawned on me; it wouldn't be hidden in here.

He was hiding it from her.

So it would be somewhere she wouldn't stumble on it by accident. I dropped my bag by the door and went outside to the truck. I looked in the bed of the pickup, and sure enough, the golf clubs and cooler were still there. I reached in and flipped the cooler lid open in a moment. Surprisingly, there were still several ice-cold beers waiting inside. My bruised and swollen upper lip slowed the celebrating, but I managed to suck one down despite the discomfort, tossed the empty can back into the cooler, then jumped inside the truck and turned on the cab light. The vehicle had a solid bench seat with a woven seat cover over the entire backrest and the seat. Behind my calves was a pocket that ran the length of the seat face, for rifle storage. I felt around just in case, but I knew it was probably empty. I did come across a box of brass for the revolver, though, and set them aside. I dug through the glove compartment but came up empty handed. I put the search aside and jumped out to grab another beer. I would need some fortification in order to keep going tonight. I pulled open the tab and tipped it back, carefully this time. The sky had cleared up, and the stars were out in full gala; the temperature was dropping quickly. The roads might get slick if it got much colder. I jumped back into the truck and set my beer down in the cupholder. It most certainly was meant to be there. I flipped open the ashtray.

Keys. Hot damn!

That made my night, but my search was not over yet. On the keychain were one square-headed key and one round one. I slid the square key into the ignition and turned. The V-8 roared to life. I flipped on the lights and opened the door, leaving the engine running to warm it up. I walked the perimeter of the truck and checked all of the lights. I opened the driver's door and slid my leg in to hit the high/low light switch on the floor. The 4x4 was in pretty good shape, all things considered, and ran like a champ.

I flipped on the heater and the CD player. Led Zeppelin came through the speakers, and "Stairway to Heaven" was just getting started. I switched off the dope light and sat quietly, finishing my beer. I laid my head on the steering wheel and tried to come up with a new plan, one that could be executed tonight and in short order. I feared the cops might wise up and come by, or they might post security at the hospital, if they hadn't already. Either way I needed to get moving, my auntie-mom could pull up at any second and blow all my ideas to hell. Again.

I dropped my forehead back onto the steering wheel despite the need to keep moving and listened to Jimmy Page cut loose. I didn't know much in life, but I knew music—all kinds, and classic rock was a favorite. Led Zeppelin led the charge in my transformation from boy to man along with the Rolling Stones. The Beatles couldn't hold a torch to such royalty, and it disgusted me to think they were ever given a crown. They were ushers for the truly gifted, nothing more. Turned out that Dick and I had a handful of things in common after all.

My spirits were lifting, and I was jamming along with the boys, and I whacked the steering wheel to the beat of the drum. The square horn button that covered the center of the steering wheel suddenly dislodged. I looked down and grabbed it, pounded the rest of my beer, and went to pop the button back into place when my bounty appeared!

I laughed out loud as I pulled a small bag of white powder from the hidey-hole.

Once a junkie, always a junkie.

I killed the lights, grabbed the keys, and shoved the treasure in my pocket, then headed back toward the house. Before I did, though, I put the golf clubs in storage, and a gas can and shovel in the back of the truck. I grabbed a flashlight and went back to the truck toolbox, looking for the giant zip ties I had seen there last summer.

I spotted the bag and pulled out a handful of them and looped them through the belt buckles on my pants. They had to be close to a half-inch thick and at least thirty inches long. They were designed for permanently fastening flexible air ducting to metal fittings, but Dick used them for all sorts of other things. They were sturdy and impossible to break by hand, once installed. I scanned the toolbox to see if anything else useful might catch my eye, then I threw the flashlight in and shut the top of the toolbox. I was taking too long, and I knew it. I could feel time pressing up against me, why I did not know but the urge to hurry began creeping in.

I jumped back into the truck and fired it up. I left the headlights off and pulled onto the street. I went down around the corner and pulled to the side of the road into the gravel and put the vehicle in park. I jumped out and ran back up the hill to our house. If my aunt was at the hospital, she wouldn't be coming back home that way. Hopefully, she would be too drained to even notice that the GMC was gone.

I went inside and locked the door, grabbed my bag, and headed back downstairs.

I couldn't help myself. A hot shower would only take a minute or two, and I needed it, badly.

I set my bag outside the basement door and went for the shower, knowing I was running short on time.

It was 11:30 p.m., and I sat outside the hospital in the green machine. I watched my aunt climb into her car from a distance. The fight went down around 6:00 p.m., then time took on a life of its own. I had no doubt tonight would resonate forever. I was going to make sure of it. I checked the pistol to make sure it was loaded, and I fingered the extra-large zip ties around my belt.

If he couldn't walk, I would have to find a wheelchair. My thoughts danced with joy and excitement. My body was energized, full of life from a bump of Dick's stash. I was filling my own gas tank with intoxicants, preparing to commit murder. Premeditated. It was just unfortunate that he hadn't died earlier. Kill or be killed. It was that kind of a life now, and I was committed to it.

I slid out of the truck and shut the door quietly, then holstered the gun in the waist of my pants. It felt wrong. Heavy with a lie. The weight of justice wasn't in it. It was for the hand of lesser men who knew nothing of bravery. I opened the door to the truck and tucked the gun under the seat, then shut the door again.

I pulled on my gloves and tugged at my hat. I felt a dark heart and a crooked grin grow. I leaned back against the door, watched the hospital doors, and let the cold night air wash over me.

I pulled out my pack of smokes, slid one between my lips, and smelled the tobacco of the unlit cancer before I peeled a match from the book, closed the cover, and struck it against the friction strip. The sulfur flared to life. I watched as it burned, then brought it up and lit the tobacco. My mind was on a single track. Focused. Clear. Aware. Sharp.

It would be time for a full-blown celebration soon enough.

I looked back at the hospital doors thinking about the best way out. Front doors were no good. Side door was probably locked. I'd need a wheelchair. I let the puzzle pieces work in my head and started walking toward the entrance when no other options presented themselves. I had to get in before I'd need to get out.

It was a small town and a sleepy night. The cold and the stars pierced the quiet darkness that embraced a country town at midnight. I took a final draw and flicked the butt across the empty parking lot. I watched the embers scatter as they hit the pavement.

I strolled boldly through the front doors only to be met by an empty reception desk, the moving shadows on the wall behind it painted by the flicker of a small TV. I hit the up button on the elevator as I passed by and continued striding confidently. I turned the next corner in search of a wheelchair. I quickly poked my head into a few rooms to no avail, and then quietly turned back to the elevator. I caught the doors just as they were sliding closed and let myself in. The reception desk across the hall still sat empty. I watched the glow from the TV as the doors slid shut.

There were only two floors that held overnight patients, so I went up as far as I could. Starting at the top and working my way down, I got off on the fourth floor to find dim lighting and locked doors. I wasn't sure what each room held or where the staff was, but I tried every door. The only one that opened was a small bathroom that led nowhere. I needed to hurry up; my buzz started to fade so I hit the stairs going down in a hurry. My feet echoed throughout the stairwell.

I hit the next floor just in time to see an employee turn his back and continue his rounds. I let the door close behind him and watched through the rectangular window. He walked down the hallway and took a right into another room. I leaned against the door and turned the handle slowly. Without a sound I crept through the door, set it gently back into the doorjamb, then quick stepped into the first room I saw the nurse walk out of. The lights were dim, and the curtain was pulled in front of the door. I could hear a wheezing, rhythmic breathing and the slow, steady beep of a hospital heartbeat. I peeked around the curtain and saw a curly, gray-haired woman with a thin blanket pulled up to her chin. Her eyes were closed, and she looked lifeless, but the machine she was attached to told a different story. I scanned the room, and my gaze stopped on a brown, folded-up wheelchair.

The old woman's breathing was labored and shallow; her life was surely close to the end, but the corners of her upturned mouth spoke of untold joy. The depression that sucked at my soul begged to trade places with her. To be her. For this life to be over with. The promise of the end stood tall and proud. Hope was forever a promise of things to come but never present. It was what could be but never was. It was a lie that we all told ourselves when life hurt. I saw it clearly now. Hope wasn't an eternal well to draw from; it was a bridge of lies over the river of truth. I had to fight off the urge to smother her, to give the old woman what she surely must have been smiling about: hope that the end was near.

I was disgusted by life and watched the world turn dark again. I peeked my head out the open door and began zigzagging from room to room, furious. My renewed anger and contempt drove me on. The time to finish this had come.

After several minutes of looking, I finally found the man I was looking for in the room at the end of the hall. I crept in for a closer look. It was worse than imagined. Newly stitched skin took center stage across his upper lip and nose. The one side of his mouth was split and badly swollen. It matched his eye sockets. Both were grotesquely swollen and discolored. The left brow had a dozen stitches up and across, and he wore a gauze patch over the top of his forehead. I looked at him and smiled, knowing that he had earned every bit of it. I imagined that behind the torn-up lips were a few missing teeth. His breathing was fine, though, and his heartbeat seemed plenty strong. I was the remedy for that.

I shot my head out the door and looked around. Nobody. I wasted no time and went to the old woman's room for the wheelchair. I felt the pull once again to do her the favor that God wasn't willing to do. If I had time maybe I would come back.

I grabbed the wheelchair and raced back down the hall. He must have been heavily sedated as I wrestled the still-breathing body into the wheelchair. I pulled a zip tie from my belt and lashed his hands together in his lap. I linked two ties together and wrapped them around the chair and his body, satisfied when I heard them click and fasten. I grabbed a blanket from the bed and threw it across his lap and torso to hide the makeshift shackles.

We made it to the elevator undetected. Down we went, and the doors opened. I wheeled him out and heard a squawk, then a beep from the dispatch station. We stopped behind the corner in case the noise brought attention.

"Third degree burns. Face, neck, and chest. Condition is critical. ETA two minutes." The noise stopped as a light on the wall began to blink red.

I had to move, but my legs were concrete. I had to get him out, but I knew. It was too late. I knew that call was for me, and my heart sank like a stone.

I stared at the man in the wheelchair and backed up, shaking my head.

Blood and fire.

Head on a pike.

You missed the reap fire boy.

My mind was reeling. The clock on the wall had turned over to Saturday, and Friday was no more.

I looked up in time to see a nurse coming around the corner. She saw the sleeping man in the wheelchair and did a double take from him to me then back to him again.

I gasped for air and begged. "No. Please, no. Please, please, no. God. Please, no," I kept repeating and mumbling. The nurse looked again at the man in the wheelchair and came to me.

"Please, God…no. No, God…no. Not this. Not this. God, please…"

"Son are you ok? What happened?" the nurse asked. "Are you hurt?"

My voice was barely a whisper. "It's not me…"

"I couldn't hear you honey. Are you ok?" She lifted her radio and was just about to speak when the doors to the emergency entrance broke open and a gurney came crashing through.

"Please, God, no. God, not this."

On the gurney lay a boy whose upper torso had been cleansed by fire. The blistered and charred skin lay waste to his once-beautiful face. His eyes were closed, his breath barely there. He rolled by, his spirit leaking out slowly before he ever even truly lived. Another boy close by felt his spirit break. The last threads of love that bound him to this world were finally severed.

In the world where gravity holds us all down, Dick narrowly escaped certain death, living to die another day. My flesh and blood the one that burned instead.

10

CLARITY

I shot up in my bed, as I escaped from the most painful part of my childhood. Dick was out there, alive and breathing, while others had not come away so lucky. It was all too clear what I had to do, what had to be done to save my soul. The bed was soaked in sweat as I felt around for my phone, snagged it from under the pillow, and climbed out, heading for the shower.

All the suffering was leading to this. I knew it in the beginning, but the madness skirting around in my head made it difficult to pin down.

I had to find Dick. I had to kill him. It was that simple.

I leaned my head against the shower wall and let the water cascade down my naked body, the last scene at the hospital from those many years ago still rich in my mind.

"You have to do what?" my wife said in a short, dismissive tone. I had been up since 2:00 a.m., and the clock spun by. In that time, I put together a loose plan and needed to act on it quickly.

"I have to go back," I said, referring again to the small town I once lived in.

It was just after 5:00 a.m., but the shower and our daughter climbing into our bed shortly after woke my wife up. Both of us were sitting in the living room, drinking coffee. Our brown, leather U-shaped couch from Costco kept us on opposite ends. She was not a morning person and stared at me in irritation. Since January and taking the job with the university, our lives were supposed to be improving. They most certainly were not. She knew about my past, the darkness and the struggle for sobriety, but didn't know how far it went. She didn't know I was participating while at work, daily at that, until changing jobs in January. The six-figure salary from the trade I was in, prior to teaching, gave us a comfortable life—certainly not extravagant or excessive but comfortable. Our house was small starter home in the suburbs from the '60s, but over the last decade, we made it a home, updating and renovating with sweat equity. Our vehicles were paid off, and we had no other debt. Our life wasn't excessive; there was no need to keep up with Joneses. I was going to have to take a leave of absence from the university, but to be honest, that job wasn't going anywhere. I needed to get back to my craft and away from the Cabalifornians regardless. The world and the no man were both telling me it was time to go.

"The therapist agreed, last time we talked about it, and said it might help, that I might be able to close the book if I went back. I haven't slept in months, I can't focus, I can't work, and I just can't live like this anymore. I have to do something, and it has to be soon. Like now," I said, knowing I wasn't going to let it go. She had been changing the sweat-covered sheets and washing them a few times a week. The evidence was there; I just needed to nudge her along without making things worse. I felt bad for her and our children, I had become a vacant father and husband. I was going through the motions, but it was mechanical. I felt like posting a help wanted sign to see if I could fill the position while I dealt with the devil. It was no doubt a difficult time in our relationship, and the end wasn't yet in sight.

Her face softened a little, and she sighed.

"Ok, do what you want." Then she held up her coffee cup, motioning for a refill, and went back to the tablet in her lap.

It was the kind of approval I expected, but it was approval nonetheless. She should probably divorce me while I was gone.

Twenty-four hours later, I was in my truck heading north on I-5. Last I heard Dick was still floating around the northwest somewhere, and I had no reservations about piecing a plan together along the way. The no man relented on his maddening pursuit of my past and let me sleep a full night for the first time in months. The addictions were muted, and with the Cabalifornians in the review mirror, I felt a growing surge of hope.

"Expect what God has promised, chile; das what hope really is." Memaw smiled and slowly slid another slice of applesauce cake toward me. My eyes were wide with anticipation. I loved her and her applesauce cake too; despite what I was, and where I came from, she loved me back.

"What do you say, Joey?" she asked with kind eyes. Prodding for an answer. We did this daily at lunch. "Thank you, Memaw, and thank you, Jesus!" I shouted loudly, never taking my eyes off the cake as it got closer to me. The old woman giggled and hid her mouth behind her hand.

"Amen! Thank you, Jesus," she said in return.

Her delight came from the happiness in the boy as he received his cake. Her husband was a good man with a bad habit of bringing home stray cats. The boy's mother, Lilly, likely never laid a sober eye on her child and in the end probably didn't care. The heroin poisoned her soul and wasted the life given to her by the creator. Jacob and Memaw raised a large family of their own and then moved on to the alley cats and their litter. Often times, Jacob was able to find them some help—a friend or a relative—and worked to get them on their feet and headed in the right direction. The house that Jacob and Memaw built was filled with love and compassion. They had helped dozens, if not hundreds of people reclaim their lives over the years, and it was their passion and calling. She looked at the last of her younglings and smiled a sad smile. Her husband had passed recently from a heart attack, and Joey was the only youngling left in the house. He would be the last of Memaw's adopted family. With Jacob gone and her own health waning, she cherished her time with him, knowing that her race had been run. She took the time to impart as much of God's word and wisdom onto the younglings as she could, knowing it might be the only time they were ever exposed to the Truth in their life. She gave her heart and soul to those kids, and only God knows what happened to many of them.

A small smile tugged at the corners of my mouth as I drove on, thoughts of memaw filling me with gratitude.

The drive north out of California was nothing to be envied. It was flat, empty, and lifeless. The speedometer said eighty-seven, the limit was seventy-five, but the faster I got out, the better I felt. My wife had a half dozen things planned for her and the kids before I even left. I think secretly she was glad to see me go. I would have been too.

I was going to start looking for Dick where I left off: the hospital and the tiny town sixteen hours to the north in Washington state. I planned to drive until I got tired and sleep in the truck or find a hotel. In my heart, I would always be a street urchin with minimal needs. I drove on in silence, listening to the hum of the tires on the road.

I realized how I felt. It was at peace. I wondered if it was the peace of Memaw's God or the peace of AA. The tenants of AA seemed an obvious path to Jesus without saying his name out loud. Sure, they said God, but anything could be a God to anybody. "Higher power" was really the AA lingo, but in the end it was a direct path to righteousness and to Memaw's living God.

Alcoholics Anonymous was a dollar-a-meeting group therapy. Sitting with people who struggled with the same thing I did for an hour a night, sometimes two, was working its magic. It was more effective than rehab, $25,000 a month cheaper, and could be instituted just about anywhere.

I once heard a guy tell me rehab was better because he didn't have to say his name and admit his addiction. I wondered how desperate the guy was to get sober and whose dime he was living on—it certainly wasn't his own.

Pride came with a cost unless it was coming out of somebody else's pocket; even then, humiliation would exact a toll.

Several hours later, I pulled into a Chevron, just off state highway 205 in Happy Valley, Oregon. The sign said "Clackamas Town Center," but I wasn't exactly sure where I was. In either case, my phone said I had seven hours to go.

Damn.

I pulled up to the pump and waited with my door open.

"What can I getcha?" the girl with her hood up said. She had red eyes and hard lines on her face, several earrings in each ear, and uneven front teeth, one slightly discolored. Her blue-green eyes, though, were warm and friendly. When she smiled, it made her face light up. She was hiding her attractiveness rather well beneath the hood and scars.

"Regular, please," I said as I handed her my credit card. I got out of the truck, shut the door, and stepped away, watching the young woman go through her routine. Her hand shook slightly as she slid the card into the reader. She almost dropped it, fumbled, then slid it into place. I heard her mumble under her breath and hit a few buttons, then she turned and handed me back my card.

A smile appeared, and she gave me a gratuitous "Have a great day!" The smile that time felt cheap and strained.

"Thanks," I said, and she turned and walked away. I heard another mumble as she moved on to the next customer. I went in search of a bathroom, stretching and shaking my legs loose. The gas pumps were full of cars, and the small gas station was littered with people inside and out. A traveler sat outside with a cardboard sign: "Anything helps, moving on." His furry companion lay its head on his leg. The pup lifted his head and eyed me as I walked by. He seemed to whimper a little as if to ask if I had anything to give.

It would sure help, mister.

I dismissed his plea and kept walking.

I pulled the door shut behind me and locked it. The light was flickering, and the commode had seen better days, but it didn't bother me. I turned the sink on and let the water run. The mirror was chipped, and the black backing was showing in places. I splashed cold water on my face again and again, trying to refresh the good feelings I had from the morning. As the day turned over, my feelings settled in, and the reason for the trip began to weigh heavily on my mind.

To kill. I wasn't going to turn back, and I knew it, but it still meant taking a life, and that was unfortunate. It was mostly unfortunate that many years had passed, and I had missed my opportunity earlier in life—twice at that. I likely would have been excused from the deed then. I would not be now. I had a half a plan and would need some luck for the rest to fall into place. I was less likely to get caught if it seemed like a random killing, a spontaneous event. I swished some water around in my mouth and spit it out, slapped another handful on my face, wet down my hair, and finished my business.

The pup with the big eyes was watching as I came out of the restroom. He whimpered again, and for the second time I ignored his pleas. Oregon had legalized possession of hard drugs, and I questioned how many of the sidewalk sitters, transients, and homeless were under the influence. Some were obviously tuned while others may have been on the nod. The pup's master looked to be a nodder. He was sitting up with his chin on his chest, drool coming out of one side of his mouth and eyes closed, or rolled back in his head. The needle wasn't sticking out of his arm, but it was a few inches from his limp hand and fingertips. Somebody somewhere thought this was a good idea. This was how you fixed the war on drugs. You gave in. You made it legal. The Portland area had become a cesspool of violence, drugs, and filth. It was slowly becoming the West Coast culture supported no doubt by the Cabalifornians and the devil's empire. Humans made choices—bad ones at that—then wanted to blame God for not stepping in. I went back inside the station, dropped off the key, made a couple of hot dogs for the road, grabbed a water, and headed for the door.

The pup was staring hopefully when I set one of the hot dogs down next to him. A sniff and a couple of bites later, it was gone. Poor little guy was starving. He looked back asking for more, so I took a bite off the one I bought for myself, chewed a little, took another bite, then gave the rest to him. He wolfed what was remaining of the second one down and watched me again, waiting for more deliciousness. I opened the water and poured some into the small bowl next to him. At least there was a bowl. The nodder came to briefly and mumbled something incoherent. The dog looked back up, appreciating the nourishment and went to the water dish lapping up the water quickly.

I began walking back to my truck and saw the gas station attendant talking to a boy on a bicycle. They were on the far side off the ice bin, which sat between the nodder and them, standing at the corner of the building. She was smoking, and he was on a chrome Redline with green mags, hand grips, and wheels. I was flooded with memories of my own Redline and how much I loved my bicycle as a child—the freedom it gave me. I went back to my truck, climbing in quickly, then resumed watching the attendant and her friend. She looked older than him, a few years easily but less than ten for sure. The boy was smiling and laughed a lot, an enthusiastic soul. He seemed familiar, but I couldn't pin it down. The female seemed far less enthused. She yawned and pointed back toward the pumps. Maybe she was just tired. The boy nodded and smiled again. I was enthralled now by the minute details and what the conversation may have been about: Her in her black boots, black jeans, and red hoodie, a cigarette between her right index and middle finger, which were barely sticking out of the cuff of her sleeve. Him on his shiny silver-and-green bike, big smile and doe eyes looking toward her, watching every move she made.

Then the friendly pup, just thirty feet away, began yipping and yapping. It was an incessant, alerting yap. The boy and the girl both looked. The nodder had fallen back against the wall and slid into the corner of an ice machine and gas station wall. His head was tilted back, and his mouth was wide open. The pup looked directly at him, barking, then turned away and tugged at his rope, barking some more. The pup repeated the sequence three more times quickly. Something was wrong. I watched the girl, the gas station attendant, hesitate, then flip her cigarette on the ground and stomp it out as she walked toward the nodder. The pup got more excited as she approached and began bouncing all over the place, yapping. The girl walked up and gently kicked the guy in the shoe. Others walked by, ignoring the situation altogether.

"Hey, man. You ok?" She surveyed for a reaction, then made another couple taps with her foot. "Wake up, man; you can't sleep here. We told you that last night. Hey, man!" She raised her voice at the end and kicked him hard this time. Nothing. She looked at her friend, and he shrugged. I was out of my truck now, mostly so I could hear, but I was working my way closer, a little at a time. The young woman looked at her friend, and he shrugged back in response, still smiling. She must have felt me getting closer because she turned and made eye contact. Her eyebrow raised in question. I lifted my hands, palms up, and shrugged as well.

"Just freaking great," she said. "Hey, Ben!" she yelled toward the other attendant, waving her hand at him to get his attention, but he was all the way across the lot and had a full island of cars. He waved her off.

"He looks dead," I said quietly and stopped walking forward, standing at the edge of the curb. The woman and the boy were on the sidewalk in front of the ice machine, and the dog was still yapping away. I squatted down in front of him and put my hands out, calling him to me. He came over, got close, and stopped barking. He was shaking and looking at his nodded-off owner. I pulled the rope from underneath the owner and stood up with the dog. His name tag said King.

The woman swore again and reached in to grab the guy's shoulder. To give him a shake.

The nodder shot to his feet.

The woman fell backward, screaming. The boy caught her as she reeled away in fear.

"YOU!" he screamed and pointed at me. "YOU MUST PAY! YOU MUST PAY THE REAP FIRE!" he yelled. We were almost face to face, and I could see his eyes blazing away with lunacy and heroin.

"THE REAP FIRE, THE REAP FIRE! YOU MUST PAY THE REAP FIRE!" He stuck a long, dirty finger in my face and laughed like a loon. I took a step back, and the man began to spin slowly in circles.

"Pay or burn; pay or burn. You missed it once and lost your turn. You missed it once and lost. Your. Turn." He ended the jingle, facing toward me again with a long, filthy finger in my face. His crazy eyes swam in his head, then he laughed hysterically. He held his belly and let the onset of genuine madness consume him. He fell back into the sitting position and laughed long and hard, holding his hands over his belly. The woman and the boy backed up, and I moved off to the side with them, watching the man try to catch his breath, wondering what had just happened.

"F…ing druggies," she said, obviously familiar with this kind of behavior. The reap fire nodder coughed again, unable to catch his breath. The coughing turned to wheezing, and he began clamoring. He curled into the fetal position, wheezing, then coughing. Foam and spittle were coming from his mouth as he struggled to breathe. His face was turning purple, and his nose began bleeding. Then all of a sudden, it stopped. His body convulsed once, then twice, his eyes fluttered, and his head twitched.

"Holy shit!" I reached into my back pocket for my phone and realized I'd left it in the truck. I dumped the dog into the girl's arms and ran for my truck. As luck would have it, a police cruiser was pulling into the gas station. I ran at the cop car, waving my arms above my head.

"The guy just died!" I yelled and pointed to the gas station. The cop had his window down, heard what I said, and flipped on his lights, pulling past the islands up to the front of the store. I watched from behind as he got out and stepped through the small crowd forming around the nodder. The attendant and her friend were nowhere to be seen. I thought that was a good idea and went back to my truck, shaking and unsure of what the hell had just happened. The reap fire rhyme repeated in my head.

Pay or burn; pay or burn. You missed it once and lost your turn. You missed it once and lost. Your. Turn.

I was shaking as I slid the keys into the ignition and still shaking when I pulled back onto the freeway. F…ing druggies was right. The urge to rejoin my kind became stronger than ever, and the good mind I felt earlier in the day vanished, leaving no trace as my feelings plummeted into fear and loathing. Twenty-plus years had gone by, but the words of the reap fire took me right back to the struggle of my youth. The evil in the world had just become tangible and real.

11

FEDWICKS

Murray Fedwick was a jack of all trades. He owned the local butcher shop, dabbled in taxidermy, owned a service shop, and drove one badass utility truck. His truck was his pride and joy. It was a three-year-old 4x4 Ford F-350 crew cab, with locking custom bins that covered the sides of the bed, a ladder rack that had two ladders on it, a custom canopy, and one helluva cow catcher bumper, winch included. It was pearl black, with one red stripe down each side. It was a moneymaking babe magnet, but the babes were not all that interested in Murray, even with the truck.

"Fedwicks," Murray drawled into the phone. "Hi, Murray. It's Kim up at the Gold Rush. I was wondering if you could come take a look at our ice machine. The bin is empty, and water is leaking from up above."

Murray smiled at the sound of Kim's voice and the thoughts that came with her. He had a lot on his schedule but wanted badly to squeeze her. In his opinion she was the best-looking gal in town. She had a part-time man that came around now and then, but Murray was certainly convinced his charm would eventually get him nowhere.

"You bet, Kim; I can come." *Anywhere you want, babe*, Murray thought with an ear-to-ear grin. "I can be there in a half hour or so," he said.

"Great, Murray; see you then," she replied.

"See you then," Murray said and hung up the phone.

"Ryan!" Murray yelled. "Hey, Ryan, I got another call. You're going to have to watch the shop." Murray heard the freezer door slam and the shuffling sound Ryan made when he walked with his butcher's apron on. Ryan's linebacker frame appeared in Murry's doorway shuffling along.

Ryan Fedwick was Murray's only kin. He was nineteen and uglier than sin, in Murray's humble opinion—so ugly his own ma didn't even want him. When Murray found him, he had a web of snot covering his face and looked like he had been crying for hours. He was huddled down against the doorway at the butcher shop, face red and swollen, a frightened child alone in the world, hanging all his hopes on an unknown father's love.

Murray took him in and raised him alone for sixteen years. Ryan thought Murray was the best dad in the world, and he may have been just that.

"Damn it, Rye. You know not to come in here all messy. This is the showroom, bud; customers don't want to see blood. They want to see steaks."

"Sorry, Dad," Ryan said and looked at the floor. "Go get cleaned up; hurry up. I gotta go; Miss Kimmy needs to be serviced," Murray said, smiling wide. Murray gyrated his hips and began pumping his arms next to his waist.

"DAD!" Ryan said loudly as his face bloomed red. He turned and walked off.

The showroom of the butcher shop was pristine and spotless. The cold cases offered displays, the current cuts for sale. They moved product for such a small town, and it kept Ryan busy. The butcher shop was basically Ryan's now, and Murray let him run it for the most part. Murray was still the captain, though, and he ran a tight ship that was strict on cleanliness and order. He inspected the windows on the cold cases slowly and with care as was his daily ritual. He lay down in the lobby and pulled out his flashlight. He reached underneath a cold case and swept the paper towel across the floor. It came back clean. He took the Murrayscope to the show windows. Not a smudge or water spot showed anywhere. No dust or dirt on the windowsills. He ran his finger across the top of the doorjamb. Not a speck of dirt. He checked the inside of the bell above the door. Nothing but brass. He looked around satisfied. He built the butcher shop with his own hands years ago and kept it in immaculate condition. He nodded at his son in approval and walked out after the inspection was complete.

The black beast rumbled down the road. The inside was in flawless condition just like the butcher shop. Murray loved his truck almost as much as he loved his son. He had earned his life and made sure to take care of his things along the way. It was all hard work, and Murray, being the man he was, never lost sight of that.

The stereo was belting out The Rolling Stones, his favorite band, loudly. He passed into the school zone and slowed down. His shop was out at the edge of town. It sat at the bottom of Sherman Pass on highway 20. Ryan made deliveries into Colville, a larger neighboring town, sometimes twice a week when needed, so the location was almost perfect.

Murray hung a right at Clark Street and headed downtown.

Town sure looks good after the fire.

He glanced around at the Victorian store fronts. Several buildings had caught fire a few years back, and when the town rebuilt, they decided on a western, turn-of-the-century theme. Rustic Victorian. Murray made money hand over fist that year. He hung another right just before the drug store and parked. He looked at his watch: 9:15 a.m. He was a few minutes early.

He went to the back door in the alley and pounded on it with the bottom of his fist. Kim opened the door.

"Hey, Murray," she said and flashed a quick smile.

"Hi, Kim," he purred. He tried to smile his best smile, but it fell flat. She had already turned her back and was moving inside.

Murray got to work as Kim disappeared into the back.

"The water valve was sticking, causing it to freeze up. I cleaned this one out best as I could, but it won't last. I will order a new one for ya when I get back to the shop," Murray said, trying hard to keep eye contact. Kim was a real looker and didn't mind showing off the goods.

"Thanks, Murray. I don't know what we would do without you. With Prospectors coming up, it's our busiest time of year besides hunting season." Kim's family owned the Gold Rush, the local bar and grill. She pushed forward and gave him a hug. He could feel her swollen jugs press against him. Her perfume engulfed him. He didn't want to let go but knew he had to before she realized what was happening.

He stepped back abruptly.

"Can I ask you something, Murray?" Kim said.

"Of course," he replied.

"Why are you still single, hun? I have been in and out of this pit for thirty years, and I have never known you to have a girlfriend, and I can't for the life of me figure it out. You're a nice guy. Your son is a great kid; everybody loves him. You seem to be happy; your business is successful. You must be doing something right. So why the solo act?" She laughed. "You're not hiding any bodies out there, are you? The butcher shop isn't a meth lab, is it?" she looked hopefully at him with a teasing grin.

Murray was shocked. He laughed nervously, trying to think of something to say.

"I dunno what to say. I guess I'm just a workaholic. I don't have time. Between Ryan, the butcher shop, and keeping the town running, I stay pretty busy." He smiled, trying to lay it on nice and thick. He was flustered by the change in conversation and felt there was nowhere to hide. He picked his tool bag up, meaning to high tail it out the door. She watched him intently. Her eyes glowed at his answer. She put her hand on her hips and pushed her chest out.

Wowzers, would ya look at that. Must have a knot in her back. "Sorry, sore back. Waiting tables and all that," she said, excusing the lag in conversation. "Well, when you have time, Murray, let me know. I know everybody in this town and might be able to help you make a new friend." Her smile lit up the room. She hugged him again, pressing her point a little further.

"Thanks, Murray. I better get busy." She let him go and walked away. Murray was lost in her scent. He headed for the door, wondering what that was about. The intoxicating perfume left him thinking of all the things he would like to do to Kim, then he got irritated, knowing he would never get the chance and dismissed the thoughts in frustration and moved on.

His next stop was the hotel right down the street. They had some issues with a couple of wall heaters, and it needed to be taken care of today, according to the owner. He left his truck and walked down the main drag, tool bag on his shoulder, deep in thought.

"Hey, Mur, how ya doing?" The voice belonged to his buddy Mark Adams. He almost walked right by him.

"Marco, my man. I am doing swell this fine day. The solar working yet?" Murray had added a sub panel to his shop and wired in all the solar earlier that winter and was taking a friendly shot at Mark.

"Not yet; not yet. I might have to cut down a few trees."

Murray laughed. "I told ya it was a bad idea; shoulda bought a genie." Murray put the palm of his hands up and shrugged.

"Ya, ya, ya. It's not summer yet; there is still time." Marco smiled. He knew he was probably hosed and likely would never recover the cost of the panels.

"Hey, I will see yuh tomorrow, ya? I have a full schedule today and need to get over to the hotel," Murray said.

"You bet, and make sure you bring some twenties this time," Marco replied.

Murray went back to his thoughts and walked on. The town was getting all dressed up for Prospector Days, the annual celebration and the official kickoff to summer. It's why Murray had so many calls to run in the next few days. He also had to help Ryan pack the truck for a run over the pass. He ambled along and went back to his conversation with Kim.

Maybe she was hitting on me. The way she stuck her jugs in my face like that, praise God. I am way too old for her. Aren't I? Gotta take some chances eventually, can't live this way forever.

His resolve after almost twenty years was finally starting to crumble. Murray opened the hotel door and walked inside, whistling Dixie as he went.

Ryan Fedwick was covered in blood: his apron, his goggles, the walls. It was everywhere. The pig was still squirting, but it was starting to slow. He laughed inside, but his face never changed.

Hope my dad doesn't show up. He would never let me live it down. Rye's tongue shot out and licked around his lips, slowly savoring the taste. *Has to be warm. Tastes better.* He watched the squirting slow down to a trickle. He walked over and ran his finger along the bottom of the cut. He let fresh warm blood cover his finger, then quickly popped it into his mouth. This was his castle, and here he was king.

Today the king demanded blood.

The king gets what the king wants.

It was a powerful thing to take a life, and Rye Fedwick was an expert. He had been slaughtering animals since he was a child. His dad never really had the stomach that Rye did. His dear old dad would look away when the fatal blow landed. Rye always looked the animal in the eye.

Watched the flame burn out.

He had fantasies about killing people—well, maybe one person specifically, but thought he wasn't smart enough to get away with it. Aside from that, he would never have the courage. Rye was clinically shy, had severe agoraphobia and panic attacks, and was prone to uncontrollable tics when stressed. His maladies plagued him since the day Murray found his "snot-covered face."

Murray had told Rye the story on several occasions, the truth at that. He always went into detail about the amount of snot that covered Rye's face. Murray called it incredulous every time. Rye was stuck under it. As soon as Murray pulled off the mask of snot and took him inside and cleaned him up, Rye fell fast asleep in his pa's arms. It was the first time they met.

Rye looked around his torture chamber. It had all the fixings of real one: The hook rail on bearings with all the carcasses lined up. The blood. The stainless tables, the sharp, gleaming edged tools. The stench of death. It was the one room in his castle where he felt whole. Nothing bothered him in here. Ever.

He could hang a dozen bodies or so in this room. Currently, he had six, and the last one was draining out. A local ranch had to make room, so they rounded up a half dozen and dropped the trailer off. Live pigs and all. Rye took care of the rest. Blooding a pig was somewhat cruel, hard work. In the old days they would try to knock the pig unconscious then hang them live and bleed them out. Rye thought he was smart when he talked his dad into getting a shock stick. It was like a cattle prod but made for dropping pigs without killing them. Once they were out you could hang and blood them in just a few minutes. Rye loved it. The popular opinion was to kill the animal before hanging and blooding, but Rye knew better. It soured the meat if the heart stopped pumping before it was drained. Had to drain it out as the heart slowly stopped pumping.

The torture chamber was a block wall room. Three walls, all the way to the ceiling were block. The fourth was block as well but had a doorway covered by flexible clear-view panels when the door was open. The door itself was six inches of insulation fiberglass and stainless. It was also automated, with controls inside and outside of the door. Murray had talked about installing a lock once but never really saw the point. Murray custom built the butcher shop before Rye was born. He was a general contractor before he moved to Republic. It was functional and practical but way ahead of its time.

He surveyed the room again. The blood was flowing into the floor drain in the center of the room. Rye pushed a button on the wall; he heard the drain line valve actuator switch positions. When he was washing the room out, it drained into the sewer line. When he was blooding something, it drained into a collection unit. Murray had thought of everything. There were several pendant lights hanging from the ceiling. Murray hated fluorescent. The thick concrete walls made the room entirely soundproof. Rye hung the hose up after washout. He was giddy after blooding and gutting that many animals. It had been a while since anyone had needed a slaughter. Most people round here did it themselves. He pushed the pigs into the walk-in cooler and would get back to them later. First, he had to deal with the guts, and oh boy, did he have some ideas. He knew Murray would want to use most of it to make sausage casings and chorizo, but he would never notice if a pound or two went missing.

Rye never finished high school, but, in his eyes—Murray's too—there was no need. His dad taught him everything he needed to know anyway. He was becoming a fine butcher, could run the backend of the shop, kept the books, and was keeping the shop in better margins than his dad ever had. Unfortunately, he lived his life as a social outcast.

He knew what people thought of him. He knew what they said when his back was turned, which was twice as bad as what they said to his face. He didn't lack emotions either and was tired of playing defense. He had spent his entire life trapped under his social shortcomings. It tore him apart over the years. Rye didn't blame the people as much as he did the town itself. He knew the town was poisoned. Regardless, the kids treated his well of suffering like Kool-Aid. They drank much and often. It was a sickness that spread over the years, and he watched it get worse. Small towns had a way of staining a person's soul if one couldn't fit it.

He didn't talk until he was eight years old, which really gave him a difficult start. He had a few people that stuck up for him in the beginning, but even those friendships faded over time. He was the brunt of many jokes, the affection of everyone's dark heart. They aimed their poison at him for years. It soaked in. In small town America, if you didn't fit in, some way or another, you were forced to live as an outcast. All he ever wanted was to fit in. Go on a date. Play on a baseball team. High five his teammates. The animal in Rye ate up all his pain, swallowed his grief daily. It was a long and lonely road for Rye Fedwick, but tonight was going to change all that. Rye had spent the last three years working on controlling what ruined his life, and after months of research, he felt that he found a cure.

Rye grabbed the plastic bag full of intestines and a gallon jug of blood from the walk-in cooler and put them in his truck. He went back around and locked up. The shop was spotless just like his pa had taught him.

Now, if I can just find one of those wolves.

He climbed into the old Ford work truck Murray gave him and slammed the door.

It was Friday night, and Rye was heading to the cabin. The old Ford had new tires on it and hummed loudly on the highway. The truck rolled on. Rye reached down and flipped on the headlights, deep in a daydream about another life.

It was beautiful.

Life made him a cold-hearted butcher; he hadn't asked to be this way. It was God's plan for him, he supposed. He stuck his arm out the window and raised it up to the sky, extending his middle finger.

Still, Rye was excited to get to the cabin. It was like his body was in constant flight, but he really wanted to fight. That is exactly what this trip was about. He had been planning it for months.

He knew his mother was an Indian woman, but that was about all he could get out of Murray. He had hoped to find some kind of clue or some kind of cure to rid his body of his diseases in her heritage because all other resources had been exhausted. Murray had gone so far as to take him to Seattle to see some of the best doctors in the country. They had succeeded at very little.

Murray had taken him to one of the largest libraries in the Seattle area on one of the many trips and it was there he found a quiet soul. He started looking into the ways of a medicine man and it captivated and intrigued him, and the more he studied, the more he believed he would find the answer. That was before he learned about meditation and how to control his own body. He believed now that his breathing was powerful enough to keep him from losing control. He just needed to find the last piece of the puzzle.

The heart of a wolf.

Across many libraries and countless hours, he had pieced together some Native American folklore about the heart of the West's most social predator and how it could heal him. It could make him whole again. A medicine man from the past told him the story in the library one night.

Easy, Pinocchio. It might not work.

The legend said it cured the boy who couldn't talk, not the boy who smelled like death and tweaked uncontrollably. *It has to work. It* WILL *work*, Ryan thought, imposing a stiffer will. He dropped back into the daydream of the beautiful life as he drove on.

It was the eerie hours of the morning when Rye left the cabin. He had packed the wheeler the night before and was ready after a cold breakfast. The early morning brought a cold mist that hung in the sky. The moon was still bright, and the shadows stood tall across the dark land. Rye belonged here. He sucked in an icy cold breath and held it. It felt good. Summer was on the way, but winter wasn't letting go just yet; the two titans continued to battle over spring. He climbed off the wheeler after an hour with a face that was numb.

The dark still clung to the trees, but the sky was getting brighter by the minute. Rye grabbed his gear and started walking. He was planning on spending a few nights, but the pack was a little lighter than he anticipated. He was about as far from the civilized world as he could get in northeast Washington. His mind was racing with excitement and unease. He had heard many wolves across his time in the outdoors, but he had never actually hunted one. He spent many hours considering this trip after he read the story of the Walking Arrow.

Effort was not the problem. Trapping a live wolf, then eating its beating heart—now that might prove a little trickier.

Rye had come to Eden's saddle. The wolf pack was nomadic and lived life on the move in the summer. They seemed to winter locally though. He had seen the pack the spring before at this exact spot, then found their tracks again last winter when he came in on skis. He thought they had a den and were somewhere in the area. He brought his tree stand in a few months ago and set it up on a heavily used game trail. It was easy enough to find a good trail to set up on in the summer, but the winter snow left no doubt who was running the trails and where. He also knew the females would be birthing from the winter mating season. They would be holed up by now, with the males doing the hunting.

Rye pulled the bag of pig guts from his pack, then froze. The hair on the back of his neck stood at full tilt. He slowly set the bag back down and put his hand on his father's .45, which was holstered on his right hip. He could feel the eyes on his back. His sixth sense was screaming at him to move, but his breathing kept him calm. He thumbed the buckle and slid the weapon halfway up the holster. He slowly turned his neck then his shoulders and searched for glowing eyes.

"WHO?" the orange-eyed owl asked. Rye's neck twitched, then his face.

The owl on the branch scared the bejeepers out of him as it took flight. His heart skipped several beats, then tried forcing its way out of the bone-and-gristle prison. Rye had a full-on meltdown and let the tics and twitches have their way. His eyelids blinked rapidly, and his head bobbed back and forth in a twerk- and jerk-like rhythm. He managed to get his hand off the gun in case it moved out to his fingers. It rarely ever did, but he was avoiding blowing a hole in his leg just in case.

The woods went quiet again, and he listened to the undercurrent of life as the owl landed in another tree a few hundred yards away. His spasms slowed, then without another word left him on his own again. Rye took a few deep breaths, and the enemy inside him slept once again.

He set the bag of guts down and started his labors over again.

A few hours later, his work was done. He could have left and hoped the live trap rig did the job, but he felt the warm blood and guts would attract attention quickly. He climbed the tree and settled into the stand.

Dawn was cresting through the mist. The rainbow of colors across the vapor in the air had an intoxicating effect on Rye. The steam coming from the ground as the earth warmed and the mist cleared only added to it. The rugged country gave Rye something that humans never could. The mountains gave him solace and peace; it was the balance.

It's why the medicine man spoke to me.

Rye drifted into the twilight of sleep, warm and at peace.

He heard the soft steps on the rich woodland soil, and his ears perked up.

Something's coming.

He listened intently but kept his eyes closed. The noise vanished. He listened again. He could feel the beast now—whatever it was—off to the left of the trap twenty-five yards out. Alone in the forest and the quiet, Rye could feel the web of life.

All things are connected.

The rainbow mist of dawn was breaking up. A ray of sunshine dove through the trees to the forest floor. Rye still couldn't see the animal on the ground. The soft steps had picked back up, though. It circled the trap warily, managing to stay hidden in the trees. Rye knew the males would be hunting for the bitch and her litter.

She must be close. It's only been a few hours.

The pig blood had been poured around the trap. He heard the wolf sniffing around but still couldn't see it. Its head slowly came into view. He closed his eyes to breathe and caught the panic at the tip of his teeth. He opened his eyes again and watched the wolf continue to circle the trap. His circles were growing smaller. The timber wolf could taste the blood and was weighing the risk. Rye had put what he thought was just enough cover across the top of the trap to hold the weight of the entrails. The wolf sensed it. A few times he stretched his neck, reaching for the intestines, but he wouldn't take the fatal step. Rye's stomach rumbled. The wolf paused and sniffed the air. He backed up from the pile of guts and impending death. He turned and cast a final look back, then loped off. Away from the trap.

Damn...He knew. How could he have known? What did he smell? Rye looked at the trap again. It was perfect. Rye was anything but discouraged.

He got comfortable in the stand after lunch. He modified it last fall so he could safely sleep in it. He pulled his harness tighter so it would hold him in the same spot. After another forty-five minutes, his eyelids fluttered again.

At first the picture was fuzzy, but it slowly came into focus as he fell further away from the world. The wolf king sat on a throne of horns and hide as a man. The darkness swirled with a thousand brilliant colors. He saw the king again; this time he was kneeling before someone or something. His face was dripping blood.

Rye snapped his eyes open at the cold. It pierced his body like needles. The action of the trap below him and the trashing brought him to the surface world quickly. It was almost dark, and the wolf had returned. The temptation was too much.

The beast hung dying. The steel bear trap teeth were dug into the animal's jaw and face; the custom eyelet on the trap had a rope tied to it and was strung around its neck and up to a large branch above. The body was strapped to the tree, exposing the underbelly of the beast. The obsidian knife he found a few years ago had done its part. The heart beat once, and Rye sank his teeth deep into the soft, tender tissue. Hot blood ran down his face as he took another bite, then one more for good measure. The taste did not deter the man from chewing and swallowing quickly.

12

STONES

The logging truck blew by horn wailing. Jamie's shriek of terror drowned it out. The brake lights lit up, and the eighteen-wheeler bucked, trying to slow down too fast. The Jakes were thumping wildly, and the tires barked briefly against the pavement with the brake pedal jammed to the floor. The truck had a full skid and too much momentum.

Across from Jamie's new driveway sat her son, head down against the handlebars on the motorcycle. The bike was sitting halfway up the drive opposite hers. The motor wasn't running, and her son wasn't moving. The log truck had managed to come to a full stop down the road finally, and the driver was getting out. The door slammed.

"HEY, KID, YOU OUTA YOUR EVERLOVIN' MIND?!" the driver yelled. He was storming toward me. I was shaking and couldn't quite talk yet. I could feel the moisture between my legs.

"KID. HEY, KID...I'M TALKING TO YOU...YOU HAVE A DEATH WISH?" The angry trucker was getting closer but was still a hundred yards away. Jamie gunned it across the highway and pulled me off the bike, cradling my body to hers. She put me on the four-wheeler, kissed my head, and held me tight. I could feel her heart beating wildly. She just sat there, holding me against her. The trucker continued storming our way. My mom just sat and rocked with me in her arms. Some part of the angry logger's tiny mind must have finally understood the situation. His steps lost some bluster as he neared.

"You alive, kid?" he said, finally realizing I might be hurt or unable to think right. "You came out of nowhere, sport. You're lucky my front bumper doesn't stick out any further," the trucker said and tried a nervous laugh.

Jamie looked up. "Thank you." She went back to holding her baby boy. My senses were starting to come back around.

"Holy crap," I mumbled and tried to unwrap the anaconda arms my mother had surrounding me. "I couldn't stop, and I was going too fast to jump. I didn't see the driveway across from ours until the last second. So I went for it. Holy crap." My voice cracked and tittered. Our hearts were slowing down a beat at a time. The trucker stared at me, then looked at my mom again. He shook his head again.

"Next time try the brakes," the trucker said, scoffing. The venom in my mom's eyes backed him up a step.

"Thank you," she said again. Her voice was thick with fury. The trucker opened his mouth to let some more stupidity show, then thought better of it. After a final glare and a shake of his head, he turned and walked away, mumbling with anger.

"He had a good point," my mom said, then laughed with relief.

"I know. I tried the brake lever. It almost killed me." My mom laughed again and hugged me some more. "Oh, Paulie, the excitement never ends with you, sweetheart, does it?" She kissed my head and finally let me go. She noticed the wet pants but didn't say anything.

"We better get back. Your brother is probably going nuts." She paused and looked down the driveway. "Speak of the devil." My brother was pedaling toward us, new motorcycle helmet and all. "Go sit on your bike. Hurry up," she said.

"Hey Pee, did you crash? I thought you were dead for sure…I bet Mom will never let you ride again, will you, Mom?" He took off the helmet and set it on the four-wheeler. His eyes were wide with excitement. "Since stupid isn't dead, can I ride now, Mom? Can I?"

"Sure, bud, as soon as we get home. Don't call names," she said. The excitement was wearing down. The arrival of Bryan and his lack of interest in my near death brought normalcy back.

"Mom, Pee can ride my bike back. No way you're going to let him ride again, are you? He doesn't even have a helmet." I sat with my back turned to my brother, not saying a word. I didn't want him coming anywhere near me; he might see the wet pants if he did. Mom was quiet for a minute, obviously working out a solution. She rolled the wheeler down to the bottom of the drive.

"Let's load your bike up. We can strap it to the rack on the back. Then you can take it back and go ride in the pasture but stay in sight of the house. I will ride back with your brother," she said trying to keep Bryan away from me.

"AWWRIGHT!" Bryan exclaimed. He was fully absorbed in getting to ride and didn't look my way again.

"Don't go too fast. Those bungees won't hold the bike on very well. And for God's sake, be careful." She kissed his cheek before he slid the helmet back on.

"You know this is the brake, right?" she said as she pushed down on the foot pedal.

"Ya, Mom; I'm not stupid," he replied. The wheeler was an automatic. Thumb throttle and brakes were pretty much all there was to it. He pushed the electric start button, and it fired up.

"See ya, dummy!" he hollered as he rode off.

Mom came over. "Ready to try again? Or you want to push it home?" she asked.

"Can you show me how to use the brakes?" I replied.

"Of course," she responded. "Slide forward a little."

With that we began rolling home.

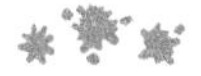

The last day of school was finally here. We rode the bus for the last month to our new house. Same school, same class, same bus, different house. I was in the process of making a new friend on the bus.

I was lying under his seat waiting for him to step on a paracord snare I made earlier in the day. I crawled under three seats to get to him, and I wasn't about to blow it now; the rest of the plan was in my backpack and with my brother. This was the part that had to go right, or we might be screwed. He had to be sitting down in order to slip it over the toe of his shoe. I could see the back of his legs, ankles, and shoes. He kept standing up and sitting back down, so I waited until he sat down again. The toe of his shoe touched down, then came back up. I slipped the loop over his shoe and pulled it just enough to keep it on there.

C'mon, c'mon, stinkbag. Just stand up now and stay there. He heard me. Holy smokes, he actually heard me.

I stayed still and watched the stink stand up. Mission complete, I army crawled backward under the empty seat, spun around, then crossed the aisle back to the other side. I got back to my seat and slithered into it. We were down to the last few stops. The stinkbag had been picking on my brother and me since we started riding the bus. He apparently needed some fresh meat. Bullies were often cowards, and this one was no different. He picked on the younger, smaller crowd always one at a time.

Today was his day of reckoning. The stink was going to get his license soon, so this was likely his last day on the bus. He made sure to let everyone in earshot know he had a car waiting for him. I wasn't going to let him get away without at least one memory that would last forever.

The bus came to a stop and let all but one of the other remaining passengers off.

One more stop, and it would be just the three of us. I made eye contact with my brother. His eyes were big, and his face was flat. I opened my backpack and pulled out the rest of the plan, setting a Tupperware container back into the bag, leaving the zipper open.

Don't you chicken out, I thought at my brother as the door closed, and we started moving again. I sat back in my seat and began counting down.

Twenty-two, twenty-one, twenty… My eyes were closed, and the lighter in my hand shook just a little.

C'mon, Bry, don't be a wuss. Twelve, eleven, ten, nine… oh boy, here we go…

I lit the extended fuse on the firecrackers and heard Bryan start singing loudly.

"The wheels on the bus go round and round, round and round…"

I quickly and gently tossed the pack of lit firecrackers across the aisle and underneath the seats between stink and me. The extended fuse gave us just a few extra seconds. We had worked on the timing the last few months and had burned through our supply of firecrackers in doing so. The bus stopped, and the door opened. The string of bangers fired off inside of the bus like a machine gun.

BANG! BANG! BANG!

It became rapid fire as the rest of them burned off. The stinkbag jumped then ducked down in his seat. He poked his head out the side of the seat to look behind him.

C'mon, Bry, I thought, and the loud boom of the m-50 my brother lit went off, right on time. Stink jumped up and looked around, confused and slightly stung from the small blast. The bus driver was ducked down in the corner; the noise made him think somebody had a gun.

"Hey, buttface," I heard Bry say.

The stinkbag looked up from his seat and was hit in the face by a water balloon filled with a gooey concoction of sugary molasses. The bomb exploded all over him. Bry ran for the door. It was all the stink could take. He roared and chased Bryan down. The cord caught his foot, though, and slammed him down face first. It looked like he went limp. I was right behind him, shaking up my Tupperware container. I saw the cord snap loose of his shoe and recoil behind him a foot or so. Perfect. I popped the lid and dumped the ants on his head as I passed over his moaning body.

"MY ANTS! MY ANTS! Oh no, he made me drop my ants!" I cried and stomped on his hand as I went for the door. "That guy threw firecrackers at me! I'm telling my dad," I said to the bus driver with a whimper. He was confused and very angry.

"He is in big trouble, young man. Big, big trouble," the bus driver replied, his jaw muscle clenched tightly. He stood up. I skipped off the bus as I heard the driver telling stinko he was in quite a pickle.

Hello, summer!

We ran fifty yards down the driveway, and as the bus pulled away, both of us fell to the ground, howling with laughter. "Pee, bro. You are a magician! I can't believe it worked. That was so awesome. That dude totally deserved it." Bryan was excited. He really thought it was something else. He rarely partook in my magical stunts of mischief and revenge.

"You think we will get caught?" he asked. He was animated with excitement, and his face changed quickly. It went from elation to worry in an instant, showing the fear of getting in trouble now.

"No way, bro. I told the bus driver he tripped me. I dropped my ants and acted like I was going to cry. Then I told him he threw firecrackers at me before I got off. He said the stinko was going to be in big, big trouble." I laughed at the thought of it as Bryan just stared at me; he couldn't believe it. The depth of the plan scared him. The fear in his face faded into pure joy after a few seconds of realization.

"King Pee, I am your humble servant." Bryan scoffed and bowed down in front of me. He held out his hand toward me. "Backpack." I put my backpack in his hand. He slid it over his shoulder and stood up.

"Race ya home!" I said and took off running before he could think twice about carrying my backpack the mile and a half down our driveway.

My mom was getting ready to go to work, and she was taking us to town with her. It was Friday, and the town fair started today. School had been out for a few weeks now. She had a short shift this morning and wanted to let us run around Prospector Days. Bryan and I were both excited and waiting at the car when my mom came out.

"C'mon, mom!" Bryan yelled. He was sitting in the car with his feet out the window. He was looking in the mirror at the volcano on his face. He pinched it together between both pointer fingers, and it ejected a stew of blood and puss, squirting onto the mirror he was looking into. Without a thought he flipped the visor back up, leaving the mirror in a sad state.

I lay in the back seat watching him desecrate his face and my mom's car. I wanted to go to town and check out the town circus, but I also really wanted to ride. The last six weeks or so, I rode every day, and I was getting pretty good.

Either way I tried to talk Bry into staying home and riding, but he wanted something in town. He didn't tell me what it was, and I hadn't asked.

We were driving down the highway to town. The windows were down, and the sunroof was open. It felt like it was going to be pretty warm today. Mariah Carey was belting out one of her latest jams. My mom was checking her makeup in the rearview. Bryan wouldn't shut up.

"So, Mom, when is our hunter's safety class? When it's over, do we get our own guns? I think we need to take a gun to the class so we can show them we know how to be safe. I bet it's lame. Grampa has already taught us everything we need to know. Ask him..."

Mom glanced at the road and hummed along to Mariah. She kept pace with Bryan's questions.

"August. Yes. We will see, and I'm sure it is lame, but you can't get a hunting license without the certificate. I am sure your grandpa has already taught you everything you need to know, so you shouldn't have a problem with the class...PJ, finger." She looked in the rearview and made eye contact. I had a real nugget I was mining for, and my finger was buried to the knuckle. I pulled the nugget and the finger clear of the mine shaft and launched it out the window.

I spent as much time as I could out running around in the woods and the dirt roads. The powerline road that ran through our property went for miles and miles. It wound its way into town eventually, I supposed. I hadn't made it to the end yet, but I would find it eventually. I also found a cave up by the lake that was quickly turning into my own.

BOOM!

The noise shocked me out of my daydream, and the car pulled to one side. I looked at my mom in the mirror and saw mild panic on her face.

"Shoot, dammit. I think we just got a flat." She had both hands clenching the wheel, and the Subaru was rumbling along haphazardly. The road felt rough, and the repeated thumping left no doubt the tire was blown. I continued watching the rearview as she managed to get us pulled over.

"Guys, I can't be late. Can you help me get the tire changed?" She looked worried as we pulled off the road.

"The pit crew will take care of it, Ma," Bryan said. He was being way too nice. "Ready, Pee?" Bryan said and opened the door. I climbed out and looked at the tire. It was the driver's rear. Mom popped the trunk and started handing out tools. The lug nut star wrench was the first thing she pulled out. She handed it to Bryan. He put it on the first lug nut, made a grunting sound, and tried to spin it. I watched him try again.

"Help me, stupid. It won't turn." He tried again and grunted some more.

"Wrong way, dummy," I said. He let go of the wrench and stepped back. I flipped it so the other arm was higher then stepped on the lower arm. It didn't move.

"Grab that side, Bry. You pull; I push." Bryan grabbed his end and started pushing down. "Bryan, that's the wrong way! Pull up on your end; I will push down on my end. One…two…three!" We went for it. Both of us were straining, our faces turning red. The lug nut broke free and spun.

"Dammit," my mom exclaimed from the trunk. "There is no jack, guys. Where is the frickin' jack?" She mumbled some really bad words, and I heard more shuffling from the trunk. The spare was lying on the ground, and the trunk was bare. There were some metal poles that looked like they could be the hand crank for the jack but no jack. My mom had turned and was walking down the highway toward the truck coming our way.

She waved her arms above her head back and forth several times. The truck pulled in behind our car.

"Hiya," said the stranger. "Need a hand or two?"

"We sure do, the back tire blew, and our jack seems to be missing." My mom put on her best smile and played helpless. It transformed her face from mother of two to vixen in distress. She was a career waitress and walked a hard road in life. She knew how to use what power she had.

The stranger smiled and said, "Of course. Let me get my jack." His eyes lingered on my mom hungrily. Rye and I went back to the lug nuts like the little gremlins we were. We popped the other four loose, then got out of the way. The stranger pulled a jack from the toolbox in the bed of his truck and was sliding it under the car.

"It's coming, ya know. Prospectors Days." He got hung up on the esses. The gap in his teeth made him sound like a snake. His jack hand had a large swastika tattooed on it and was pumping away. He had the car off the ground in no time.

"Yeah, the boys are really looking forward to it," my mom said, her voice purring.

"Republic was a mining town long time ago. Called Eureka Gulch way back when." He shot a stream of tobacco juice across the ground and pulled the flat off, then continued talking. "The idear of Prospectors was ta honor the town history. Wha' people dunno is the real history of the town is blood, fire, and greed." He laughed and gave my mom elevator eyes. She played innocent and smiled back, listening, her eyes asking the man to go on, like she really wanted some dirty gap-tooth redneck picking up on her, on the side of the road, in front of her kids at that.

A cloud moved in front of the sun, and the sky got dark. A cold breeze picked up.

"The people round here don't talk about it much. Too many spooks and kooks." He spat again and winked at me. I watched his crazy eye rolling about lazily. He grabbed the spare and pulled it out. I watched with awe-like wonder; he smelled like a man who knew a secret and forgot to use soap. It wafted in, then back out.

"The town has been burned down and rebuilt a few times. Hunerds of people have died since the first time it happened way back when, and mark my words, lady. It's gunna happen again." His head jerked to one side. "They say it's the dead miners, crooks, and lawless come back for their bounty."

"Awesome," I said, jumping in. I couldn't help myself. I knew a good story when I heard one. He finished up with the tire and pulled his jack out from under the car. The wind picked up, and the cold air swirled. I shivered, and the goosebumps pricked at my skin. My brother was having a similar reaction. I looked at the sky; it was dark and gray. Wasn't it just sunny?

The man's voice grew dire and quiet. "If I were you, lady, I would get as far from this place as you can. Keep them boys outa town and away from Prospectors if you like 'em breathing. I wouldn't be going maself if I didn't have bidness that needed to be settled." His eyes flared to life at the last of his words. He threw the flat tire and tools in the trunk and slammed it shut. "Good luck," he said. All interest in my mom was gone. Her charms weren't enough to keep the darkness in the stranger from boiling over.

"Thank you so much," my mom said and tried to give him a few dollars. He ignored her offering.

"Keep it. You're going ta need every penny ta get them boys outa this shithole. Trust me: you don't want ta be anywhere near this town. The devil built this place on hate, and it grows here. Hell is a real place, Momma, and you're standing on the edge of it." He spat again, staring her in the eye. His lazy eye rolled around slowly, then stopped and stared at my brother and me. He turned and walked back to his truck. I watched as he climbed in his truck, pulled onto the highway, and rambled away.

On his back window he had a sticker with a rifle scope crosshairs on it. It read THIS IS MY PEACE SIGN.

My mom shuddered. "That was pretty strange huh?" She checked her mirror and pulled onto the highway. Her eyes showed a fleeting trace of fear, then dismissed the crude man.

I ran down the street, away from the parade and hubbub of town, my heart pounding. If I could keep this up long enough, I would be able to find Bryan or get back to the crowd.

"YOU'RE DEAD, PUNK! YOU HEAR ME?" said the stinko from the school bus. I accidentally dumped ants on his head, threw firecrackers at him, almost knocked him out, and stomped on his hand. Oopsie. Guess he hadn't forgotten yet. At the moment, he had me cornered in a residential area. It wasn't really a neighborhood; it was a bunch of really small houses packed into a tiny lot just behind the park. It had one-lane alleys that weaved the way through and around the houses. The fences were all wood and six feet tall. I could hear his labored breathing.

I waited and listened, catching my own breath. He was a fat boy and really had no chance of catching me. I spent all my free time riding, running, hiking, jumping, and fighting with my brother. Fatty had no chance unless he cornered me. I smiled. I peeked under the truck again. I could see just his feet for the second time in my life. I bear crawled on my hands and feet under the truck toward him. He was totally gassed. I could do this for hours. He walked around the other side of the truck, then kept going. I climbed out quickly on the side he was just standing on and peeked around the back of the truck. He was standing bent over, one hand on the tree, still breathing hard. I picked up a rock and weighed my options. The front door of the house was open, and the TV on. The tree stink was leaning on was on the edge of the alley, the house looking right at it. I moved around the Bronco so I could just see inside. Sure enough, there was a person lying in a recliner, watching TV, I supposed. Quick as a snap, I lobbed the rock at the front window and ran like my butt was on fire. I was a full house away by the time I heard the commotion. I assumed the guy charged out of the house and caught stinkbag red handed.

Boy, did I know how to make friends or what?

By the time I hit main street, the full-blown sprint had turned into a light jog, and I was giggling hard. Candy was raining out of the sky—what luck. I darted around and scooped up a few treats. There were Rodeo Queens, horses, cowboys, loggers, and miners everywhere I looked. I unwrapped the taffy and popped it in my mouth. Delicious. I walked down the street a couple blocks, then crossed behind the parade and made my way back up the other side of the street, headed for the Gold Rush.

I saw my bro and stopped. He was talking to a girl.

That's why he wanted to come to town.

She had long blond, curly hair and was laughing at something stupid he said. I walked over and interrupted the blossoming love affair. "Hey, dummy," I said. He spun and walked toward me, his reflexes that of a brother who really didn't want his younger around. Faster than any cat I'd ever seen. He grabbed me with the Vulcan grip.

"Get outa here, puke, or I'm going to wreck your day," he threatened, quietly pinching down. His voice was just above a whisper. Saved by a southern belle.

"Hi," said the blonde. My brother eased the pinch. I stood up straight and smiled my biggest smile.

"Well hello there, madam," I cooed and kissed her hand.

"This is my little brother, Paul. He was just leaving. Weren't you, Pee?" The death grip was back.

She giggled, "My, aren't you a little gentleman? I'm Sadie."

The grip was gone. Bry knew it wasn't going to work. The ladies loved my charm. I bowed and smiled. She laughed. Bry gave me a hairy eyeball. The parade was wrapping up, and the local law was the last bit of the entourage. The sirens blurped every now and then, and the lights flashed. There was only one car; the rest were trucks and Broncos. Looked like they had a gaggle of "inmates" towing the line. The black-and-white striped uniforms and the chains on their feet gave it away. Johnny Law walked in the back with the bullhorn, barking orders at the chain gang as they threw candy to the crowd. One of the inmates looked familiar, but I couldn't quite put my finger on it.

Bryan's southern belle drawled.

"Aww, that's the cutest thing I have ever seen." At least I thought that's what she said. The sheriff with the horn was walking a little pup tailored in inmate stripes and a hat to match. Almost as soon as Sadie spoke, the dog squatted. I looked at Bry, and we both laughed hard enough to split seams. I watched as a Republican walked out on the street and said something to the sheriff. The copper asked a question, and the man pointed toward the park. He shook his head and handed the bullhorn and leash to the last inmate who had heard the conversation. Then he walked off toward the park, radio up to his lips. That was my cue.

"The pleasure was all mine, my most beautiful goddess," I said as I took her hand again. This time I shook it vigorously, then went for a high five, but she missed it.

"Adieu," I said at last.

"Goodbye, little prince," she said and faked a sigh. My bro put his arm around my neck in a show of brotherly love.

"Be right back," he called and walked me away from his sweet little tart.

"Pull that crap again, and I will kill you," he said and cranked down on the headlock as we made it to the corner.

"Wait. Let go!" I said impatiently.

"The guy from the school bus is here. He saw me at the butcher tent and tried to run me down. I had to punch him in the biscuits to get away," I said and unwound the headlock.

"Shoot," Bryan said and looked over his shoulder at his new girl. She was watching the pup prisoner.

"That's not all. He chased me down into the houses on the other side of the park and cornered me under a truck. I think he threw a rock at me and missed. It went through somebody's window on accident. I barely got away," I lied.

"WHAT? Dude, you're kidding me. Tell me you're kidding. Your ass is grass, Mom is going to kill you." He looked at me, then stepped back a little and laughed.

"Hey, bro, we are in this together, remember?" I said, reminding him. His balloon deflated slightly. "I'm going to tell Mom I was with you the entire time, ok? You and your sweetums," I said and gyrated my hips. He glared at me for a second, then agreed.

I turned and headed for the Gold Rush, the restaurant where my mom worked.

It was hopping busy for a Friday evening. The real loggers, miners, and townsfolk were out in force. It looked like most of them made it to the Gold Rush after the parade. Good thing Mom had her running shoes on. She saw me across the room and smiled, then shook her head slightly: *Too busy.* I went back outside and sat on the bench in front of the bar and grill. The sun was shining, the birds were chirping, and the grass was growing. I kicked my feet up on the other end of the bench and got comfortable. A few minutes later, I was starting to doze off.

"Hey, Paul." I knew that voice and slowly slid my hat back up so I could just see him. It was Eric, my mom's ex-husband.

"Uh, hey?" I said in confusion.

What is he doing here?

I looked back down the street, hoping to see Bryan, but he had disappeared like a fart in the wind. I was cornered, and this time I didn't have a rock to throw or a car to hide under. My contempt was all but impossible to hide. I had spent much time fantasizing about Eric getting hit by a car or a sledgehammer or catching on fire. Turns out when my mom left him, she probably saved his life. I looked him in the eye.

"What are you doing here? I thought you were in Oregon," I said.

"I came up this morning. I had some business in Spokane, so I thought I'd drop by." He smiled at me. He was playing nice, trying to be my friend. Spokane was almost three hours away. I didn't say anything else. I looked away and pretended to be interested in the bugs on the sidewalk.

"Your mom around, sport?" I was about to say no when the door to the Gold Rush opened. Out walked my mom. She wasn't shocked to see him.

"Hi. How are you?" she gushed, and her eyes flashed. She only held back because I was sitting right here.

"Good, Jamie, good. Glad to be off the road finally," he said and winked at her. She gave him a hug, and he kissed her on the cheek. It made me want to puke.

"I bet. I can't believe they let me out on time. We are slammed," she replied and looked at me, my discomfort ever growing from their conversation. Eric leaned in and whispered something in her ear then ran his finger along the side of her face gently. He was looking intently at her. She giggled and looked back at him. They whispered some more back and forth. They must have forgotten I was sitting here.

I jumped up, taking my cue. "Mom, can I have some money?" I didn't need to stick around.

"Sure, hon," she replied and started to reach into her pocket.

"I got it," Eric said and pulled out a thick stack of bills. He held out the stack long enough to pick a twenty off the top.

"Here ya go, bud," he said and smiled at me. I had to thank him but really didn't want to. I was just about to walk off when the sheriff came around the corner with stinkbag and some other guy. The other guy was a little older than ol' stinko. You could see the muscular build underneath the plain white tee he wore. I thought he looked familiar. He walked apart from the other two, keeping his distance.

"Evening, ma'am," the sheriff said as he walked up to my mom. Eric stepped back just a bit. He wanted distance between him and the cop. Criminals have natural habits.

"Officer," my mom said and looked at the other two. Muscles was staying back from the conversation, just watching for now. Mostly he was looking at me, though. My discomfort was growing in leaps and bounds. So much for a good day.

"I'm Sheriff William Keating, and this is Josh Coleman," he said, gesturing to the teen who had tiny red scabs all over his face. My mom glanced at me; her eyes were hiding a scowl. No doubt she already knew; it wasn't the first time we had been here, after all.

"I'm Eric Black, and this is my wife, Jamie," he said and stuck out his hand to the sheriff. "This is our son, Paul." My head exploded. That did not just come out of his mouth. I thought about taking a swing at his biscuits right then and there.

"What happened to your face?" Eric knew his way around people and the law. He sized up the situation instantly and was already taking the offensive, trying to figure out what buttons to push. It was his only admirable quality by my estimation.

"Ants," the Coleman kid said with a look meant to drill holes in my head. His voice was just short of fury. I continued looking at my shoes but couldn't keep from smiling at his answer. Eric caught the exchange, and so did mom. The smile broke my foul mood, but the anger was still seething beneath. Coleman felt no different, and I didn't think it would take much before punches were thrown. Now was not the best time to have a blowout.

Eric stifled a laugh, then apologized as an afterthought to his rude question, continuing to control the situation as best he could.

"Can we talk for a minute?" questioned Keating. His face took on a serious tone.

"What can we do for you, officer?" my mom replied. She was being kind but forceful. Her question said-Cut the BS and get to the point, man. She was also no stranger to the badge.

"Well, it seems Mr. Coleman and your boy may have had a dispute. Boys will be boys, but the altercation—if we can call it that—ended in a broken window," the cop said and looked at me. "I'm totally innocent," my eyes said in return. Hiding the malice, I felt, was almost impossible.

"That little puke threw a rock through the Howards' front window. Mr. Howard is trying to make me pay for it," growled the stinkbag. Coleman's eyes were still shooting bullets. Keating put up his hand to quiet the boy.

"I asked Mr. Fedwick to come along so we could get to the bottom of this," the cop said, tilting his head toward muscles. "It seems he may have witnessed the event." I tried hard to keep my jaw from crashing into the cement. I was screwed. The stinkbag glared at me. I acted scared and tried to hide behind my mom, but really I was just short of taking a shot at him or Eric. The sheriff noticed the tension and gently guided Josh to the other side of him, so he was in between us. Small-town law. This is exactly how it operated. No courts or lawyers; just a friendly conversation. The sheriff wanted to talk somewhere quiet. He asked if we would all mind heading over to his office; it was only around the corner. This wasn't going to end well. I was going to have to fess up or stick to my story. I couldn't see any other way out. I decided on plan C as I walked over to the cop shop.

Eric put his hand on my shoulder and held me back just long enough for the others to move out of earshot.

"Did you do it?" my mother whispered as we followed the sheriff and his posse. I gave her the silent treatment for a few seconds. Eric walked on the other side of my mom.

"Wife and son?" I whispered back with as much venom as I could muster. Eric looked over and made eye contact with me.

"Ants?" he questioned with a raised eyebrow, curiosity and amusement showing on his face. I couldn't help but smile again at the thought and shrugged.

The sheriff had a legal pad and a pen, and we were separated into two rooms. The stink bag, Josh Coleman, sat in one by himself waiting for his dad to come down. Rye Fedwick sat at the table with the sheriff, my mom, Eric, and me.

"Mr. Paul, can I ask you a few questions? Is that ok, Mom and Dad?" The last word burned my ears. Mom and "Dad" looked at each other, then nodded. It was a moment of pure clarity. I was going to have to kill him.

Eric was watching the cop with interest. I was watching him with disgust.

"Mr. Fedwick is our local butcher here. He runs a nice little shop on the edge of town, out toward Sherman Pass. Ryan, this is Jamie Black and her husband, Eric. Jamie works over at the Gold Rush," the sheriff said, making some introductions.

"Nice to meet you both." Rye stood up and shook hands. His face may have slowly turned red, or it could have been the lighting. He sat back down expressionless.

"Rye was dropping off some product to their booth and heard some yelling. He looked around, and next thing you know, he sees Mr. Coleman in a foot chase with Mr. Paul. That about right so far, son?" He said this still with the nice-guy voice. I nodded my head in compliance. No talking; that was the rule when dealing with the fuzz. Eric had an eye on me. He was trig when it came to dealing with the cops and wasn't going to let me hang myself, as much as he might want to.

"So, what Mr. Coleman said and what Mr. Fedwick said don't exactly match up. Now I ain't calling anybody a liar, cuz that wouldn't be proper, but..." the cop drew a pause and held it, watching me closely, the country twang in his voice audible. "There is only one truth, and it's my job to find it. Mr. Paul, would you mind telling me what happened from there?" the balding, round law man said. He had taken off his cowboy hat and set it on the table. I was floored. I wanted to talk and saw an opportunity, but I wasn't exactly sure what muscles said. I knew it must be different enough than what Coleman was spewing, so I decided to take a shot and go for it. Instead of answering his question, though, I went for the backstory.

"That guy is a bully. He rides my bus and picks on my brother and me all the time," I whined. I could still pull off the poor little kid, but I was growing up too fast for it to last much longer. I continued the scared little boy routine. "The last day of school he lit firecrackers and threw them at me. Ask the bus driver," I cried, my voice rising a few octaves. I left out the rest of the story.

"It's ok, son; you're not in any trouble." The sheriff reached across the table and patted my hand. "I just need to figure out what happened to the window for now."

I glanced at muscles again. He looked down quickly. No help there. "I don't exactly know, sir, honest." Then I shut my mouth and looked as scared as possible. Eric jumped in after a minute of silence. "What do you think? We good here? Paul is obviously the victim of a much older boy bullying him. He isn't even a teenager yet. How old is pockmark out there? Seventeen? He better not be eighteen; I will tell you that much right now. If he is, we will be pressing charges right away." Eric, the doting dad, was pressing the old man, forcing him to defend or dismiss his case against me.

"Easy now, easy. Like I said, I just wanted to ask Mr. Paul a few questions. According to Mr. Fedwick, he saw Mr. Coleman throw a rock at your son as he ran away from him," he said, then looked back at me. "Did you see Mr. Coleman throw a rock at you?"

I nodded then added, "He was yelling at me! He said, 'You're dead, punk! Do you hear me? Dead!' Those were his exact words. I just kept running and heard the crash of the window behind me."

The sheriff hooked a thumb at Ryan Fedwick. "That's what he said too." Rye smiled at me. It made me think of a lion getting ready to eat. I stared at him for a minute. He looked away, and his face turned red again.

What is up with this guy? Why'd he lie? Is his face turning red, or is it the lights?

I looked at the beefy butcher and wondered what he was hiding and why. He had his eyes closed and was breathing deeply.

We walked out of the pokey free to roam. My mom was thanking Eric, and I guess I should have been too. I couldn't get over it, though. I hated him; it was venom in my veins. It just kept growing and getting worse, infecting other parts of me. The guy beat the shit outa my mom a few times, he almost broke my neck once, and he threatened to kill Bryan. That was just the beginning. We lived with him from the time I was a tyke until just a few months ago. Now he was coming back around. It was all too clear what I was going to have to do. I watched them laughing and touching. It burned. I could feel the hate fuel the inferno inside of me. Hunter's safety, hunting season, guns. The thought stopped crossing my mind and glowed like a neon sign. At least I knew the sheriff already.

Ryan was going back to the butcher shop. He had loaded up the rest of the product and helped Murray close down the tent. The night was finally over. Murray never asked Rye to work the tent, not once in the last five years, until earlier today. Murray had to run up to the hotel to look at another unit. Rye kept quiet and watched the crowds. Then, in the distance, he heard the younger Coleman kid yelling at someone. The voice was unmistakable. He stood up and looked around and caught movement on the other side of the park and watched.

He watched a smaller kid come sliding into view underneath the Bronco, then he stopped and stayed still. After a minute or so, he saw the younger Coleman huffing to chase the kid down. Coleman yelled again and went around the back of the Bronco. He stopped at the tree right in front of the Howards' place, trying to catch his breath. Ben Howard was a bit of a drinker, and Rye figured he was probably sleeping one off. In a small town like this, everybody knew everybody else's business.

The kid climbed out from under the Bronco and picked up a rock. He slowly poked his head around the back of the Bronco and peeked at Coleman. Then he looked at the window on the house.

Holy smokes, he is going to do it.

That was all the time it took. The next thing Rye knew, the window crashed, and Ben Howard was standing over Coleman. The kid that threw the rock was long gone. Rye missed the first part of the action in front of the tent. Coleman said the kid hit him in the biscuits.

The little guy has got some stones.

13

BART

I was sitting in the back of my mom's Soob a couple nights later. My face was red, and my voice was several octaves above normal.

"WHAT THE HELL ARE YOU DOING? ARE YOU TRYING TO GET US KILLED?" I screamed at my mom. "IF NOT YOU, THEN ME! IF NOT ME, THEN BRYAN!" I was furious and letting it all out. No way was Eric going to be a part of our lives again. My mom stayed calm.

"Paul, you saw him; he is different now. It won't be like that again. Besides, he isn't moving back in."

"Stop freaking out, Pee. It's just going to be us, right, Mom? Do you see him in the car?" my brother said, defending my mom like always. I needed out of the car right now.

"STOP THE CAR, MOM. STOP THE CAR AND LET ME OUT!" Mom had been through far worse with us. The car was just too small, and I was completely flipped out; she had to let me out. I was screaming at her from the back seat, and it was right in her ear.

"Ok, Paulie. I am pulling over." She pulled the car over and put it in park. I jumped out and slammed the door. I walked out into the field next to the road and screamed. Mom knew I was right. Eric was no good.

But he was different now. He acted differently, he looked different, and he treated her differently. For now. The new house complicated things as well. Eric had a hand in helping her get it, just to show good faith, show her how much he had changed. In her heart she knew I was right, though. Eric was no good. She looked at the clock on the dash. It was almost 11:00 p.m. She was exhausted and wanted to get the boys home. I was still in the field yelling and throwing dirt clods.

"How long you think this will last, B?" she asked, turning her head toward her older son and tucking herself into the car seat.

"I dunno, Mom. Pee is a psycho. Eric is lucky he hasn't figured out a way to kill him yet," Bryan said and yawned. "Pee is wicked smart, Mom. He isn't like other kids. You should probably put him in military school for his own safety. Hey…if you do, can I have his motorcycle?" Bryan looked back at Jamie and smiled. "Love you, Mom."

"Love you too, hon." She smiled sadly and laughed, then watched him recline his seat and close his eyes. I had stopped yelling but was still out in the field talking to myself and kicking at who knows what. Mom sighed and pulled herself out of the car.

"Paulie, c'mon, honey; let's go home. We can talk more about this in the morning, ok? Just sleep on it tonight." She smiled softly at me. I shot lasers her way—no chance I was going to let this go. I looked back at the car and saw Bryan sleeping in the front seat.

"Fine," I said and started walking to the car. I got to the rear passenger door and put my hands on the roof of the car. I stood there for a minute, trying to calm down. I watched the building across the highway. The front door was open, and the lights were on, but I didn't see anyone around.

Small towns in summer, I guess.

I took another deep breath, then climbed in the car.

"Ok, let's go. Hey, Mom…" I was going to apologize.
"WAIT. STOP."

"Paul," my mom replied sternly, her voice tired, tired of me. I slid over to her side of the car and opened the door and climbed though the car instead. I looked again. Yes, it really was. There was a human tied to a pole across the street.

HO-LEE-SHIT.

I started babbling. "There. A person. The pole. There is a person. TIED TO A POLE!" I was climbing out of the car. I crossed the highway quick and quiet to see if I was right. I kept one eye on the door to the building and my other eyes on the flagpole and the human. The moon was bright, and it was a clear summer night. I could see the person's head bobbing slightly. It looked like crying.

"Paul!" my mom yelled. Then she saw what I was heading toward.

"Get your ass back here. What is that? Holy shit, what is that, Paul? Get back here now!" she whispered and yelled and the same time. I only had another ten yards to go. I could see the tape around his hands holding him, wrapped backward around the pole. My mom was shushing at me in the confusion. She could clearly see he was a male strapped to a flagpole. I was completely engulfed in this nightmare, and I kept my eyes moving the entire time. The big guy strapped down had me beyond words. My mom was shaking Bryan awake in her panic; she had no clue what to do. Every sound and every step had me ready to blow like a volcano from the inside out. I took another six steps and could see his face clearly.

"Hey, dude, you alive?" His head whipped to the side. A rattlesnake couldn't move that fast. His eyes were ominous and malevolent. They glowed with ferocity. Then his face changed instantly. I saw two different people in one body. It was a transformation—too much. I turned to run, but he grunted and tipped his head a few times. Looking down. The duct tape on his mouth. I weighed my options, but standing here waiting for somebody to show up and kill us all wasn't one of them. I got within striking distance and slowly reached my arm up to his mouth. I grabbed the tape and jerked it off.

Rye loaded the truck a few nights later, went back to the butcher shop, turned on the lights, propped the front door open, and waited.

Bart Coleman was a year older than Fedwick. They had known each other since first grade. It was love at first sight for Bart. He couldn't keep his hands off Fedwick. He teased him, pushed him, tortured him, and eventually broke him. Worst of all he got the rest of the class—the rest of the town, it seemed at times—to join in.

Bart's legacy immortalized him. In high school he went on to win three state championships in wrestling, was a four-time all-state defensive player of the year in football, and pitched the only no-hitter in school history. He was the best athlete the school had ever seen. Everybody in town loved him. Well, almost everybody anyways.

Rye sat with the door open. It was warm and smelled good outside tonight. Rye had succeeded in much lately, and it was all part of his journey for growth. He lied about the younger Coleman out of spite and opportunity. He thought it was convincing at that. Sheriff Keating seemed to buy it, but he always had a soft spot for Rye. Keating's own son died a few years back in a car wreck. They were cut from the same cloth. Jerry Keating was a shy, quiet boy who never really fit in. Bart made sure everybody thought he was gay. He had even gone so far as to break into Jerry's locker and tape up pornographic pictures of men and their naked parts. The school was watching when Jerry opened it up. Public humiliation burns for years. Rye thought of Jerry. He missed him. He was Rye's only real friend; they had too much in common not to be friends, especially in a tiny town where hate was grown.

Rye heard the rumble of a truck and then a door slam. He took a deep breath; he knew who it was.

In walked Barthalomew James Coleman. He had only been out of high school for two years, but by the looks of it, college was treating him well. He was in better shape now than he was then, and he was a brute of a man. His bright-green eyes sparkled with mischief.

"Rye, Rye," he said and stared him down. Ryan stared back. It was the first time in his life he had ever looked Bart in the eyes.

"Bart," Ryan said and fidgeted.

Bart was standing in the doorway. His silhouette filled the empty space in the frame.

"So my brother told me a story tonight, dicklick," Bart said calling him by his boyhood title. "He said you lied to the cops about him throwing a rock through a window. Is that true, Rye Rye? Did old dicklick do a dirty? I, for the life of me, couldn't imagine you having the guts to do such a thing. Lying to the police—hell even talking to the police, for that matter. So I had a conversation with myself. I said, 'Barty, ole boy, now why in the world would dicklick make up a lie about my poor little sixteen-year-old brother? Why in the world would my good buddy Rye Rye Fedwick do such a thing?'" Bart tipped his head in a questioning pose and stared hard at Fedwick. "Then it dawned on me that the butcher bitch—that'd be you, stupid, just in case you didn't understand—might still have some feelings about me." Bart walked to the counter. Rye was watching him intently. The wolf's heart was working; he knew it. He could feel it. He had never been able to do anything when Bart was around except faint, cry, piss himself, and run away. He could feel the panic starting to well but was totally committed. It was for Murray. Bart was only a few feet from him now, the counter the only thing separating the two. Ryan continued leaning against the wall. The panic was rising, but he kept it in check for now. His eyes laughed at Bart and his stupidity.

"Wow, dicklick, you have changed, haven't you? By now you should be red faced and crying like the little bitch I left behind. And look at that you even put on some muscle, didn't you? Oh my, everybody, little dicklick Rye Rye Fedwick's balls finally dropped. Well, I'll be damned." He paused, eyes glowing with hate, arrogance, and curiosity, watching for a reaction. Rye stood his ground. "Now be that as it may, I am goin' to…EEEESPECIALLY being as we are childhood chums, give you a chance to make things right with my little brother." Bart's tone was mocking and superior. Rye took a breath. He had been waiting to do this for years.

"Did you hear me, dicklick? Or you deaf now too?" Bart asked, a big smile on his face, eyes glistening with contempt. He was leaning forward aggressively, hands on the counter. Rye's whole body started to shake. He could feel it coming on, the flush of emotions, the fear, the panic attack. The red face. He couldn't let it happen. He choked it off, swallowed, and just stared at Bart. The flush tried again, and Rye pushed it back down. He was gaining control over it, after years and years of agony, he was finally going to be able to control it. He smiled at Bart and stepped forward.

"Up yours, fart."

Rye did it! He actually did it!

It was such a simple thing for most people, but Ryan Fedwick had just reached a milestone he never thought possible. He saw the opportunity to get Bart here, where he was safe, and took it. Not only did it work but he told him off and didn't pass out. Rye had never felt anything like it in his life. He was over the moon at his courage. His mind began a victory lap, and a smug smile (another first) took up residence on his face.

In all his glory, he failed to remember who he was dealing with.

The incoming fist certainly reminded him.

Quick as a blink, Bart's right hand hit Rye in the eye socket. Then Bart's left cracked Rye across the jaw and dropped him to the floor, lights swimming all around him as darkness slowly settled in. Bart walked around the counter, grabbed Rye's legs, and began dragging him outside.

Rye came to, realizing slowly what happened. His first thought was he had succeeded, then he remembered Bart hitting him. He failed to account for how quickly Bart would get violent. His pride deflated like a popped balloon.

"Dicklick, hey, dicklick." Bart whispered and slapped him two times more than he needed to. "So dicklicker is a tough guy now, huh? You got some words for ol' Barty? Listen friend, between me, you, and the trees, I have always wondered when you would snap. AND THEN… When you do, you call me a fart?" Bart howled with laughter, then finally composed himself. "Jesus Christ, dicklick. I expected a little more than that. Hell, when Jerry Homo lost it, he at least broke all the windows out of my car. I mean, it was something. Did he get the satisfaction of telling me to my face? No, no, no. Poor old Jerry Queerbait. Heard your little boyfriend finally got what he deserved. Rest in pieces, little faggot," he said, exaggerating his sadness at Jerry's death.

They were outside the butcher shop. Rye wasn't sure how long he'd been out, but his shoulders were starting to burn with feeling. His hands were taped behind his back. He was sitting on the ground, against the flagpole next to the butcher shop. It was a twenty-foot pole that was buried six feet into the ground. The flagpole was in between his hands and back. He wasn't going to be moving anytime soon. His boots were missing too.

"So here is what we are going to do. Since you sorely disappointed me…you're such a big guy now toooo…" Bart shook his head in mock disgust, stifling a laugh. "Why didn't you at least try to deck me, you pussy? You really are just a sad excuse for a man, to tell the truth. Regardless, we are at a crossroads here, dicklick. So I will tell you what I am going to do." He patted Rye on the shoulder, mocking empathy. "I am going to let you spend the night out here. How's that sound?" Bart was as happy as Rye had ever seen him. This wasn't part of Rye's plan. His face flushed and ticked. The right eye fluttered and twitched. His neck muscles spasmed, and he hit his head on the flagpole over and over. "There's my sweet little Rye Rye. I missed that lil' fella." Bart walked over and pinched one of Rye's cheeks as the mild head banging twitch continued. The sound was a dull thump.

"But that's not all. I have a surprise for you. Like the way you surprised me with your naughty mouth, you little fart you." Bart burst into laughter again at his own joke.

Ryan was melting down. His body shook and shivered with twitches. He couldn't control it and wasn't even going to try. Misery had been his closest friend for so long, and had been missing of late, that Rye just opened his arms and welcomed her back home. He could always count on Misery. At least he wasn't alone.

Bart pulled a knife from his truck and grabbed the roll of duct tape off the tailgate.

"You just happened to get lucky, dicklick. I saw the duct tape on the floor of my truck right before I walked in tonight. If it wasn't for that, you might be nursing a sore jaw in the comfort of your own little dumpster. Stand up," Bart said and grabbed underneath a shoulder and forced Rye to his feet.

Bart seemed to know exactly what he was doing. Rye stood up, and Bart stripped back some tape, held up the roll a few inches from Rye's face, and slapped the sticky side against Rye's forehead and began taping his head to the pole first.

After several wraps, he said, "There we go. Hopefully no wild animals come, huh, butcher? That'd be a sad way to go. My dad said he seen some wolves up above the lake there, up by Boulder. Wouldn't that suck?" Then Bart hit him in the stomach. "I just want to make clear that tomorrow or whenever you get out of here, you're going to go see queer bait Jerry's daddy and get the story strait. Can you do that, big fella?" Then Bart hit him again. The blade was out in a flash. Bart waved it in Rye's face slowly. He pulled the collar of Rye's shirt out and started slicing down the front. He slit the sleeves and pulled the shirt off, tossing it aside.

"And this, big guy, is a special special just for you. I know how shy you are with the ladies. So I am going to do you a solid tonight. I am going to take all your clothes–pants and chonies too. That way your little prick can flap in the wind. Maybe even a broad will show up and see what you have to offer the ladies. I love picking on you, I really do, but college has taught me some really great new things. You ever been with a girl, dicklick?" Bart stared at Rye's bright, fear-riddled eyes hard, letting it sink in. He held the knife between Rye's legs, putting just enough pressure on it.

"No? I figured as much. Not really your cup of tea. Well if you get the chance, you should give it a try, and by try, I mean just take what you want. Great sport, satisfaction guaranteed." Rye was as angry as he was afraid. Bart unbuckled Rye's jeans then slid them off. He ripped off Rye's boxers while walking away, gathered up Rye's clothing, and threw it in the back of his truck. Then he went inside. Rye started thinking he was going to get impaled in the backside. Bart came back out with a handful of clothing or anything that could be used as such.

"Ok, dicklick here is the second special of the special special. My gift to you on this splendid night. I am going to go back into town to get wildly drunk. Then I'm going to bring half the town back out here to party while you're taped to the flagpole. Did I mention the entire gang is in town tonight? NO? Well, there you go. Reunion at Fedwick's later tonight. Until then, be well, friend. Be well." Bart bowed and then climbed in his truck. He sprayed Rye with gravel as he spun out, heading back toward town.

Rye cried quietly, and Misery held his hand.

"Thank you. Please, please, just cut me loose. This is my butcher shop; there is a knife under the register. No one else is here. Hurry, please. Please," the man begged. He had a black swollen eye and a bruise on the side of his face.

His butcher shop?

He looked like he was in a lot of pain. Mom and Bryan crept up. They both reached out to grab me, trying to pull me toward them.

"Paul, we need to get out of here, ok? We need to go right now. This, son, this is none of our business, and we need to go right, right, right now." Mom was scared and her voice trembled with fear. She also knew when she saw real trouble. This was men's business, and she was a 120-pound mother with two little boys. No chance they were staying.

The man begged. "Please, please, my name is Ryan Fedwick. You can call my dad. Murray Fedwick. He owns this place. Everybody in town knows him. Please just call him. Please. PLEASE," he begged some more.

"Mom, it's the guy from the cop shop. Fedwick. The guy!" I said, getting excited over a naked guy strapped to a flagpole. I knew I recognized him.

He lied for me.

The thought hit me like a punch and forced blazing feet to the ground. I was far too fast to catch and avoided the grasping hands from behind. I bolted in the door and over the counter, grabbed the knife, and was back out in a wink. Too scared to move any slower, I pushed the blade against the flagpole and slid it down, keeping pressure on it. I ripped the tape off the pole, then stepped back with my mom and brother, holding the knife toward the naked man.

"Oh God, thank you," Rye said. He was still in his birthday suit. The Blacks stared at him. I kept the knife out and stood in front of mom and Bryan.

Rye pushed the duct tape up off his head then rubbed his wrists and flexed his shoulders, trying to work out the soreness.

"We need to go, Paulie, right now. Mr., we are leaving. You never saw us; we never saw you. Good luck," Jamie said and started backing away.

I didn't move. "What happened?"

"You should go," said the naked muscle man.

"You lied to the cops earlier. Why?" I asked, still holding the knife out. "You lied, then you ended up naked strapped to a pole?" I muttered in disbelief.

"Go, kid, before they come back." Enough said. Tonight had been too much, and I was shutting down. I dropped the knife, and we all ran.

He felt the change before he opened his eyes and looked at his rescuer. Broken Ryan Fedwick was no more.

Rye went back into the butcher shop, and slid on his muck boots. They were the tall rubber boots he wore when slaughtering. He grabbed spare keys from the office in the backroom and headed for his truck, naked as a jaybird and hungry for blood.

14

THE NAKED EYE

"Dammit, John! I told you the gas gauge was broken," Sara said, fuming, and slammed the door. The old Jeep rocked back and forth. John was watching her and thought her nose flared when she was angry. He liked it. He was having a hard time not laughing as he watched her pout. The summer squall had let up, and the stars shined down from a clear night sky. The Jeep sat on the side of the highway just above Curlew Lake. John and Sara had a family cabin not far from there. He had been planning the weekend getaway for the last month but had been trying to get Sara out of the house since the loss of the baby. He knew Sara was yelling at him over that and not the truck. It had been her dad's before he passed, and they were restoring it to its original condition. This was the maiden voyage after the rebuild. It ran great when it had gas. Sara was the gearhead of the family, and she was pretty sure the float in the gas tank was cracked, which meant a new tank, not just a new float. She wanted to take it to the cabin but forgot to tell John about the problem, so when he checked for gas, it read full. They left Spokane a few hours earlier only to run out of gas just short of the cabin. She knew it was her fault but was frustrated. Her dad and then the baby. It had been three months since the miscarriage, though, and John was gently trying to get her to come back to life.

"The cabin isn't far from here. We have a gas can in the barn with the wheeler. I will go get it and ride back, ok?" he said. "You can wait here or you can come with. Stretching the legs a little won't hurt. Besides, you said you wanted to do some hiking this weekend." He flashed a smile, and despite the humor in her rant, he had to work from keeping the tone out of his voice. Her anger at him, for things he couldn't control, was wearing thin. He rummaged around and pulled out a flashlight from the Jeep, grabbed a cold beer from the cooler, and popped it open.

"Really, John?" she said, still fuming. He looked at her and reached back into the cooler, then handed her one. She stared at him for several seconds, then took the peace offering. He grabbed his hunting pack and strapped it on. She grabbed her dad's walnut walking stick and opened the beer, took a long drink, and then said, "You better put a few more in the bag."

"I love it when you talk like that," John replied, surprised, and immediately slid the pack from his back and began loading it up. He finished up and walked around to the tailgate, opened it, and sat down. Sara joined him.

"Sorry," she said quietly.

"Love you," he said in a grunt and pulled out his phone, trying to avoid any kind of emotional conversation.

He plotted a course to the cabin on his hunting app. She watched and leaned into him. "We have a few miles to go. Through the woods, down to the railroad tracks, and then an easy walk to the cabin from there. Or we can take the long way around, ten-ish miles or so and stay on the road." Sara drained her beer, belched loudly, her attitude improving, and stood up.

"The woods. One for the road?" she asked, heading for the cooler. She needed an adventure and knew John would rather be in the woods. Both grew up in the area, and she no doubt could find the cabin from here without John or a phone. The lake was almost directly east, which meant the old railroad tracks were down there somewhere. Hit those and take a right. Keep going until they hit Eagle Tree, and then the cabin was right there.

"Sure," he said and tossed his empty can into the back of the Jeep. She handed him another, and they started down, off the road, into the woods. The trees were sparse, and the moon was full, and it was all downhill. It made for easy trekking. The lake was in the distance, and it was a beautiful summer night. John felt some reprieve as he heard his wife humming quietly along the way.

A while later they arrived at a bluff that overlooked the lake. Sara sat down and patted the seat next to her. John slid off his backpack and sat down. A wolf howled in the distance, and the moonlight bounced off the lake. They were still above the lake and could see the entire valley. Sara felt good for the first time in months. She rummaged around in her black-and-red-checkered vest pocket, then pulled out a small vial. John watched, somewhat shocked, but knew when to keep his mouth shut. She was the driving force in their life, and he needed her to get back on track. If that meant smoking pot on a late-night hike through the woods, then who was he to jaw about it? He watched as she sparked the lighter, and the doobie burned. She inhaled deeply and began coughing almost right away. He laughed. She waved him off as he pulled another beer from the pack. She finished her coughing fit, then took another drag, passed it his way, and giggled. When they met in college, Sara was a pothead—a whipcrack smart, gorgeous, driven, and passionate pothead, but she was a pothead nonetheless. In the last fifteen years, they had married, built a successful real estate business, and attempted to build a family. The latter they were failing at miserably, and John had already come to grips that he would never be a biological father. Sara, on the other hand, was determined to experience heart-wrenching failure over and again. They were on the sunset of a second miscarriage after a stillborn a few years ago.

"Been a while, huh?" John was curious when the last time she smoked pot was. It had been legal in Washington for quite a while now, and Sara didn't mind cutting loose with her gal pals. She was a mystery sometimes, and he liked it that way.

"It wasn't legal then," she said and took another puff. John was never a big fan—a beer buzz worked just fine for him—but he took an obligatory puff for commune with his wife. Dope was for hippies and those gosh damn liberals. He watched her snuff it out and slide it back into the container. She looked at him and smiled. The intoxication worked its magic, and she was free from her demons for now.

Another howl, only this one was a little closer. "Time to go!" Sara jumped up and smiled big, laughing at the look on John's face. "Can you hear that?" she asked.

"Hear what? The wolves? Long ways away. Don't worry," he assured her.

"Not that. The humming. It's like a song," she said and listened hard, putting her arms out, shushing him.

John had the hearing of a hawk. "I don't hear anything, maybe a truck on the highway, running water? Maybe the weed?" He gently poked at her and smiled.

"No, John John. I can hear it. It's close." She grabbed his hand and started moving, pulling him along toward the lake, heading down the hill into the woods. They made their way around the rock bluff, and John heard running water nearby but couldn't see it.

"We are getting closer, John John, c'mon!" Sara teased and laughed. The humming song had turned into a soft pulsing in her mind. It called to her; she was giddy and felt a warm rush of excitement. The rock wall to the right began growing taller as the downward slope of the hillside increased. The game trail they were on was leading them up right up against the slab. The rushing sound of water disappeared as they continued down the trail, deeper into the forest, then underneath the bluff they were sitting on minutes ago. Sara could see a glowing sparkle up ahead; she was being pulled along now. It felt like she was floating down the tight trail as it wound around the rock. A split in the massive formation left an opening, a crevasse, just wide enough to walk into.

"Sara, wait a minute. I have to get my pack off," John called out, but Sara was drifting away. He didn't like small spaces, and though the crevasse was open at the top, thirty feet above him, it was only a couple feet wide at the bottom.

"SARA!" John said again, this time with force, commanding his wife to stop. He could no longer hear her footfall up ahead. He backed up to the entrance and slid the pack off, pulled out a headlight, and slid it on. The moonlight bounced off the vermiculite in the stone walls, slightly lighting the way ahead. John moved on, unable to see his wife ahead.

Sara was a hundred yards ahead, following the crevasse trail down a much steeper grade. She heard the traces of her name being yelled from behind but couldn't stop now even if she wanted to. The path up ahead grew dark. She looked up. The crevasse trail was no longer open above. She was officially spelunking and moved forward in the dark with her hands on the walls ahead of her. She felt compelled to keep going, excited to see what was at the end of the trail. She had to turn sideways now and couldn't see much of anything but pressed on; time was left further behind with every step. She could feel the life ahead of her and continued to weave her way down through the winding abyss.

Then she stepped into an opening, deep in the earth.

Awe flooded her body. The water below her glowed with muted bioluminescent twinkles of orange, green, and pink from the depths of the pool. A waterfall cascaded down from the right, and an opening in the earth, the forest floor above, let a column of moonlight in. The stone slab banks around the underground pool were littered with foliage at the water's edge. A cloud moved in front of the moon, and the shaft of light cut off; the pool below glowed in fluorescent colors. She had never felt so good in her life. The massive cavern was calling out to her, inviting her in, asking her to stay a while.

"John. Hey, hun, can you believe this?" She had heard him walk up a few minutes ago. He was in shock. John Abrams spent a lifetime in the woods in the Northwest and had never seen anything like it. The cavern height from pool to ceiling must have been around a hundred feet, and from where John was standing, he thought it all of eighty feet to the other side. The mist from the waterfall left a rainbow vapor trail across the atmosphere in front of them. The smooth walls from floor to roof were rare in this part of the world, and he couldn't place it off the top of his head.

Then he felt it: Warmth. Drops of hot water against his cheek. He moved behind Sara to the left, walking across the stone slabs that covered the banks, and made his way down from the waterfall to the pool. He squatted down and dipped a hand in. It was hot. Sara went with him and watched. He smiled a big smile and started taking off his clothes. Sara did likewise. The couple entered the pool naked a minute later. John felt incredible himself. He didn't know if it was the obligatory toke or the underground Eden they were swimming in, but he may have never felt better in his life. He dipped under and swam to her. She pulled him up and wrapped around him.

An hour later, Sara's eyes were glowing brightly as she climbed out of the pool and began drying off. She picked up John's shirt, wiped herself down, then threw it his way. He lay in the middle of the pool, face up, vacant eye sockets staring nowhere at all. His broken neck ensured he would never see anything again. She threw the rest of John's clothing into the pool with him, then finished tying her boots, popped an eyeball in her mouth, and made her way out of the cavern with a new bounce in her step.

The Gold Rush was starting to fill in. Bart had a following everywhere he went when in town, and tonight was no different. There was a handful of men and women, watching him, hanging on his every word, trying to be a part of the crowd. He felt superb after his little meet and greet with Fedwick. He loved being the center of attention and soaked it up like a sponge. College wasn't like that for Bart. He wasn't the best wrestler at the school or the best player on the team. He loved his tiny town, because here he was somebody. Here he was still a king.

The front door to the Gold Rush banged off the threshold loudly. In the doorway stood Ryan Fedwick. He was as naked as the day he was born except for the muck boots.

"COLEMAN!" bellowed Fedwick. His body was a rippled mass of muscle, glistening with sweat. Every cord tight and showing, roaring, hot blood pumping through his veins.

The women gawked and stared, but Ryan Fedwick had nothing to hide. Bart stepped out of the ladies' restroom followed by a raccoon-eyed tart. She stared in awe, stopping in her tracks. The entire bar fell deathly quiet; all eyes were on Bart and Rye. They were only ten feet apart. Bart stared at Rye in all his wild-eyed glory.

"Well, I would have never seen this coming. How...?" But then Bart stopped as the bewilderment gave way. He embraced the coming violence and let the rush run through him. He sensed the crowd watching his every move and lapped up the attention.

"So you finally want to take a shot at the champ, huh? That right, dicklick?" Bart laughed a short bark of a laugh, cracked his knuckles, and rolled his head from side to side. A few of the other patrons snorted along with him, but most were caught up by the intensity the naked man brought with him. The center of the room cleared out, the corners of the bar packing in with people willing to risk injury for a legendary night that would live on forever. Fedwick stared at Bart, waiting for him to make his move. He knew he wouldn't have to wait long. Bart was never long on patience.

A chair slid across the floor, breaking the silence, and Bart moved like lightning, closed the gap, and wound up his right hand, catching Ryan across the jaw. The blow was glancing, anticipated, and Fedwick spun with it, shooting out a hard trailing left elbow. Bart's nose exploded in a spray of blood, the return blow right on target. Rye growled at the sight of fresh blood. Bart didn't recoil, to his credit, but the bloody nose made his eyes water. He roared and shot in on Fedwick, hoping to get to his domain on the ground. Rye's movement was fluid, timeless, and seemed well practiced. He caught Bart flush in the face with a knee, and it stopped the takedown cold. Bart hit has back and scrambled away. Fedwick paused his attack and circled, Coleman stood up slowly. In a blink, Rye fired away with a combination of punches that ended with a headbutt. Bart fell backward, and Rye broke from the attack, letting his victim suffer.

"THIS IS YOUR GOD?" Fedwick roared at the crowd.

One of Bart's boys dared pick up a barstool to swing at Fedwick from behind. The attacker almost had enough time to get it off the ground, then Rye turned and hit him like a train. He wrapped up the arm with the barstool and hit him with a second straight shot to the nose. The noise of cartilage snapping loudly brought a chorus of oohs from the onlookers. Bart pulled a blade, bringing another round of gasps from those still watching. Rye grunted and broke the second attacker's arm and spun him in between himself and Bart, stopping the knife. The loud snap made the crowd realize it was time to get out. Someone was going to die here tonight. It only fueled Bart's fury, and he swiped the blade quickly across Rye's cheek, drawing a small flesh wound. Rye smiled, the predator in him looking for the kill. Bart kept the blade moving back and forth, keeping it in between the two of them unsteadily. The Republic hero was looking for a way out. He was bleeding badly, had a loose tooth, and could barely stand. He had never been in this position and was starting to panic; his arrogant confidence was leaking out. A picture of him with his throat ripped out, bloody chunks of meat and muscle strewn across the bar with Fedwick's bloody face buried in the gaping hole, popped into Bart's mind. Rye looked at him and smiled, his eyes blazing, and showed his perfect white teeth with flecks of blood spotting them. In a heartbeat Rye snatched Bart's hair and hit him three times with his other hand before Bart even realized he moved. The knife slid out of Bart's hand as he went limp. His face was crushed and broken, and his blood was everywhere. Rye grabbed Bart and threw him on the counter. He wanted to rip his throat out.

"D-d-d-don't move, Ryan," Sheriff Keating said, gun drawn. He was standing just inside the doorway of the Gold Rush. He was wild eyed with fear and sadness. He had known Rye Fedwick his entire life and couldn't shoot the boy if he had to, and he really might have to. There may have been a few onlookers still lingering in the back of the house, but most of the other patrons in the bar had found the exit. The snap of the broken arm and the wailing of the sirens meant trouble.

"I know these boys have hurt you, Ryan. They have hurt you more than words can describe. Jerry told me, Rye; he told me everything," the sheriff began pleading immediately. The sadness in his soul was leaking out of his mouth. His voice cracked and trembled. His esteemed career was hanging in the balance, but the guilt in his soul tipped the scales.

"I'm sorry, Rye. I knew, and I never did anything about it. It's my fault. It's all my fault. I never stepped in. I never stopped it. Rye please, please, don't kill him. Please don't be like them, son. I know if Jerry were here, he would tell you the same. Please, Rye, put the knife down." The sheriff shook with grief, the tears were dripping down his face now, impossible to hide. His sadness begged Rye for mercy; his eyes pleaded for forgiveness.

Rye took the knife and licked the blade clean on both sides and eyed the sheriff warily. Then he moved in a flash.

"RYE, NO!" the sheriff screamed but could not for the life of him pull the trigger.

Rye slammed the knife down into the bar next to Bart's head. He grabbed Bart's ankle and jerked him off the bar top onto the floor for good measure as he walked over to the sheriff and put his hands out in front of him, palms up in surrender.

Rye looked at the sheriff. He had to work to get the sheriff to look back at him, to look him in the eyes. The weight of the guilt, borne from time being unwound, was heavy indeed. Rye, naked and bloody, took the sheriff's free hand and went down on both knees. He kissed his hand, looked back up, and smiled.

"All is forgiven, Bill. Jerry loves you." Rye let the hand drop and stuck his wrists together, palms up and hands open prompting the lawman to do his job.

Later that night, Sheriff William Keating sat at home with a bottle of whiskey and his dead son's photograph, knowing that he would truly never be forgiven after all. He never cried harder in his life.

15

LOCKS & KEYS

The Gold Rush was packed the next morning. Jamie had the breakfast shift, unfortunately for her. The short turnaround from the night before left her groggy and out of sorts. The local customers were all in a hubbub about last night. The Gold Rush had a few fights since she started working there. She had yet to sink her teeth into the gossip. The flagpole man was still etched in her foggy mind.

"Morning, Mark," she said as Mark Adams walked in and sat down. He was one of her regulars.

"Hey, Jamie. How ya doin' today?" Mark said and smiled.

"Tired. Those damn boys are just full of excitement." She sighed, thinking about Paul.

"That's what I hear. Hey," he started and leaned in a little closer, "did you hear about last night?"

The flagpole man.

Jamie perked up a little and slid in the booth across from Mark. Her heart fluttered. "No, well. I mean it depends on what part of last night you are referring to. I heard there was a pretty bloody brawl in the bar but no details yet. I'm still asleep." She pointed to the bags under her eyes. Mark reached across and patted her hand.

"It gets easier, sweetheart." Mark had two grown boys.

"I hope so." Jamie's eyes flashed, the flirt in her finally waking up. "What happened? Do tell."

"Well, I heard it involves a flagpole and the sheriff." Mark had a sad look on his face. "Rye Fedwick told his dad that Bart Coleman showed up at the butcher shop to say hello and somehow it ended with Rye taped to the flagpole outside."

Oh no.

Jamie snatched up the little bit of energy she had and leaned forward.

"Who is Bart Coleman?" She wanted to know what kind of trouble she and the boys might be in for helping Fedwick.

"He graduated a few years back. His family runs the mining outfit out there offa the highway. Big time jock, a high school legend in our quiet little town really. Been rough with some folks over the years—not a real nice guy from what I hear." He watched Jamie and kept going. "Murray said that Rye was taped to the flagpole, the flagpole out front the butcher shop, and was naked. He got himself off somehow and finally snapped, I suppose. He showed up here in shor' boots and nothing else. He beat Bart bloody and broke another fella's arm." Mark was almost beaming. He couldn't stop the gossip in him, regardless of his love for the Fedwicks. "Murray and I have been peas in a pod for long as I can remember. That Coleman kid was a real jerk to Ryan when them boys were growing up. He deserved it, and Rye was the right person to finally give it to him. Maybe the sheriff's boy if he were still around." Mark beamed with pride like it was his own son. Jamie thought for a minute.

"Coleman. Does he have a younger brother?" she asked.

"Yes ma'am, and I heard little Paul had a run-in with him yesterday as well." Mark smiled, and she chuckled. The apple doesn't fall far from the tree. She wondered what the dad was like.

"Murray also said Paul walloped the younger Coleman a good one below the belt." Jamie hadn't heard this but was far from surprised. "Guess them Coleman boys both got what they deserved. 'Bout time," Mark said and smiled again at Jamie.

Her head was spinning. What Paulie lacked in size and experience he made up for with smarts, ferocity, and determination. She sighed again.

"So why did Fedwick get taped up?" Jamie asked, wanting to exonerate her family of any wrongdoing.

"Like I said, Bart has picked on Rye ever since they were tykes. Murray almost moved them to Colville, on the other side of Sherman Pass, but at the time just couldn't afford to do it. Poor guy. Anyways, it was just another shenanigan kids get up to around here. Nothing beyond some bad-mannered fun, I guess."

Jamie was a little shocked. "You call that fun?" she said, remembering the bruises on Rye Fedwick's body from the night before.

"Boys will be boys," Mark said and shrugged. She was convinced of that. Paul was headed for that life one way or another, most likely in very short order too. She shuddered at the thought of him being the predator and not the prey and knew there was no stopping it.

All of a sudden, she wanted to cry. Her baby boy had to grow up in this life. Wherever she went, this life went with them. Her chin quivered.

"You ok, sweetheart?" Mark asked, overtly friendly again.

"Just tired, I guess." She sniffled, thinking of her boys. She found out later that day the beating Rye put on Coleman was serious, and she couldn't help but think of Paulie and how much worse he might do. It was only a matter of time and size. It broke her heart the rest of the way.

I managed to catch a ride to town with our neighbor. It was a couple hours before Mom was off, but I was headed for the Gold Rush anyway. I wanted to let her know I was in town, so she didn't head home without me. I walked in and sat at the counter. I was watching my mom work and kept my head down. She looked tired. I felt bad because I knew it was at least partially my fault. I knew I could make it easier, but she was the grown-up not me. I heard another waitress talking to the cook.

"There was blood everywhere; the butcher was naked as the sunshine. They prolly should keep the bar closed tonight." She paused, then let out a muffled laugh. "I heard it was a big one. The fight was all over the bar." I leaned in, attention narrowed, turning up my hearing. "He walked in and said the king has rose or something crazy like that. He stood in the doorway butt naked 'cept boots, and then he put a man-size whooping on that Bart Coleman. I'm just sayin', Coleman, he prolly deserved it then too. I heard the sheriff picked up the naked feller and took him in." The old bird prattled on to herself as much as the cook, while she rounded the corner out of the kitchen.

I'd heard enough. "Hey, Mom!" I said and waved. Her face dropped when she saw me. It hurt to see her look at me and react like that.

"I am going to go run around town, see if I can get in some more trouble, maybe get to know the sheriff a little better." I smiled my biggest smile. She was trying to figure out if I was serious or not. "C'mon, Mom, lighten up!" I teased.

"I'm off at two thirty; be back by then." She kissed me on the top of my head and went back to work with a sad smile.

Don't worry, Mom. I know exactly where I'm headed.

I walked into the cop shop and went to the front desk.

"Hello, I am here to see the butcher," I said and looked around.

"Who?" she asked. She must have missed the memo on small towns being friendly. She squinted her eyes and watched me closely. Her voice told me she was irritated with my statement. I didn't exactly have a lot of cards to play.

"I need to see Ryan Fedwick. The butcher that got in the fight. I have some information for him and his lawyer." It was a total shot in the dark, and her eyes narrowed even more. She picked up the phone without responding and talked quietly into it. After several uh huhs and one ok, she dropped the receiver back into the cradle.

"The chief will be down in a minute. You can wait over there." She motioned to a row of wooden chairs.

"Mr. Paul," the chief said as he walked up. The vulture at the desk had a look of disgust on her face. "What can I do for you, son?" he asked, raising his eyebrows.

"I need to see Ryan, sir; I have some information," I said.

"Is that so?" responded Keating. "Well, so far as I know, his case, if you want to call it that, is pretty much cut and dried. He hurt another fella purty bad last night. In fact, I caught him red handed. Quite literally at that." The sheriff folded his hands together, looked down, and picked at a nail.

I thought for a minute.

"What if I told you he was taped to a flagpole at the butcher shop? What if I was the one to cut him loose?" I said, taking the long shot. "Sir, before I can tell you anything else, I need to talk to him."

The sheriff's eyes gleamed with excitement. He stroked his beard, thinking deeply about what I said and Rye Fedwick's charges. He watched me for a minute and let the silence get uncomfortable. He must have decided I was telling the truth, or I couldn't really do any more harm at least.

"Ok, son, stop by my office before you leave, though. I need to hear the rest of that story. Miss Dolores, can you please walk him down to the paddocks? Thank you." He looked at the old vulture and smiled. She cut him a short grin, which looked painful on her face.

"Let's go, kid," she muttered.

The door shut behind me as her instructions echoed in my head. I walked slowly down the line of empty cells. I had a feeling I was going to end up here at some point anyway. It made me think of Eric.

The last one on the left had the only occupant. He had on jailer socks with traction on the bottoms and an orange jumpsuit. He was lying down with his arms crossed. It looked like his eyes were closed.

"Hey, butcher," I said loudly, and the words echoed. His eyes opened, but he remained lying down. He tilted his head to one side and looked at me. "I told the sheriff you were taped to the flagpole," I said and then stopped. He didn't move. "I imagine if you told the sheriff what really happened, he might cut you some slack. You have a witness now." Rye lifted his head, then sat up, putting both feet on the ground.

"What do you want, kid?"

"I want to help," I said.

"Why?" he asked, still looking at the floor.

"I haven't lived here all that long, and I am trying to make some new friends," I said unable to hide the smart-ass in me. It was innocent enough. "And anybody who lies to the cops, gets taped to a flagpole, then ends up in jail might need a friend too, but before I offer my services, what's your story?" I said.

Rye looked up and stared for a long time. Then he started talking and covered his history with the Colemans quick as a cat.

"I told you, Sheriff, we found him taped to the flagpole naked. My mom and I were arguing, so she stopped the car to take a breather and let me out. That was when I noticed him, standing there naked."

"Well, son, it makes sense, I suppose, but I am going to have to talk to your mom. Why don't you bring her over here when she gets off work?" I knew that was coming, but it still didn't feel good. My mother would have to be dragged in here by wild horses.

"Mom, Sheriff Keating wants to talk to you," I said quietly. The look of shock on her face hit me harder than I expected.

"WHY? Paul, what did you do now?" She hissed, The look on her face was wrought with suffering. She was losing faith in me. I was twelve, almost thirteen, and more trouble than I was worth.

"I dunno, honest. I bet the butcher told him we cut him loose from the flagpole," I lied and stared back. I just needed her to go over there. If she didn't, I imagine the sheriff would come find her and tell her I was in the jail. I didn't want her to know that until the sheriff closed the door. Then she would have no choice but to tell the truth. If she did that, I was assuming muscles would be set free, then maybe owe me a favor in return.

I was free from the moral stance of being a good human. I was a criminal and now a liar. I wondered briefly if there were any boundaries I wouldn't cross, then dismissed the thought. If my people were going to live, it was up to me.

"YOU WENT INTO THE JAIL? ALONE? YOU KNEW TO STAY OUT OF IT! I TOLD YOU TO LEAVE IT ALONE!" Jamie was hot; her fear from the other night returned in full gala. I was usually the one to get like that; this time, I saw where it came from. We were in the car on the way home after she had talked to the sheriff and told him what I said was true. I got pretty much exactly what I had anticipated and assumed my new friend was on his way to freedom. My mother, on the other hand, didn't exactly see it my way. She was all venom and fire. Seemed familiar.

"Mom, I told you. It was just some dumb jock from high school that did that to Fedwick," I said. "It was high school stupidity. A prank." She was constantly getting phone calls regarding stupid pranks. We were always in the middle of something. There had been several phone calls home to date; nothing had been proven, though, at least not yet.

"PAUL, ENOUGH," she yelled again. "You are home until further notice."

16

P & J

At 4:00 a.m. I woke and stared at the clock. Paul was ultimately the first thing on my mind. His story dissolved like mist in my mind but he, himself, stood out like a lighthouse on the shore of the beach. I lay there wondering if I was him in another universe. I thought of him and his family as the memories of the most recent dream faded away. It was like I was living alongside him. Watching his every move as his life unfolded but at the same time I was him. I was in his head and could see his thoughts and feel his emotions. It was eerie yet comforting. Our shared life only added to the confusion in my own head.

I reached up and pulled an ear plug out, and the muted sounds of sleep ceased. Reality flooded my hearing. A quick shower and shortly after, I was heading for my truck, coffee in hand. It was a two-and-a-half-hour drive to Republic, and I still wasn't sure what I was going to do. I figured I would go to the hospital and have a look around, maybe head out to Curlew Lake after that and sniff around the old stomping grounds. Something would come up. The no man led me here, and I was counting on that more than anything.

Twenty-plus years had passed, but it would have been hard to tell by the looks of the town. It seemed more like a relic than a town in the American West, but the demons left behind certainly still haunted this place. I stared at the hospital door—paint worn and fading, hinges rusted—and wondered how much life could have changed, how different it would have been had I been successful two decades ago. My emotions swirled.

I owed the reap fire and missed my turn.

I could feel the no man leaning on my soul, so I picked up my coffee and got out of the truck to stretch.

An ambulance pulled up to the emergency room door, and I leaned back on the truck watching. The driver hopped out and went around back, opening the rear cargo doors. Her mate pulled the gurney out, and the wheels popped down as it cleared the cargo bay. It was empty. The clack and snap of the gurney was loud in the remote solitude of the lifeless morning. The vehicle was still running, and the rear bay doors were left open as they wheeled the gurney inside, disappearing from my view. The street urchin in me had never seen the inside of an ambulance and was curious, so we wandered over to have a look.

I was shocked to see it mostly empty. I expected medical gear, tanks, neck braces, and the like, but what I saw was a stark-white, blank canvas. It looked like the gurney sat off to one side, and all of the medical gear was neatly tucked away in storage bins and shelving—vacant and sterile. Curiosity disappointed, I turned and made my way toward the emergency room entrance when the door slid open again. I stepped aside as the medics came back through with a loaded gurney this time. The passenger had a bandaged-up head and face with a neck brace on and was lying down.

"The doc said Spokane," the male medic said. "It was a big fight down at the bar a couple weekends ago. Another guy got his arm broke, but this fella took the worst of it. I heard the guy that started it was naked too."

The man's partner replied, "Naked, huh? Well, that's a first. This town is full of the devil. Ain't the first time I said it, won't be the last. I can't wait to get out of here. Three months to go!" She shuddered slightly. "One… Two…THREE!" they said in unison and pushed the gurney into the waiting ambulance.

"Whew! He is a big one, isn't he? You remember last year when them two fellas got into it?" She thought for a minute, then said, "The one where the guy ended up dying on the way to the hospital? What was his name? Ventosa or something like that. That sunofagun still haunts me, his eyes turning red like they did, then whispering at me. Too creepy, man. The devil, I tell ya," the woman said and shuddered again as she latched the gurney in, then shut the doors.

I listened as the ambulance drove off, thought about red eyes and death and a naked man in a bar room brawl, then went back to my mission, There were a handful of Ventosas in town way back when, no relation, but I was thinking of swinging into the library anyway. Hearing that just confirmed I should do a little research when I had a chance. I stepped into the hospital doors, saw the intake area empty, and darted past, moving further into the emergency room, looking for any clues from my dreams.

I left the hospital with little but memories and spent the rest of the day exploring the old place down by the lake. After a few hours of searching and walking the railroad tracks, I finally found what I was looking for. The growth in the forest had covered it up, making it difficult to find, but the rock outcropping that stuck out, visible from the railroad tracks, was still there. The tip of the outcropping stuck out like the tip of a nose. Behind it and up the hill a hundred yards or so was a stream that ran down the mountain into the lake. I listened carefully to confirm I was in the right spot, and I could hear the familiar gurgle of a waterfall before I started climbing. Relief washed through my body as I climbed over the edge and saw the entrance to my old haunt. I felt like I was being welcomed home. I turned from the cave and looked back over the lake, catching my breath and taking it all in. My soul relaxed, the knots it had been tied in for the last several months loosened and I finally felt like I could breathe without a legion of demons standing on my chest. I watched the treetops sway gently in the breeze and the lake ripple to the familiar touch of the same. I could feel the remote and isolated location of the cave, the lake and the tiny town tucked in the northwest. I closed my eyes and took another deep breath just letting the peace of the moment wash over me.

"Hello?" The voice behind me materialized from thin air. I jumped and whipped around, heart beating wildly, and my hand instinctually fell to the holster at my side. My moment of peace obliterated by panic.

Wide eyed and staring back at me, clutching a hand-carved walking stick, was Paul.

The seams of reality split wide, and the doors of the unknown burst open, spilling the impossible into my world. Another double take followed, my hand curled around the gun at my hip, ready to draw. I bobbed again, then stood still as stone in shock. His reaction mirrored mine briefly, then his eyes flashed, and his lips upturned into a knowing smile as understanding spread across his face.

The boy stayed perfectly calm, his silhouette standing in the entrance to the cave. He was no longer a dream but standing before me, flesh and blood.

"I've seen you before. Watching me. You're the guy from my dreams. I knew you were coming. Err, assumed, supposed maybe is the best word for it." the boy said and stared back with a wondering, crooked smile. I heard the sound, but the words didn't register. I continued to stare in disbelief. The lub dub hammering away in my chest from the fright was starting to slow but the disbelief was not.

His life. My life. Our life. It was all wound together. My chaotic mind was struggling to find a foothold.

"No, that isn't quite right either…" Then the kid took a step toward me. I drew and held my other hand out.

"Hold it there, son. I don't know what's going on here, I don't want to hurt you, but I have been dreaming of you or somebody like you for months, and now here you are standing right in front of me. I don't know if you're real or imagined. If I shoot, and you bleed, I know you're real. My God. Are you real? Have I completely lost my mind? I'm sure your name is Paul right? Of course it is. What the hell is going on here?" My voice was low and threatening; the truth was in it despite the kid's innocence. He stopped moving midstride but spoke up.

"I thought for sure, at one point, you were dead." His excitement at understanding gave way to the gun, reason, and the unknown. He put his hands up and slowly bent down, laying the walking stick on the ground, then he stood back up slowly and kept his hands open. He stepped over the walking stick and rolled it behind him with his foot. There was certainly no ill intention on his part, and he was making it clear, but the boy seemed to have some resolve and continued with questions of his own. I was dumbfounded that he obviously recognized me, and it quelled any potential itch in my trigger finger.

"Is the other man dead?" he asked with apprehension.

I had no idea what he was talking about, my body stiff from the unexpected, but my brain finally engaged, and I stepped forward, holstering my weapon slowly in good faith. This kid meant no harm. Paul of my dreams or not.

"I'm not sure what you're talking about. Have you been dreaming about me? I know you but…? Obviously, you have." I was stumbling all over myself, my thoughts and words still crashing together. I caught my breath this time, forcing the situation into hand, driving my mind to slow down.

"The no man? Do you know him? Has he been showing you things? What dreams exactly?" My voice cracked from the dust in my throat, but my wits were finally returning. I let my backpack slide down off my back and pulled out my water bottle to fight off the cotton mouth and shock, continuing to stare hard at the kid. I needed something tangible and my throat was dry as chalk.

The boy was watching intently. I took a long drink, watching him all the while. After several seconds of staring hard at him, I took another and he politely waited until I put the water bottle down, watching me in return. Then he stuck out his hand.

The collision of the two different worlds left wreckage in Joseph's mind, but the separation was distinct and obvious now. They were two different people, with two different lives existing together on the same earth.

"I'm Paul," the kid said, his face twinkling with excitement as he stuck out his hand. He was a dozen steps ahead of the man standing in front of him, his eyes blazing with raw, intimidating intelligence. Twelve or twenty-five, what simmered in the depth of the young man was wisdom beyond years. He was special, and only time would reveal to what extent, but Joseph, still recovering from the shock, was intimidated by it.

The man closed the distance cautiously, reached out, and took Paul's hand slowly with trepidation, he felt it then squeezed and covered it with his other hand, sandwiching Paul's in between his two hands and holding it briefly. Paul's blue eyes sparkled with life but Joseph's hazel ones were only filled with skepticism and frustration.

"Nice to meet you in person? I hope anyways. I'm Joseph." he said as a light rain began to fall. "Are you alone? How did you get here?" Joseph asked, unsure of the boy even after they touched.

Joseph stood in the mist as the rain began to fall, watching Paul, who naturally moved underneath the overhang of the cave. Paul said he was alone, his motorbike was parked in the forest below, and he'd found the cave earlier that year. The large stack of wood inside showed him to be an industrious caretaker.

"I will get a fire going, if you don't mind," Paul said as he shivered, and the rain picked up. Huge drops began hammering the open bench in front of the cave.

Joseph nodded at him, offering no resistance, and continued to watch the boy intently. Paul retrieved a homemade fire starter of wax, lint, and egg carton, then placed it in the fire ring. He quickly made a teepee around the fire starter, using split kindling from the stacked wood, then produced a lighter from his pocket. Joseph watched him closely the entire time, still not quite believing what was right before his eyes.

The cave was large with smooth, reddish-brown hematite walls, like a river carved it out thousands of years ago when the glaciers melted. The ceiling was twice as high as a man's head, and the distance from wall to wall double that. The mouth of the cave had an opening as wide as Joseph could stretch his arms, but he needed to duck slightly upon stepping through the entrance. The rear wall had a seam that ran from floor to ceiling. The crack was carved smooth and wound an elongated *s* in the wall. The top of the crevasse was maybe eighteen inches wide, narrowing as it fell to the floor. The fire ring was still where Joseph left it many years ago, only a few feet from the back wall, and the smoke vented through the top of the crack—exactly like when Joseph was a kid. The crack sucked the smoke in like a vacuum and was a natural draft vent dumping the smoke outside. The wind could blow, the rain could fall, and the storm could rage, but once you were inside the cave, the outside world faded away. Joseph ran his hand across a smooth wall, and it reminded him how much he loved this place, how much he missed it, and how it made him feel. It was unique, palpable, and gave him a slightly buzzed feeling. He stood in the entrance and let the feeling wash over his body inside the cave. The emptiness when he stepped out seemed distinct.

"I did that too," said Paul as he glanced up at Joseph, while feeding more wood into the growing flames. "Weird feeling, isn't it?" He could feel the intensity of the man's eyes on him and wondered if he should be looking for an escape instead of a tête-à-tête. This was his cave though, and his curiosity at the man was redlining. He casually slid his walking stick next to the hay bale he used as a seat, the stack of wood hiding the motion of his foot. Just in case the man wasn't right, he would need that stick.

"I used to come here all the time as a kid. Practically lived here for a while. I built the fire ring and carved a bunch of stuff on the walls," Joseph said, then flipped a thumb over his shoulder, motioning to the markings on the wall.

Paul watched him closely and nodded his head in understanding, agreeing and smiling big.

"You think it's some kind of magnetism? Or maybe voodoo instead?" he asked as he finished adding wood to the growing fire hoping the sarcasm came out funny. Paul was no stranger to the violence of men. He was a natural charmer, like his mom, and had learned that his charm was the best approach first. It often deflated potential conflict, but in the event that it could not, it would catch the aggressor off guard. If an explosion of violence was necessary, the eruption had to come with a friendly and welcoming smile. Hard times from a hard life taught survival tactics that worked and worked well.

"It's something. Good mind, ya know?" Joseph said, missing intoxicants badly. He smiled sadly at the reference, wondering if the kid would catch it. The dream boy and their lives, how intertwined and similar they were, reminded him there was no chance the kid would miss it. The thought gave Joseph a harsh gut check. He watched the kid make the fire and felt terrible for him all of a sudden. Joseph had a son a handful of years younger and couldn't imagine his child growing up like he or Paul. It all hinged on Paul being real, though. Joseph's recent sobriety and the struggle to get there left a bad case of the hot fantods in his mind. The thinning reality left behind something far worse, though: Joseph was no longer sure he could trust himself—at least not entirely. And the boy really could be a phantasm produced by the stress of addiction, his breaking mind, and the relentless pursuit of his past by the no man.

The fire flicked and popped, the sap from the pine giving up its life to the heat, shooting sparks against the wall. The cave was warming up, the storm outside began to howl, and the lake in the distance showed white caps rolling across it.

"The hay is a nice touch. Must have been a pain to get up here, huh? Anybody else know about this place?" Joseph said, softening the tone. If the dream boy was real, he should probably treat him as such.

"Not exactly. Stringing the rope through the trees and attaching the pulleys, now that was a total pain. Once I got that part done, though, I have been able to get pretty much whatever I want up here." Paul motioned to the stacks of firewood lining one wall.

"My brother knows about this place too, but nobody else that I know of. I asked him once if he could feel the cave. He said this place gave him the creeps, then insisted we go hunting. I haven't talked to him about it since then," Paul said and started to speak up again, then lightning reached out toward the lake, and thunder boomed. The storm was increasing in ferocity, and the day became dark and cold. The mild discomfort between the two was dissolving. The familiarity through the visions, dreams, and nightmares bound them, and Joseph could feel it, which was part of his problem. It was all too easy.

Paul held up a finger on one hand, the fire was burning bright, and the shadows were tall on the cave wall, then he walked over near the wood pile, moved his helmet and backpack, then rummaged around. A few seconds later, strips on the wall started glowing, lighting up the alcove. The flakes in the rock twinkled and reflected, shimmering dimly. It added to the feeling of the cave and gave it a dazzling effect.

"LED strips hooked to a battery. I keep it charged with a small solar panel my neighbor gave me," Paul said as he stood up and came back to the fire, plopping back down on his hay bale chair with a package of beef jerky and a water bottle. He smiled big again and shrugged, then held up the bag toward Joseph, offering the beef jerky after fishing out a few pieces. Joseph reached out for the bag of jerky. The kid had a friendly smile on his face, and Joseph relaxed a little more, then dipped his other hand into the bag of jerky. In a flash, Paul had the staff in his hands and swung it hard at Joseph's head. Joseph managed to lean back just a little before it cracked him across the temple. Joseph fell back onto the hay bale and hit his head against the wall as consciousness slipped away.

Paul dropped the stick and jumped around the fire, retrieved the gun, and rummaged through Joseph's pockets quickly. He patted him down, then grabbed Joseph's backpack and rifled through that. He found some paracord, to his surprise, then pulled a knife from a hidden pocket in the pack. He hurried over to Joseph, looped a trucker's hitch in the paracord, and tied his hands behind his back, smiling at the opportunity of the found rope. Then he went back to his side of the fire, sat down, and calmly continued with his jerky and water. The gun sat on the hay bale next to him. Joseph might be an ok guy, but Paul wasn't interested in taking chances after the man pulled a gun on him. Paul could feel the instability on the man and if they were going to have a heart to heart, maybe even be friends, it was going to be on his terms.

"Not every day you get to meet yourself," Paul said several minutes after watching the man's eyes flutter and open. Joseph made eye contact with the kid after looking around and regaining his bearings.

"Is that what you think I am?" Joseph questioned groggily. He had come to, and his hands were tied behind his back. He was lying on his side across the straw. He could feel the growing knots on his head and badly wanted to touch them. He should have known, but the comfortable and easy life he had built with his wife and children no longer held the horrors of vicious or violent cycles. A padded life had made him soft and slow over time, his guard had dropped, and the kid had capitalized immediately. He could feel the blood trickling down his temple and struggled to sit up.

"Are you? A different version of me? The first time I saw you, I was playing catch with my brother," Paul said. "It was fleeting, like I saw you step through the mirror in the back hall one day and then you were gone. I thought my eyes were playing tricks on me. I have seen your face or a reflection of it in the glass windows in town. Car windows, bathroom windows. At first it scared the wits out of me." His face changed at the memory. His eyes grew hard, cold, and distant as Joseph watched him speak.

"I have had the same dream a dozen times or more. Different variations, but the premise is the same and every time we…" The boy stopped, then started again, "When I say we, I mean I am inside your body with you. We. I can watch your thoughts, and you can hear mine if I send them out, but you are not exactly aware I am there, I don't think. Are you? I can jump into the captain's chair and drive, run the show, but if I am not careful…Something else shows up. Inside you. With us. Whatever it is, it scares the crap out of me. It's some sort of rage monster, I think. Have you ever seen the movie *The Hulk*? Sort of like that," Paul asked, then stopped talking. He slipped another bite of jerky in his mouth, but his hand trembled just slightly.

Joseph stayed quiet after watching every tick and change in Paul's face as he spoke. He was mostly convinced Paul was real now; the swelling, pain, and blood coming from his head brought about the revelation faster than he thought possible. His mind was still cloudy, but he sensed the kid was afraid. Not of him but of the savage that he thought lived within maybe. It slowly dawned on him that was why he probably hit him. After the silence between them had grown thick, Joseph spoke up again. The words were heavy and came out slow.

"The bullet is still probably in that house, I have had the same dream I think.... Can you at least untie my hands? This is really uncomfortable, man. I am not going to do anything weird. I just wasn't sure you were real, which is why I pulled the gun in the first place. What good will a gun do against a shadow? I dunno but I was willing to find out. I... have been dreaming of you for weeks and months now. It has sort of wiped out my life... but the knots on my head and the blood have convinced me that you must be real.... The beast's name is Jamis. He was a protector one of us created, maybe inadvertently, maybe not. The violence started pretty early in life. He liked to fight; I never did, but I wasn't really given much of choice, I suppose. I wasn't sure if he was yours or mine, to tell the truth, but when I looked back into the past it didn't matter. He was there either way. I have been struggling to separate our stories. Don't sleep much anymore, and keeping things straight, especially the last few months, has been brutal." Joseph stopped talking, flicked his eyes at Paul and then away. Paul had a hard look on his face and seemed to know exactly what Joseph was talking about. The kid's eyes lit back up, and the look softened to a smile.

"Lie flat," Paul said. He jumped up, skinned the knife from his pocket, flicking it open in one fluid motion, then walked over to Joseph, who had tipped on his side. He rolled flat on his stomach and caught some more pain from his head for the effort. The kid cut one loop free and was back across the fire, gun in hand before Joseph moved again. Joseph pulled his hands free of the restraints and sat up slowly, wincing at the pain. He gently touched the side of his head and felt the lump, then pulled his hand away, fingers bloody. He put his head down in his hands and sat still, then touched the back of his head gingerly, fingers probing around silently.

"You gonna be ok?" Paul asked. The unspoken between them was acknowledged in that moment. Joseph understood why it happened. Paul was sorry for the pain, but it had been that kind of life for both of them. Friendships forged through experiences were the best ones after all.

"Yup," Joseph said, keeping his head down.

He heard some rummaging, and the kid said, "Catch." Joseph looked up, and Paul tossed him his water bottle from his pack, then a first aid kit. Joseph was relieved at the sight of it.

"So you have the Hulk living in your head? Or maybe he is living in mine? Can you make him come out? You ever change color?" Paul laughed, trying to break the uncomfortable tension. "Do you think I am you? Like a younger, smarter version maybe?" Paul teased and laughed again, adding levity, but kept the gun close at hand. The bondage was a bonus discovery anyway.

Joseph grunted sullenly as he cleaned up his head. The kid no doubt was a charmer with courage in spades. Give him a few years, and he would be formidable for even the best and the brightest.

"Since you are sitting across from me, I'm no longer unconscious or dreaming, then you must not be me. It doesn't seem likely anyways at this point, to be honest, besides, I am much better looking," Joseph said, giving a hard time back to the kid and answering his first question.

"Minus the new additions," he added, then pulled away the gauze pad and looked at the small blood stain. He shifted and looked at Paul for a reaction to his glib response. Paul smiled and shook his head in disagreement. The similarities were obvious, but so were the differences.

Joseph was thirty-eight and had a lifetime of experiences, and it showed on his face. He was six foot, thin and muscular. His dark complexion, dark hair, and dark features gave him appeal, but the too-oft broken nose, furrowed brow, and hard eyes showed character beneath. A challenging life left some hard lines, and at almost forty, they were all starting to show.

Paul, on the other hand, still had the soft face of a child. His icy blue eyes sparkled with life, intelligence, passion, and mischief. He was shorter than average height for his age and still skinny; his preteen body had yet to catch up with his mind.

The makeshift den was warm, and the rain outside was comforting. Joseph was leaned back against the smooth stone of the cave wall, sitting on the pad of hay, his long legs stretched out toward the fire. His hiking boots were set to the side, and his socked feet were absorbing the warmth of the flames. He could see the whitecaps on the lake, and the wind whipped the treetops around outside.

He and Paul talked for a long time, the obvious draw being their childhoods, though Joseph's was long over, and Paul's wasn't finished yet. Joseph's head was no longer pounding or bleeding, but the knots were still tender to the touch.

They focused on Paul, Joseph steering the conversation back to him, answering questions about his own life with more questions about Paul. Joseph wasn't about to tell Paul why he was really in Republic. He told him about the no man and how he felt pulled back to the tiny town, told him about his family and much of his own childhood. Neither could pin down why they were dreaming of each other, but several suggestions were made. Joseph told Paul it was the no man, but the no man wasn't familiar to him. Still, it didn't change Joseph's opinion. As the day turned to twilight, the storm broke, and Paul saw a chance to get home without getting soaked.

"I'll be back in the morning," Paul said. "You staying here tonight?"

"Yeah, I planned on staying a few nights. I thought I might get into a shootout with a mountain lion or a bear if anything, but I definitely didn't expect to get thumped in the head by the kid from my dreams," Joseph said, still in mild disbelief.

"Tomorrow then." Paul smiled and saluted, grabbed his helmet, and walked out, then spun back around with an afterthought.

"Hopefully you don't use this while I am walking off," Paul said and handed him the gun, then turned around, once again displaying courage in spades. Paul was trusting Joseph, and it was not a small act. Joseph, coming from the same world, understood it clearly.

He holstered the weapon, then grabbed his pack and began setting up his bed. The Thermarest on a pile of straw would be more comfortable than the hotel bed he crashed in last night, and cheaper too. He stoked the fire and began making a quick meal. The shadows danced on the wall as his mind spun away. Shortly after dinner he fished out a couple more Tylenol, then laid down. Within minutes, his eyelids fluttered, and he welcomed the euphoric feeling of falling asleep.

The cave had a heartbeat all its own, and Joseph could almost touch it. He could feel the pulsing at the bumps on his head as he drifted away. He saw the no man offering him a hand, asking to pull him deeper. He reached out and touched it as he fell away.

He needs me. Paul needs me too. That's why I'm here.

Then a deep sleep carried him far away.

17

STATIC

Joseph lay with his back against the cave wall, the hay, air mattress, and sleeping bag cradled him, enticing him to stay within the warmth and comfort. The summer sun was still below the mountain in the east, but the sky was growing ever brighter. A red-and-gold thrush sat on a limb not too far from the entrance singing sweetly for his missing mate. He glanced at his watch.

Five fifteen a.m.

He assumed it would be a few hours before Paul showed up and wanted to get some work in. He slept hard and was wide awake, the no man a brief specter as he faded into the abyss of sleep. He was certain the no man was what brought him and Paul together, which in the end only brought more questions. As he drifted into the subconscious the night before, he remembered feeling certain that Paul and the no man both needed him, but for what exactly it wasn't clear yet. The mystery in his mind didn't break during the night. The only standing conclusion: Paul was likely real, and that was still slightly questionable until he showed up again. The two tender spots on his head reminded him the kid should be taken seriously.

Joseph lay there trying to organize the litany of thoughts. The no man drove him to the brink and pushed him back to Republic. The nodder in Oregon tugged at the same thread of insanity. The reap fire was something Joseph missed as a kid, and it was spoken into his life again when he happened to be on a mission to right that exact wrong. The timing was all but impossible to deny. But the kid from his dreams stepping into his world? It just didn't fit.

He considered once again that he may just be losing his mind. The entire web of chaos in his life, all of it, was his body punishing him for living without his medication—the salve of alcohol. Separating the fringe of madness from the five senses of the world was becoming easier, though, and the haunting in his mind of the Cabalifornians had ceased to exist. The pain of addiction unfortunately had not.

The sky was light enough to walk by, so he climbed out of bed and slid on his jeans. It was chilly, but it wasn't cold. He was always an early riser and liked mornings, but the last several months made them difficult. Today he felt different, though. He felt rested and whole, like the missing piece of the puzzle was found. He dug through his pack and removed the small backpacking stove and canteen for boiling water. Coffee was like oxygen since he had quit drinking. He had a dozen or so instant-brew packages and pulled those out with his mug. Once the water was cooking, he dropped to the ground and began pumping out the push-ups. It was 120 a morning now and quickly at that. In the not-so-distant past, it was a mere twenty-five.

As the liquid began bubbling, he slid on a glove and grabbed the stainless bottle, poured water in his cup with the micro grounds, then set the water bottle back on the tiny stove. After that was done, he flipped over and started on the sit-ups. Never a disciplined man, he was certain sobriety after a lifetime of debauchery required some steel in the backbone; it was a work in progress. The coffee was perfect by the time the sit-ups were done. He went out of the cave and, facing the rising sun, took to his knees. He thanked Memaw's God for another day of breath, his family, everyone's health, and a warm place to sleep. Gratitude was becoming the norm; finding small things like ten fingers and ten toes to be thankful for had become commonplace. He watched the sun rise and enjoyed the rest of his coffee. If he were home, it would all be followed by a cold shower, but since that wasn't an option, he went in search of the creek in the wilderness.

Joseph dunked his head and stayed under for as long as he could. The ice-cold water running across his face touched the farthest corners of his mind. The morning ritual was a life raft he built and clung to. He popped his head out of the creek, refreshed and fully awake now. A few minutes later, he was hiking back down toward the railroad tracks when he heard something off in the brush.

He froze and listened intently. The thrashing sound said it was bigger than a noisy squirrel, a deer maybe, but they usually didn't make much noise. It was in the distance, and a hoofed animal seemed unlikely to make noise on the soft forest floor. Intuition said human. Joseph moved through the brush, quiet as a shadow. He moved quickly toward the noise, weaving up and down to get through the brush in silence. He caught a remnant of red-and-black checkering disturbing the quiet and stopped. He watched the reckless gait of the intruder as they plowed through the forest. It was an odd time of day for another person to be out this way and the wrong time of year.

Maybe they were scouting for the upcoming hunting season. Whatever he was doing before, he was moving fast now.

The person was a hundred-plus yards through the woods and getting closer to the train tracks with every step; Joseph's curiosity tugged at him. He looked up, hoping for a vertical climbing route in the rock bluff that would lead back to his stuff and the bench overlooking the tracks. It was a fifty-foot climb, and it had to be quick if he wanted a better look.

He put his long limbs and whipcord frame to the test, and a few minutes later, panting and bleeding again, head pounding from exertion, he rolled himself over the top edge of the bench, right next to the cave entrance.

He lay on his back, catching his breath. The palm of his right hand had a minor gash that was trickling blood. He held it up and looked at it for a minute, watching the blood drip slowly. He sat up, then stood, breathing deeply, and went into the cave to grab the water bottle from this morning. He emptied it on his hand and washed the blood away, making a fist, then wiped it clean on the back of his pants. He walked back to the open bench in front of the cave and waited.

The red-and-black flannel came into view after a few minutes, and he watched the long blond hair bounce with every step. He was a she who was certainly in a hurry, moving with an an odd gait that he couldn't put a finger on. It seemed abnormal, uncomfortable, he thought. He watched her move south along the railroad tracks and wondered where she was going. No pack, nothing in her hands, no binoculars around her neck, and no water that he could see. They were in the middle of nowhere. This side of the lake was Bureau of Land Management property, so coming out here had to be intentional. There was a cabin down the way, on a small slice of private land, but it had to be five miles from here, maybe even more. The highway was up above, behind the cave, at the top of the ridge to the west a few miles.

It was another mystery for him to solve. He watched her carry on and was about to dismiss it when she turned and looked at him. Even from the distance, he could feel the eye contact.

The palpitation caught in his chest midbreath. He felt like he'd had the wind knocked out of him, and not being able to inhale was going to make him suffocate. It was instant and consuming. He caught sight of the woman in the vest, and through a blurry vision, he was sure he saw her smile. Then she turned and disappeared from his view. Joseph dropped to a knee and started seeing spots, still unable to draw breath. He pounded his chest with a fist, and the familiar lub-dub sounded in his ears again, and he felt it in his throat. He inhaled deeply, trying to catch back up to life.

Sooner or later one of those is going to kill me, he thought. Likely an a-fib attack—he'd had them before, and occasionally, he would get a whopper, and his heart seemed to stop beating for several seconds or more. The worst of them, like this one, would take away his ability to draw breath in. The look of hatred in the woman's eyes seemed to swirl in his mind, but the beating heart brought him back to the present.

Thank God.

He took another deep breath and stayed on the ground and watched the big blackbirds in the sky spin circles over death nearby.

First the addictions and the cabal, then the no man and his past, the nodder, now Paul and the woman. He was no longer sure he wanted to pursue anything in Republic except an ice-cold beer and something—hell, everything—stronger than that. He was still lying there, soaking up the morning sun, when he heard Paul's motorcycle in the distance.

Joseph got up and headed into the cave for another cup of coffee. It was still too early to feel defeated, and after shaking off the toxic thoughts of inebriation, he was determined to make sense of it all. He forgot about the woman and started thinking about Paul and the no man.

"Morning," Paul said as he entered the cave, carrying his backpack and helmet, making eye contact with Joseph and smiling with a mischievous smile. Joseph was sitting on his bed, steaming cup nearby, notebook in his lap and pen in hand. He smiled back and wondered what the kid had up his sleeve.

"Morning. You're here early," Joseph said. The fire was barely flickering, and Paul traded his gear for a couple of pieces of firewood. He sat down on the straw bench across from Joseph and dropped the wood in the fire pit between them.

"Yeah, not much for sleeping right now," he said and shrugged, watching the fire grow.

"So…anything new come to mind?" Paul asked and looked up at Joseph.

"Only things that stand out are my past, your present," Joseph said and watched Paul as he spoke, who nodded his head in agreement, slowly at first. He really felt bad for the kid and wanted to help him, but he felt like that topic was off limits for now. The kid was unsettled but focused on the task at hand. Joseph already knew damn well what happened and decided he would right that wrong, one way or another before he left town.

"When did you start dreaming about me?" Paul asked.

"Early last winter," Joseph said. Paul's eyes sparkled.

"The first time I found the cave was on a four-wheeler trip with our neighbors. They had a cow get out, the snow wasn't deep yet, so we ended up out here, on the BLM land, looking for her. I saw a group of birds circling above, so my neighbor said we should look for a carcass, see if the wolves got her. Turns out they did, but I climbed up to the bench to see if I could get a better look. That's when I found the cave. Early last winter," Paul said.

They stared at each other for a minute, letting the thoughts sink in.

"The cave," Joseph mumbled and stared at the fire, tugging on his ear. The obvious answer; he felt foolish for missing it. His eyes flicked to Paul, who was gently probing fingers around his swollen nose. Both of them had some tender spots, but Joseph's seemed to have shrunk substantially—almost gone in fact, whereas Paul's were fresh.

"Maybe we should check it out a little more? See if we are missing something. The cave is creating some kind of telepathy? Or it's like a server that is connecting you and me? How does it work?" Paul said, talking quietly, almost to himself, staring at the fire again. "The cave *does* have some type of voodoo, some kind of force that we can both feel. Could we test it? How? What can we do? If it is some type of telepathy, can we use it consciously? How?"

"Maybe it's the rock itself." Joseph offered, feeling inferior to the young man's speed. Paul's eyes sparkled, then he got up and walked over to the firewood, pulled the old splitting maul found in the barn out, and went to the back of the alcove. He swung the axe hard at the crack in the rear wall. The tip caught, shot a spark, and split off a small chunk. Paul watched it fall to the floor, then took a few more swings, this time aiming up higher. He caught another piece and chipped it off. He scooped up the pieces, leaned the ax against the wall, and sat back down, looking at them.

"That's a good idea," Joseph said, picking up where he was going.

I had too many other distractions. The cave would explain everything. It's why the kid doesn't fit. He is part of the cave, not the no man or my past. So it was the kid that brought me here?

Paul handed Joseph a rock.

"I'm going outside and will think of a number. Try to focus."

Joseph watched Paul walk out to the far edge of the bench. He thought of the number three, closed his eyes, and sat down. He focused on the number and he tried to send it like a spear toward Joseph.

"I got nothing," he heard Joseph mumble, then excitement rose in his voice. "Wait. Was it a three? Were you thinking of a three? It wasn't really clear and sort of popped into my head at the last minute. I think I should be outside of the cave too, though."

Ok, so we have some kind of connection, Paul thought.

"Yea, just come out here, and we can sit back-to-back or something." Paul said. Joseph went out and sat down, his back to the kid. Paul thought of the number thirty-eight and sat quietly, this time letting Joseph look on his own. Joseph concentrated but shook his head slowly in frustration.

"Eighty-three maybe?" he said. "It's not real clear, like looking through a fogged-up mirror."

After several more attempts of Joseph trying to see Paul's thoughts, they switched. Joseph's attempts were only mildly successful. Paul, however, possessed some type of natural clairvoyance. As he sat there concentrating on the man behind him, he saw a dirt path that led up to a door. He knew it was the back door to his thoughts; how or why was irrelevant. He just knew. He gripped the handle and spun it slowly, the wooden door creaked loudly as he opened it into the man's mind. He stood in the open entryway and saw the numbers and more as he looked into the chaotic mess of Joseph's mind. He could see plenty, in fact, but wasn't about to tell Joseph that. He sent a thought to Joseph.

Joseph, can you hear me? Paul waited a few seconds, then a loud and clear response came through.

Paul? Paul was that you? I can barely hear you if that's you. It's like an echo in the distance.

"I can hear you just fine," Paul said out loud. Joseph stood up and turned around. Paul was all smiles, excited at the thought of being able to read minds. Joseph was starting to wonder if it was Paul and not the cave. The kid was obviously special. Joseph, on the other hand, only had minor success at best. It likely had something to do with the static in his head, but neither brought it up.

When the experiment was finished, Paul went back into the cave and chipped away at the slab until he had a nice little slag pile. He grabbed a few larger chunks, after putting several others into his pack, then handed a second, larger one to Joseph.

"What now, boss?" Joseph asked sarcastically, stretching and watching the kid work.

Paul chuckled. "I think the cave is like an amplifier. We should explore it to see if we can find anything else," Paul said.

Joseph thought about it for a minute. "If the cave is an amplifier, what is the generator? What is the source of the power? Us? If that is the case, then how did we dream of each other? I was three states away and haven't been in this cave in twenty-plus years. I know I don't have any pieces of it floating around either."

Paul shrugged. "Don't know."

But I will figure it out.

The thought popped into Joseph's head, and Paul smiled, knowing that it got through. Joseph wasn't thrilled at the thought of the kid adding to the disarray but didn't really see the harm in it.

"Let's check out the cave, then I need to get home. I am thinking I might come back up tonight and camp out, see if anything comes up with both of us in the cave,"

Paul said. He wouldn't even have to lie to his mom but wasn't opposed to it. Again, he wondered if there were any lines he wouldn't cross, and it made him question where he was headed in this life.

"Whatever works, kid," Joseph said. Maybe he couldn't read minds like Paul, but he sure could read feelings. He was an empath of sorts, he supposed, and it came naturally. He could feel Paul's guilt—at what he wasn't exactly sure, but the guilt was clear. The kid was certainly growing on him. Maybe it was the bond between them, maybe it was the dreams, or maybe it was the empathy of a hard-knock life.

They searched the area but nothing new came up.

"I need to head into town, make a phone call, pick up some supplies, then I will be back. Shouldn't take too long. I should be back by evening," Joseph said and looked at his watch. It was almost noon.

"Ok, I will be back around then too. If something comes up, I will let you know," Paul said.

"You have a phone? But I don't get service out…" Joseph started but stopped talking when Paul held up his rock.

18

BISCUITS & BLOOD

The town was getting ready to kick off the last weekend of Prospector Days. It had been almost two weeks since the big fight at the Gold Rush, and Sheriff William Keating was sitting at his desk with a bottle of Maalox for indigestion. He was proofing all the field reports and catching up on anything important he might have missed. It was amazing how much trouble could get stirred up in a town with an official population of 1,182 people during a three-weekend festival. The sheriff petitioned to close Prospector Days a few years ago, but the city council flat out denied to even hear it. It generated almost a third of the annual income for many local businesses and was really the only tourist attraction they had. People didn't exactly come from all over the world, but Spokanites and folks from the coast showed up year after year, weekend after weekend, boosting the local economy. They weren't usually the issue. The problem was that every biker, logger, miner, and redneck in a hundred miles showed up, and lots of them didn't get along too well. It was rough crowd, and the local bars often had to hire security, who may or may not break up fights, depending on who was doing the fighting and who was supplying who with what. It was coming to a head, years in the making, and Keating thought this was the year that all hell would break loose.

The sheriff wanted nothing more than the quiet, sleepy little mountain town he grew up in but would have to make it through one final weekend of misery before he got his town back. The emotional toll of Rye Fedwick's bizarre naked fight weighed heavily on the man. He put the reports down and leaned back in his chair, rubbing his face, thinking of his wife, Gladys.

She was heartbroken after Jerry died—absolutely ruined. He knew after several weeks that she wouldn't make it; she would never recover. The sadness was too great for her to bear, but he ignored it all. He spent his time at work, and despite the family and friends that surrounded her, she died along with Jerry. His funeral was a few months before Prospectors, and Gladys hung on for as long as she could, but the "big" kickoff parade to Prospectors was too much for her to take. It was always the thing Jerry (Gladys in reality) liked best, and Gladys had taken him every year until he was seventeen. He chased down some candy no matter the age, probably because his dear old ma would squeal and laugh every time he did it. She loved taffy, and it was the only time of year she would eat it. Gladys had a picture collage of her and him, in the same spot in front of the hardware store, from every season of their life together. When Bill got home late that night, he found the collage in her arms, the empty pill bottle on the nightstand next to the bed, the whiskey bottle on the floor, and a sad smile on her face. Bill reached for the Maalox again, hoping to wash away the memory.

The Coleman-Fedwick brawl was the opener to this year's mayhem. Since then, the sheriff and the handful of deputies still on board had been running nonstop. The city police were removed from duty the year before due to budget cuts, so the sheriff's department was all that was left. They inherited some facilities, vehicles, and weaponry but not much of the leftover budget to go with it. Keating was able to squeeze a few more dollars out of the city to transfer two of the city cops to his staff, but that was it.

Keating sighed and looked back at the reports then thumbed through them. He pulled one out and set it aside. Every one of them involved violence. From domestic violence, which was the most recent, to assault to attempted murder, the inmates were running the asylum now. What started as an empty lockup with Rye Fedwick as a solo occupant twelve days ago was now overflowing. Bill just didn't have the manpower to keep things under control, and he was going to have to release minor offenses, bonded or not, to make room for the devil.

The state government was a blue trifecta, and those morons, in Bill's opinion, couldn't manage a bowel movement successfully, much less a state. Blame cops, cut funding, step all over the second amendment, write laws that criminals don't follow anyway. As far as Bill was aware, murder had been illegal for a long time, but they continued to try to disarm the law-abiding folks. Like banning firearms was going to stop people from killing each other. All they had to do was look at Chicago and New York for proof those laws didn't matter shit for Shinola.

It disgusted William Keating to the core, but he managed to never let it slip. He was the sound voice of the law in this county and had been for twenty-plus years; he wasn't about to let some backward-thinking idiot ruin his sterling legacy. That legacy was all Bill had left. With retirement on the horizon and his reputation on the line, Keating wasn't sure he'd make it clear of the badge before he had a heart attack.

He picked up the picture of his wife and son, sitting on the curb in front of the hardware store, hugging as the parade passed by, and let a tear slide down his cheek. He held the picture for another second, set it down, and wiped his face, then picked up the latest report and went through it one last time. After another fifteen minutes, Sheriff Keating put it down and headed for the Gold Rush to have a biscuit and some coffee with his electorate. Then he wanted to see Jamie Black about her son.

Jamie had the second shift of the day and was still going to be late. She was in the bathroom working the cover-up. She and Paul had a blowout this morning after Paul and Eric had one last night. She just couldn't stop it from happening. She knew Eric was bad news and had put a tremendous amount of effort into distancing herself from him. Paulie told her as much, again, this morning: that Eric wasn't worth spit, and he was going to fix it once and for all. The small bruise on her face was light, and the cover-up hid most of it. She thought about the night before and just couldn't believe how fast it happened.

Paul rolled his motorcycle into the barn and put the kickstand down. He hung the helmet on the handlebars, then pushed the bay doors closed and latched them shut. The ride home, the race to beat the rain, was exhilarating and he relished the rush. He guessed maybe it was eight miles to the cave from here, most of it through the woods. The final mile or so ripped along the railroad tracks, then led up to the cave. It was a slick and wild ride back to the house, and he loved every minute of it.

He left Joseph, his new friend, at the cave for the night, confident that they were not different versions of each other, but the mystery of the dreams still lingered. He wondered if there was a purpose to the cave connecting them, or if it was just coincidence as they cohabitated the cave at different times. He knew Joseph had a secret locked away, and he wasn't able to pry it open before he left. He wasn't sure he wanted to either, for fear the beast was hiding behind the lock in Joseph's mind.

Just as he slid the last latch into place on the barn door, he heard the screen door slam up at the house, then a muffled argument ensued. It spoiled his elation. The dark world he had lived in before Republic was washing away. Eric was the sole remnant from that life, and Paul wished him away. A bitter and angry mood surfaced quickly. He wanted to kill him. His new life was great, and the universe had given him his own unique and exciting mystery to solve. The man sleeping in the cave was another, very real, part of it. The only thing left to do was get rid of Eric.

Maybe today is the day.

Paul sighed and let his anger grow, then looked around for a weapon. Today was the day then. He didn't need hot blood; the contempt was enough. He found a round metal fence pole. It was an inch and half in diameter and about three feet long. He picked it up and flipped it over, then swung it hard at one of the massive vertical support columns in the barn. It landed with a thick thunk and left a perfect half-moon indent in the corner of the wood column, even with his scrawny, skinny arm.

Good enough.

Paul turned to make his way out of the barn. Then he thought of Joseph. If he killed Eric today, it was likely he wouldn't be going back to the cave any time soon. They would end up at the cop shop for hours. He may even end up locked up somewhere. He may never see Joseph again, and the great mystery the universe had given him to solve would remain locked, its treasure hidden away from the world forever. He weighed his options carefully. He needed a plan not a reaction. He needed evidence first, proof that Eric deserved it, at least something that would muddy the waters. He dropped the metal pole and sat down, thinking of another plan.

Self-sacrifice.

So be it. He nodded to himself and steeled his resolve, knowing it was a long game now.

Jamie was standing on the back porch when her youngest son came around the corner. Eric was standing next to his truck. The bickering he heard earlier was escalating, and Eric's brow was furrowed, his face angry. She watched Paul walk toward them. He looked at his mom and smiled. Her mother's intuition screamed loud in her head, and time lurched, braking hard, then began moving in slow motion. Paul was wearing boots and jeans, and his pants were wet and covered with mud from riding his motorcycle. In the back of her mind, she realized he should not have been out there riding alone. He looked taller and thicker. His sweatshirt was wet and clinging to him, the fire in his eyes evident, as it usually was, but what caught her off guard was his gait. He was striding, confidently and with purpose, like he was on a mission. He made eye contact with her and smiled like a carnivore about to eat. He looked back at Eric and smiled again.

"Hi, Eric," he said.

"PAUL, NOO!" she yelled and held her hands out meaning to stop him, her face lit up, eyes wide in fear. The rain started coming down hard, blasting against the metal roof, above the wooden porch, like a machine gun firing away in war. Eric turned toward Paul just in time to see him cock back his arm and shoot a fist right into Eric's crotch, unprovoked. Jamie saw herself take flight in the memory and run toward Paul and Eric. She got there just in time for Eric to backhand her out of the way. She stumbled backward and fell, watching Eric drop to one knee in pain. Then from the backhand, he changed direction, balled up a fist, and hit the kid hard. Blood exploded from Paul's nose and covered his shirt. He hit his head hard against the side of the truck, then fell limp to the ground. Jamie watched as she got back up and put herself between Paul and Eric. He grabbed her by the face and slammed the back of her head against the truck. Then he let her go and hobbled to the door, half turned, and said, "I'll be back for my money, bitch." He slammed the door, started the truck, and spun out, taking off down the driveway.

Time returned, and Jamie saw her scooting toward her son in the rain, picking up his limp body, and pulling him toward her, into her lap. He came to, a heavy rain falling, washing the running blood over his face, mouth, and shirt. He opened his eyes and smiled at his mom. Jamie sat there holding him, crying, wishing for a different life.

Paul insisted he was fine as she got him some ice for his head and face once they got in the house and the bloody nose was packed. He went into his room and changed his pants, then came back out to the small living room in the single-wide trailer. He sat and looked at his mom; she was soaked and shaking. "Go take a shower, Mom. Get warmed up. I'm fine. Really." He still had on the wet and bloody sweatshirt, his face swollen, bloody, and bruised.

"Why did you do that, son? He could've killed us both. He didn't do anything, and you just walked up and hit him. Why? Oh Paulie, why, why, why would you do that? Do you want to die? Don't you have any fear?" She was shaking, confused, and scared, now more than ever. Eric wanted the money for the house. He "loaned" it to her, he said, and it was time to pay up, even though several months ago he said it was a gift. She knew it was dangerous and only took enough for a down payment but knew she shouldn't have taken any at all. She had been saving, planning, and working to clean up her life for months before that. Working Eric was the most difficult part, but she succeeded in getting the boys out of a terrible situation. Finally.

Eric had been holding back since then, trying hard to have a relationship with Jamie. She managed to keep him at arm's length, but now that the violence had started again, Eric would stop holding back. She stared at her youngest, waiting for an answer.

"Proof." And it was all he said, then he flipped on the TV and turned on the gaming console. Bryan was staying the night at a friend's house, so at least he wasn't involved. Jamie watched her youngest son in awe, not understanding what he meant; many times she never understood

Paul or the way he thought or the things he did. She was working on getting them out of a bad situation, and every time she turned around, they seemed to get deeper into the grave. He stared at the TV, ignoring her presence altogether. She gave up and headed for the shower.

She climbed out of the shower ten minutes later to a knock at the door. She peeked out the bathroom window to see a sheriff's Bronco parked in the driveway. She couldn't believe her bad luck. She hustled to get dried off.

Then her heart dropped. Proof, he said. Understanding unfolded in her mind. Paul probably called the cops before he even walked up and smiled at her. Before he hit Eric. Before he was knocked unconscious in the rain.

The cops would only make things worse. Eric had a way of working around them, and they both knew it, especially the understaffed yokels in this town. She wrapped a towel around her, forgetting the clothes or bathrobe and went for the door, but it was already too late.

"It was my mom's husband. He has done it before," Paul said as the cop looked at his face. Jamie should have known. He was always a step ahead of her, though. He had never cleaned up, and it was intentional: the swollen lips and packed nose, the bloody streaks across his face, the growing bruise, and the wet and bloody sweatshirt he still had on.

She wasn't blaming him, and it wasn't the first time that Eric had left them this way. Jamie sighed, grabbed a bathrobe, and went to the door. She invited the cop in, knowing the night had just gotten longer. The truth was inevitable, and she wasn't going to fight her son and Eric at the same time. She was being forced to take sides, and there was no question where her loyalty stood. Paulie knew exactly what he was doing, and if she went against him now, he would hate her forever. He would also likely outsmart her along the way, especially if he already had a plan. And it was becoming more apparent that he did. She trembled at the thought that her son should be feared more than Eric. Realizing that he was willingly knocked unconscious by grown man, that he had spades in resolve, and she was seeing a plan in action terrified her. Paul was on his way to becoming a murderer, and there was nothing she could do to stop it.

Except do it herself. The idea sparked the smallest flame of hope.

After pictures were taken and the cop had everything he needed, he said, "Ok, well, the restraining order is automatic. Spokane County has been notified, and a warrant has been issued for Mr. Black. You are a brave young man, Mr. Paul," he said, giving Paul the exact recognition he was going for. He just wanted the local cops looking into Eric; his history would do the talking. He also figured most of the local cops knew his mom. They were in the Gold Rush on the regular, it seemed and it never hurt to have some backup.

Then the officer looked at Jamie and said, "If you need anything else, Jamie, just call. Me and the boys will take care of this for ya." He was one of the regulars at the

Gold Rush, and she was sure he would be in tomorrow morning.

She gave him a hug then. "Thanks, Dale." She let him go. He walked away, and she shut the door behind him. Paul was already in the bathroom, turning on the shower. She knew this should have happened years ago, but it didn't, and now they were here, and he was going to solve the problem. She sat down on the couch and wondered where this life was headed. Eric no doubt would get out of jail; he may even post bond and head to their house immediately. She wondered if Paul expected that or planned for it. Eric would get his money or kill them both; it was going to be one or the other, maybe both in the end. Of that she had no doubt and knew he cared little for the law or its restraints.

Once she walked away from that life, one filled with bad choices and dependency, there was nothing he could hold over her head anymore. That was before they moved and started living an almost normal life. Now, he would try to force her back into it, and now he wouldn't hold back. Jamie previously had been just buying time, trying to figure out how to close the door on what was behind her—a way to get the money and send Eric away for good. This town was too far off the beaten path for him and would put Jamie out of reach most of the time. Paulie just didn't understand, and that was only because he didn't know everything. It crossed her mind to tell him the truth. Tell him all of it. It was likely he had already known much of it.

She didn't doubt he would figure out a solution faster than she could. Hell, she had been trying to think of something for weeks and had nothing. Proof. At least she had that now.

She finished with the make-up and slid the drawer shut, flipped off the lights, locked the door, and walked out to her car. Thoughts of her sons, getting high, Eric, and her impending doom swirled as she drove into town. She prayed Paulie would be ok. She heard his motorcycle start after he stormed out of the house this morning and wasn't going to stop him from leaving. She watched him ride down the driveway, his backpack bouncing along behind him, wondering where he was going.

Despite all that had happened, grace in her life was evident. She survived the abuse of her first husband, the boys' father, then moved herself, her addictions, and her boys on to Eric. Eventually she left him and her addictions behind, the miserable life of a desperate junkie finally killed off.

Providence.

Somehow, she also managed to become a landowner in a sleepy little town, near her family, at the same time. She had escaped the chaos not just once but twice, and now here it was, chasing her down for a third time. It was her own choices that brought her into this life, but it was grace that was leading her out.

She knew the devil and Eric were working hand in hand to drag her back to hell. The contracting business he owned used to be his craft, but now it was solely to wash his dirty money. He had enterprises set up in Portland, Seattle, and Spokane. She suspected he was involved in sex trafficking but couldn't say for sure. The kind of money he was flashing around spoke of a different kind of success, and at one point, he divulged he was washing money, lots of money, through the construction company. Then he called her his ace and told her she had been there from the start; when his chips were down, he could always count on her. Shortly after she told him she needed some space to deal with the boys and some "other" family stuff that had come up. It wasn't too long after that he said he wanted his money back with interest, and if she didn't have it, well she could always work it off. She finished the drive in, feeling stuck in a hopeless situation. The only option was to kill him, and Paulie was setting that ship to sail. Jamie gripped the steering wheel tightly and started to pray.

19

QUITTING TIME

Sheriff Keating noticed the Jeep in the Gold Rush parking lot and smiled, thinking of a different life. He and Don Abrams were peas in a pod when they were younger. That Jeep had been the source of countless hunting (and drinking) trips that Bill and Don relived dozens of times after they happened, usually during breakfast at the Gold Rush. As they got older and the trips became less frequent, Don would retell his favorites to anyone willing to listen. He had the gift of gab, and Bill Keating always secretly envied that. He would watch as his oldest friend became animated and launched into the memory, divulging secrets of the past with a wink, as he shared some of their greatest treasures with the zest of a stage-worthy bard. Don died from cancer several months back, but Bill always smiled whenever he thought of his oldest friend, though he missed him sorely.

Sara Abrams sat in the back corner booth, alone. She was pale and sweating. Several empty plates littered her table, and she was eating the food almost as fast as it was carried from the kitchen. She held up her water cup.

"Miss, excuse me, miss. Ma'am. Can I get some more water please? Like now?" she demanded.

Jamie Black had clocked in thirteen minutes ago and was already being yelled at. The mouthy broad in the corner, who was eating for a small army, was commanding all her attention. Jamie had no doubt had better days, and her temper was getting harder to keep in check.

"Uh hello, yoohoo, I am talking to you," Sara Abrams said again forcefully to Jamie. Jamie spun, walked over to her, and thumped the pitcher of water on the table hard enough to gain attention from several other customers. She looked hard at Sara, who responded loudly, "About time," with a sickly-looking grin on her face. The shuffle of chairs and bodies moving in unison to watch a situation unfold was eerie, and silence ensued. A cat fight was coming, and everybody wanted to watch.

The bell over the door jingled. In walked 280 pounds of sheriff, with his big belly leading the way, the smile disappearing from his face as his law dog hackles went up, sensing a situation. He noticed some of the customers were looking toward the booth in the back corner of the room, and some were looking at him, but none of them were moving or talking. Sweet little Sara Abrams was sitting in the booth, and Jamie Black was standing nearby; they both looked tense, like they were circling, getting ready to claw each other's eyes out. The cook, from behind the counter, oblivious to the situation, said, "Hey, Sheriff." It broke the tension, and a cacophony of noise followed as the patrons resumed life.

Keating said hello in return, then a few more hellos and pulled his hat off, hanging it on one of the pegs on the wall near the door.

"Sara Abrams, is that your dad's Jeep out there?" the sheriff said as he made his way across the room. "Good morning, Jamie," he said with a kind smile, then went back to Sara. She didn't look right, and as he got closer, he noticed the sweat, the gaunt face, and the empty plates on the table. Sara tried to smile back, but contempt crossed her face instead.

"Sheriff," she all but spat. It crossed Jamie's mind to whop her in the head with a coffee cup, but instead she leaned in and grabbed the stack of plates. "You're welcome," she said loud enough for others to hear. As she stood up from the table, she muttered quietly to Sara, "Dumb snatch." Then she smiled at her, walking away.

"Good morning, Sheriff," Jamie said and bussed the dirty dishes to the backroom. Sara growled, and the sheriff took Jamie's place next to the table. She stared at the lawman.

"You ok, hon?" he asked. He had known Sara all her life—high school, college, and beyond—and had never seen her like this. Her vacant stare and the growling noise that seemed to resonate from her were concerning. Her face flashed, changed, and a genuine smile surfaced.

"I'm ok, Bill. Been a rough year," she said, the vacant stare gone, big doe eyes lighting up her face. The color seemed to return too. Bill thought maybe it was his eyes, age, or lighting then.

"Yeah, that's the Jeep. We got the engine done last week, and I was taking it out for a test run. Somehow I ended up at the cabin. The Jeep ran out of gas on the highway, and I had to do a bit of hiking to get back to it." She shrugged in earnest.

"Great to see it on the road again. How is John?" he replied.

"Good, in Spokane, wanted to get some projects wrapped up. We had a big month," she said.

"Glad to hear y'all are doing well, and I'm gonna need a ride in that Jeep when it's all done. Don't be a stranger round here, kiddo. You know where I'm at," he said. His intuition wasn't exactly satisfied, but he knew she had a stillborn a while back and lost her dad, and the rumor was she had another miscarriage recently to boot. She and Jamie seemed to have some tension, so maybe he'd talk to Jamie instead, or maybe, and more likely, he wouldn't go looking for extra trouble right now.

"You bet, Sheriff. You bet," she responded, and her eyes flashed again as the big man turned and walked away, taking his usual seat at the counter. The bell jingled, and in walked a stranger, another yahoo here for Prospectors, the sheriff reckoned as he sat down and sighed in exasperation. He fished the Tums out of his pocket and popped a few in his mouth.

The red-and-black-checkered vest Sara wore had been given to her by her husband as a Christmas present a few years ago. Her blond hair bounced as she pushed her way through the door, leaving cash on the table.

Joseph saw her seconds before he felt her. She ignored him altogether and hurried out the door. He lingered briefly, wondering what to do, gave it another ten seconds, then went out the door after her, keeping his distance. She walked to the parking lot, and Joseph watched her climb into the Jeep and close the door. Fortunately, he had ridden his motorcycle to town. His truck was parked out near the cave. He'd thrown his bike in the back before leaving California, almost absentmindedly, and now was glad he did.

He watched the Jeep bounce over the curb recklessly, then it took a left on Clark Street and headed south. He heard a honk from that direction and thought he should get moving. The way she was driving, it wouldn't be long before she disappeared.

He followed her out 21 toward Swan Lake. The knobby tires on the motorcycle made a vibrating hum as they moved down the highway. He knew he was doing more than sixty, but she was hauling ass, and he was going to have to work to keep up with her without being seen. She swerved around the car in front of her, laying on the horn, almost running them off the road. Joseph was becoming worried he was getting into something serious, something he shouldn't be involved in, but it was pulling him along like a magnet, like the no man that dragged him here. At least he talked to his wife and kids not long ago.

If I die out here, at least they know I love them.

He felt the evil on the woman just like he did the first time. He knew—didn't think, but knew—he had to follow this woman. She was a cog in the gears that were turning his universe. His bike wasn't exactly street legal, but it had a taillight, a headlight, and a small mirror hanging from the handlebar. It began vibrating heavily as he pushed it closer to the limits. He wondered how much more the old Jeep had and began to sweat. Suddenly, the Jeep's taillights lit up, and the tires barked against the pavement, then she swung right onto a dirt road. Joseph slowed down and backed way off, then turned right and continued following her dust cloud.

The sheriff took his coffee black and kept an eye on Jamie as he sipped it slowly. She could feel him watching her, and he knew it but didn't mind. She was relatively new to town, and Keating thought she might be worth keeping an eye on. He knew her husband, or ex-husband as it seemed, needed eyes on him, and he didn't doubt her kid did too. He'd checked out Eric Black after their little meeting with the Coleman kid and Ryan Fedwick; turns out he had a history of bad decision-making. Bill thought Jamie might be worth the trouble, though. He had been in here a couple dozen times since she started and was slowly getting to know her. He also knew something was tugging on her, though, and likely it was some kind of addiction. The sheriff was no dummy; he lived in a small town and dealt with people every day. The advantage was in a small town you would get to know people over years, watch them grow, watch them change, watch them lose, or watch them win. He observed as plenty of people grew into addicts, junkies, or alcoholics and gave up their lives to a substance. He watched as the consequences stole what was left of their spirit, and then the lawman would deal out the worldly punishment when it was necessary, crushing any hope that remained. He didn't relish it, but it didn't stop him from dishing it out all the same. In Jamie's case, though, he saw something else. He saw she was already hopeless. He sensed the crushing had been done, though, and she was trying to rebuild, maybe having a tough time of it.

Jamie had to take a break. She was exhausted, and the midmorning rush was over. She snuck outside for a quick ten and a cigarette. Kim had caught sight of the bruise when she came in earlier and managed to sneak in a quick hug. They had become fast friends in the few months the Blacks lived there, and she already knew more about Jamie than anyone else. Kim slid outside next to her. It was just the old man mug club jawing away over coffee now, so they had a few minutes.

"Did you see Sara Abrams? Oh my gosh did she look bad. I never liked her. We went to high school together, and she always thought she was smarter than me. Oh, it used to piss me off. I hated her for it because she was right about it too. Now I just feel bad. Girl looked like she been through a hurricane," Kim said and lit her own cigarette. "She was in the corner all by herself. Had plate after plate. I have never seen such a little woman put away so much food in my life." Kim said she felt bad, but the look on her face said she was satisfied, happy about Sara's misfortune even.

"Oh, I know who you're talking about. She had a nasty little mouth, after she drained a pitcher of water and demanded more thirty seconds later," Jamie said. Kim was a great friend, but her parents did own the place after all. Jamie was thinking about Paul. When she called home to talk to Bryan a few minutes ago, he said the motorcycle was in the driveway, but nobody was home. Bryan said Paul was probably out at the pond. Jamie doubted it and told Bryan she wanted Paulie to call her before he left the house. She didn't expect Bryan to parent, just relay the message, but knew Bryan would tell him and likely make him call before he left again. Bryan was far more responsible than he should have been, and Jamie relied heavily on his help, especially with Paul.

"You want to talk about it?" Kim said, reading what was on her friend's mind. "You did a great job with the cover-up," she said morosely, angling for more details.

She eyed Kim but knew her hand had been dealt face up this time. Jamie could use a friend right now and she was no stranger to the bonds of sisterhood.

"Eric and Paul got into it," Jamie said. Now that her business was out there, she spilled the rest of the tea, opening up to her friend. "Paul is wicked smart, as Bry says, a mini genius man, and it scares the shit out of me.

Eric is not a genius, but he is shrewd. And violent. And possessive. He thinks he owns me."

And it scares me but not nearly as much as Paulie does. Not anymore. Not after last night.

She wasn't going to get into specifics. Kim was friendly with Dale, the cop that showed up last night, and Jamie couldn't say too much because she wasn't sure what her son was up to. Tears began to well, Kim saw, and she hugged Jamie tightly.

"I'm sorry, honey. If there is anything you need, just holler. We do have an empty cabin if you need a place to hide out for a while, until things blow over, and they will. They always do," Kim said reassuring her friend.

Jamie said thanks, and she might take her up on that. They snubbed out the smokes and headed back inside to freshen up and return to work.

Joseph was a few hundred yards away from the small building, above the road, hidden away in the trees. When he saw the Jeep swing into the driveway, he slowed, then found a place to dive off into the woods. There was no fence, and it was open enough, so he took the next game trail that headed further into the forest on his enduro. The bike barely had what it needed to be street legal and was built for off-roading. He gained elevation quickly but managed to keep the Jeep in sight. He stopped when the Jeep did, and shut his bike off, then he heard some banging, like metal against metal, then it stopped. His helmet and bike were behind a big elderberry bush, and he started creeping down toward what he supposed was a pump house or substation for the local water district. He heard the door slam down below and took a chance. He creeped in, quick and quiet, then put his back against the wall. There was a groan from inside that stopped him in his tracks. He listened hard, trying to tune in, and he thought he heard heavy, intentional breathing. Several seconds later another low moan escaped from the shed. He slid around the building to the back, where he saw a dirty window that had a small broken pane. He positioned himself just to the side of the broken glass so he could peek in. He knew the woman was dangerous, probably even deadly. He also knew Paul was going to be waiting for him soon, and he couldn't risk losing him either. They were both part of the puzzle, and he needed to know how they fit. He took a risk and looked in. The inside had plywood boarding up the window.

Damn.

The groaning continued. It seemed to be consistent, and he was positive she was alone. Had to be. No other voices, no shuffling of feet, just the breathing and groaning. Joseph stayed still, listening, trying to figure out what to do. He slowly and very quietly moved around to the far side of the building. There was a slotted metal grill on the outside of the building. It was a fresh air intake. If he was right, and he knew he was, there would be an identical one on the inside of the building. One of the steel vanes was bent in a *v* shape and rusted like somebody tried to pry it open. It was pulled up just enough to see through. Another groan, but this one was louder.

What the hell was going on in there?

He threw caution to the wind and squatted down to take a look.

JOSEPH!

He fell backward onto his butt and scrambled, looking around for whoever yelled at him. No one was around. He put his back to the wall again and stayed still, heart racing wildly, wondering if the woman heard him. There was no noise from inside the building now. He waited a full minute. It was almost like she wasn't there anymore. He crawled back over to the vent and started to squat down.

JOSEPH! HELP!

He fell back again but this time put a hand down and pivoted back to the wall, scouring the area for another person. Then he realized the person he was looking for was in his head. He felt around in his pocket, and he found the rock from the cave.

Paul? Is that you?

The last few days of Joseph's life came crashing down right then. The surreal reality of what he was doing hammered at the crack in his broken mind. He was staring at a rock, trying to use telepathy to communicate with a thirteen-year-old variation of himself that wasn't really him, while standing outside a pump station listening to a crazy woman diddle herself, whom he actually thought he should follow because he felt the pure evil inside her. After sleeping in a magic cave. All in a town that was thirty years removed from his life, a thousand miles from his wife and kids.

It was too much to take. Just too much. Joseph stopped and realized how utterly insane he was. He realized the addictions broke him, cracked him like an egg, and the mess was leaking everywhere. The Cabalifornians were in his head; the no man was in his head. Was the nodder in Oregon even real? He felt around on his head, and the lumps from the kid were gone—the same kid whom he had never seen anywhere but at the cave and in his dreams, the seemingly supernatural cave.

He stopped right then and gave up.

After several seconds of staring blankly at nothing but his thoughts, he made his way back to the motorcycle. His emotions were numb, the world silenced as he went into autopilot. Like a robot, he climbed aboard the bike, started it up, and rode back to town, looking for the first bar he could find.

Jake, the-short order cook for the Gold Rush called out, “Jamie, hey, Jamie, you got a phone call!” He waved it at her, then set the phone next to the register and went back to the grill. Jamie hadn’t heard from Paul yet and was going to be off soon. She felt relieved as she headed for the phone.

"Hey, bud!" she said, excited to hear from him, then turned around and leaned on the counter.

"Miz Black. It so happens there is growing market in the world for preteen boys these days, especially the feisty ones," the voice said in a baritone chord. His words were measured, clipped, and direct. Jamie listened hard; the words must have already registered because Kim was watching. Jamie's face flushed with fear, and her eyes widened. Her mouth was bone dry, and she couldn't have spoken up if she wanted to.

"I believe I have your attention now. If you choose not to render your services to your former employer, then you will want to produce twenty-five K, at which time any financial obligation you may have had previously will be satisfied. We can then discuss further negotiations. Miz Black, the boy has three days." The man on the phone went quiet, and the line went dead.

Jamie let the phone go and ran for her car. She fumbled with the keys, dropped them, picked them up, and dropped them again. She was shaking so bad she couldn't get the key in her hand. Paul was finally in real trouble. Eric already knew about the cops. He probably bugged her phone or was watching her house, and now somebody had her baby boy.

In a former life, Eric ran Jamie as a call girl. She was his platinum girl, top shelf, his numero uno. Twenty to twenty-five thousand a month. That was three hundred thousand a year. In trade for few thousand bucks here and there, a dump that had a couple rooms, a kitchen, a bathroom, and running water for the brats. Finally, black tar with boiled-down hallucinogenics and a hint of moly. It was called paint, and if it came through (which it always did), then she could get her fix when her kids were fast asleep, and services would be rendered again as needed. She was his golden calf, but she wasn't on the leash anymore. She conned, bartered, and cajoled him with the help of some of the others so she could get her kids out.

Jamie stopped and took a breath. Then she slowly reached down and picked up the keys, inserted one, and finally got inside the car. Her shitty choices in life were all coming back to haunt her, and it was her youngest son that was going to pay. In the end, Jamie had learned one thing for certain: if a man wanted something bad enough he would do anything to get it. Anything. She put her head on the steering wheel for a brief second, wondering what to do, then plugged the key in the ignition, started the car, jammed it in reverse, and gunned it.

Joseph was pulling into the parking lot on his bike and saw a spot right up front, near the entrance to the Gold Rush.

He twisted the throttle and was blindsided. The backend of a silver Subaru came out of nowhere and it was the last thing he saw before losing consciousness as his helmet hit the pavement hard.

When he came to, a woman was trying to drag him out from under her car. He was pinned between the bike and the car; the peg had saved his leg and the helmet his life. The woman was frantically tugging away but couldn't get anything to budge. She was crying and begging him to get up. Something about her son. Joseph laid his head back down for a second, trying to catch up, then began trying to work his foot out. The car was backed up on the bike, and the woman was too afraid of crushing him further to pull forward.

"Please, mister, get up. I will pay for your bike. I need to go. C'mon, man, I really need you to move. Right now, right now. I'm so sorry, mister, but please I gotta go. My son needs me. C'mon, I will pull you out; let me help," she said and grabbed Joseph as he started scooting back. After a few minutes of trying, he was finally able to wiggle all the way out. He was still dazed, but what she was babbling about, second after second, started to make sense. He was standing up with his helmet off, when the situation cleared up.

"Paul!" he said, yelling the name as his mouth caught up with his mind. The lady stopped, and her eyes narrowed quickly. In what seemed like impossible speed, she drew a gun from nowhere and pinned it against his head. Joseph backed up and fell down again, the bike tire catching his foot, but she stayed with him step for step. She snapped, and Joseph saw it happen.

Her teeth were clamped together tightly; she was all venom and fire.

"Say it again asshole. Say. It. Again." The broken addict in her had finally taken over. Sweet, scared Jamie

Black was no more. She was a survivor, a woman with a history of enduring. After her years of abuse, violence, addiction, and oppression, Joseph was looking at a predator whose teeth just came in and had a thirst for blood.

"Paul! I know Paul! I can help. It's a long story. I know he's in trouble. Jamie, is your name Jamie? It's Jamie, right? He told me to come find you. Pea pod, pea pod. He said to tell you pea pod," Joseph stammered. He was on the ground sitting half up with his hands in the air, eyes closed. "Don't shoot, ok?" He was really hoping the lunatic woman wouldn't blow his head off and opened an eye to see.

Her pea pod. A word that only the boys would know. She stepped back and slid the gun into her waistline, then turned and got in the car and stepped on the gas, and it jerked forward off the bike.

Joseph stood the bike up and moved it over to the building. He wasn't going to be able to ride it anytime soon. He leaned it against the building, then turned back to the car. She had backed out, and the passenger door was open, engine running. Joseph badly wanted a beer—just one beer—but knew it would have to wait.

He climbed in the car, and Jamie looked at him with narrowed snake eyes.

"If you do anything I don't like, I am going to put a bullet in your head, and if that doesn't work, I will wrap this car around a tree, and we will see who lives and who dies. Clear enough?" Her voice was snappy and short. Joseph knew she was about her business.

"If Paulie said you can help, then you must be able to, so start talking," she said as she turned and headed up Klondike Avenue, leaving town.

The man shifted in his seat uncomfortably, and a small moan escaped his lips as he did. He was quiet for a full minute.

"Paul and I have a, uh, unique friendship," he said, weighing his words carefully, watching Jamie. If she pulled out that gun again, then she very likely meant to use it.

She was doing eighty through a forty-five zone and motioned for him to continue.

"I lived here as a kid. There was a cave I used to visit. Paul apparently found the cave and goes there often," he said, getting to the shortest version possible. He watched her white knuckles and furrowed brow, looking for any sign that would tell him if she flipped. None showed, so he continued. "The cave has somehow connected us. I have had dozens of dreams about Paul and our childhoods, mine and his apparently, including you. It was always blurry and confusing, like faded memories, and they were always mixed together. I couldn't really tell where mine ended and his started. Paul was really the only part that was clear when I would wake up. I thought he was, I dunno, a different version of me for a long time—until yesterday in fact, when I met him for the first time." He stopped talking and held his breath. It didn't sound so crazy when he put it like that. "And there was/is something driving it. Some kind of uh, I dunno, force of nature or something. I can't quite put my finger on it, nor do I really understand it," Joseph said, then went quiet, hoping the gospel truth would satisfy the lunatic woman.

After Paul met me at the cave this morning… uh well… it gets batshit crazy, but he realized we can kind of see each other's thoughts. Paul is amazing at it, naturally gifted really. Does that sound believable to you, miss? Am I gonzo without the sauce? Did I mention I have a drinking problem? Two empty hands and not a beer in sight? You too? Well, heck, lets shoot back to the bar and have a few. I will tell you about the rocks and the no man once we get there. It's a great story, really, about this one time I sobered up, and all my marbles rolled away. Joseph kept the thoughts to himself and had to work to stifle a laugh even though it hurt like hell. Jamie relaxed a little, but he could feel the sharp edge on her still. She was Paul's mother, no doubt, and she had far more experience with men than he did. The only word that came to mind was deadly.

I can hear him too, but it's more like an echo in the distance. Kidnapped. Need help. Jamie. Gold Rush. Tell her Pea Pod. So far that is what I got from the kid. Good thing he is strong in the force, Joseph thought, then tried to change positions in the passenger seat, swimming in pain.

In a blink the gun was back and against his forehead. She was lightning fast, and if she wanted to kill him, it would have been over.

"Yo! You ran me over! Relax! I gotta move; everything hurts. I think I might have a busted rib or three. If you want my help, you best chill with the gun, lady," he snarled in pain, shifted, and stopped talking. His breathing was labored and heavy now that the story was out. She pulled the gun back and looked at him. His eyes were closed, and his shoulder was tucked into the seat facing her. He was half curled into a fetal position and grimaced in pain. If there was any chance she was going to find Paulie, she might need this guy alive. He leaned the seat back so he could lie down a little.

"Where are we going?" he said with a grunt.

"First to my house. Then we will see," she said, watching the man's face turn pale in the in the rearview as he adjusted again in discomfort. Then she pushed the gas pedal to the floor.

The sheriff watched as the man leaned the motorcycle against the wall, then he hobbled over to Jamie's car. There was something vaguely familiar about the man, but Bill thought that often, yet still, something tugged at him.

He watched the Subaru leave tracks onto Klondike as it accelerated away. He thought hard about pulling her over but decided instead to follow at a distance. He put the unmarked Impala in gear and throttled down as the silver car hit the corner, leaving town in a hurry.

20

THE MINE

The van pulled up to the house an hour or so after Paul got home. He thought it was his mom, but a knock on the door caught Paul off guard. The man was holding a box and had a uniform on. When Paul opened the door, the man dropped the box to expose a gun. Paul sent an SOS, walked out the back steps to the van, and was hit in the back of the head.

When he came to, he was in the van, rumbling down the road. He immediately tried touching Joseph but couldn't get through the static. He thought it may be him this time but wasn't sure. His head was still ringing from being clubbed. A while later they slowed and turned onto a rough road. Ten minutes after that, two doors slammed, and he heard the crunch of gravel underfoot as his captors walked away. He struggled into a sitting position and could just see out the front windshield. He managed to get the blindfold loose while lying down, and it fell around his neck as he sat up. Just trees. No noise either. It had been several minutes since his kidnappers left. He scooted around until he found a sharp edge, then began a back-and-forth sawing motion to free himself from the tape on his hands.

After a few minutes, his hands were free. He worked the tape around his ankles and eventually split a seam and began peeling it off. Then he stopped and listened. Still nothing. The silence was nagging at him. He looked around the van for a weapon, anything that would work, anything at all. The glove box was empty, but after digging around, he found a screwdriver under the seat.

He looked out the windows again but could see no building or anything else. He crawled up in the front seat and quietly popped the door open, then crawled out and stayed low. The latch on the door was painfully loud in the silence. Once out, Paul pushed gently on the door. He felt it pass the latching point and leaned against it as he let go of the handle, trying hard to creep. The silence was eerie, and his hackles were up.

Too loud.

It dawned on him that the silence was deafening, and it was the first time in his life he had experienced such. It was all wrong, and he knew it. He dropped down to all fours and crawled under the van so he could look around from cover. One hundred yards away, behind the van on the other side of a fence, was a guard shack that appeared empty. The chain-link fence ran the perimeter from the guard shack on both sides. The guard shack with the gate and arm were at the front, and a mountain with a tunnel was in the back. It was the entrance to a mine. Inside the fence off in the back corner was a contractor's trailer, and the door was cracked open, but again, no noise. Paul knew he should just bolt for the woods, head for high ground, and figure out where he was, but the trailer tugged at him. He climbed out from under the van and darted over to the forest nearby, then then made his way back toward the trailer, concealed in the woods.

There is something in there; I can feel it.

He watched the two covered back windows of the trailer. Quick like a cat, he zipped over to the fence, scaled it, then hit the ground on the other side. He had his back against the trailer in a few heartbeats, then sat down to catch his breath. Then he felt it.

It's the cave.

Joseph called it good mind, and it seemed to be coming from beyond the trailer, from the mine itself. He looked at the mine entrance and took a snapshot with his mind, then another of the guard shack and fencing, then another of the van in the distance and the road in. He mustered all of his mental energy and sent the thoughts like an arrow at Joseph's closed door. The cave amplified his abilities, and so did the rock still in his pocket, so he was assuming whatever was here would do the same thing. After a minute he sent another thought, hoping it would get through.

I am at a mine not too far from Republic.

He wasn't exactly sure where though. He fought the urge to go inside the trailer but knew it was a fruitless effort. He had to see what was in there, had to know for sure, and it seemed likely if he was going to find keys to the van, the trailer would be a good place to start. An ever-so-faint light started to glow from the mine shaft as evening ushered in nightfall.

Joseph was getting past the initial shock of being slammed to the ground, then run over, and now the stiffness was setting in. Everything hurt. His ribs were on fire; his shoulder, neck, and knee were throbbing; and a solid migraine settled in. He shifted around in misery in the passenger seat of the Subaru, each move accompanied by a small groan or grunt.

Jamie, on the other hand, was pushing the car as fast as she could without killing them on the windy road to her house. She wondered where Paul was and if he was ok, wondered where Bryan was and if he was ok, and wondered what she was going to do. Eric didn't care about collateral damage. Her only option was to find him and kill him, after she got her son back. She quelched the nerves that came with the thought. Paul was going to do it if she didn't.

Who was she kidding, thinking they could have a normal life? Thinking they could escape and live free. She did the best she could to pretend. She faked it all around since stepping foot in this town. With Eric, at her job, with her new friends—sometimes she even had to fake it with the boys.

She was a junkie whore, and that hellish thought wasn't going to let her go. Her past had teeth, and it bit down hard on her present often, causing her to bleed remorse, regret and sadness. This time, it brought a harsh acceptance of who she was. So be it. It would be she who spent the rest of it in prison for murder then. All she needed were the boys to be safe first.

She coasted down the driveway with the lights off and rolled up next to the barn. Paul's bike was there and his helmet. She quietly stepped out of the car and looked it over but found nothing. She had the gun from her purse in her hand and started moving toward the house. If Bry were home, she would at least see the light flickering from the TV, but there was nothing inside. No lights. No noise. Just darkness. She made her way around the single wide to the back door. No vehicles were parked behind the trailer. She crept up the door and twisted the knob slowly. It wasn't locked, which wasn't a surprise. They didn't have much worth stealing, and it was a joke between her and the boys. "What are they gonna steal?" they would say.

She pushed on the door and stepped inside. It was quiet and empty. She made her way into the living room and flipped on a light. Vacant and everything in order. On the small kitchen table was a note.

"At Mack's." Bryan was at a friend's house. He might have called the diner and left a message, but sometimes they didn't get passed on.

Jamie picked up the phone and dialed the number.

"Hi Gene, it's Jamie Black. Is Bryan there?" she said, working hard to be patient.

"Hey, Mom, what's up?" Bryan said. Her heart melted at the sound of her oldest son's voice. Now she just needed number two.

"Hey, Bry. How are you?" she said, not wanting to tell him the truth but knowing that she needed too.

"I'm good. We went fishing today and are going to go again tomorrow. Is that ok? Can I stay here tonight? Do you care?" he asked. Jamie was relieved but had to tell him—at least warn him.

"Yeah. You bet. Sounds fun. Hey, uh, Eric has some goons trolling around, stirring up trouble. Paulie had a run in with one of them. Keep your eyes open, ok?" she said.

"No prob, Ma. Is Pee in trouble? Did he sock someone in the biscuits again? You know, you really should put the little guy in military school, Mom. For his own good, you know?" Bryan said, and she could hear laughing in the background.

"You're right. Hey, Paulie and I might need to run to Portland for a few days. If I do you will need to stay with the g's," she said, referring to her parents. She kept them at arm's length in case things ever got ugly. The boys were always welcome, but she and her mother didn't quite see eye to eye. Jamie shook off the thought as Bryan agreed and hung up the phone. She felt better knowing Bryan was going to be in the woods and away from people for a few days. She hung up the phone and turned to go into the bedroom to retrieve some pain killers for Joseph.

Then she came face to face with a man that wasn't Joseph.

His eyes were wild with lust and hatred. She knew he was tuned up and could smell the alcohol on his breath. He smiled a greedy smile, then slapped her hard, knocking her to the ground. He picked up the gun from the counter and slid it into his jeans.

"Get up, bitch," he said, spittle forming in the corners of his mouth. "I told you yesterday I wanted my money. I've had enough of you and your brat. He won't be back anytime soon, and YOU," he said, putting a finger in her face, "are going back to work. Your little vacation has lasted long enough. I am a patient man, Jamie, but it has run out. Your little fantasy life ends tonight if you ever want to see your little shithead again. Myself, I am sort of hoping you don't. I'd like nothing more than to sell the little puke to the highest bidder. I knew you would come home after you got the call." He frothed in excitement and contempt.

Talking was useless. He gamed her and had the upper hand now. If she fought back, Paul would be gone forever, most likely after he left her body on the trailer floor.

"What do you want then?" she asked quietly.

Eric smiled, then laughed loudly. His spirit was filled with malice, and she knew well the look of a madman.

"ACE, YOU KNOW EXACTLY WHAT I WANT. THE SAME THING I HAVE ALWAYS WANTED. YOU!" he screamed, then hit her again. She fell on the floor in a heap, and he climbed on top of her, whispering and clawing at her clothes.

"Jamie, why won't you love me? After everything I have done for you. You still won't love me…" He was close and in her ear.

Then he sat up and roared at her, "WHY?"

Brass knuckles collided hard with Eric Black's head, knocking him out cold, maybe dead. He fell off Jamie, landing limp to her side. Joseph was holding his ribs and half smiled through the pain. Jamie scrambled to her feet in a hurry.

"He is the only one that knows where Paul is, and he better not be dead," she said and rolled over Eric's limp body, then checked his pulse. It was faint but there. She pulled the gun from his jeans and put it in her own. Joseph was leaning on the counter to hold himself up, the brass knuckles he'd kept since childhood quickly disappearing into a jean pocket. When Jamie pulled up to the house she jumped out and took to the house on a run. Joseph, on the other hand, could barely move. Just getting out the car had been a task that took several minutes.

Helluva way to thank a guy for your saving your life…

She handed him the other gun. "Keep it on him. If he wakes up and starts trouble, shoot him in the leg or something." Then she walked to her bedroom, and he could hear her rummaging around. A few minutes later, she came back with a small satchel of items. She pulled out the handcuffs and rolled Eric over, then secured the handcuffs around his wrists, behind his back. Then she took a gag out and put it around his head, the ball in his mouth, and buckled it tightly to his head. Last, she pulled out the duct tape and wrapped his ankles with it. Her frantic movements started to slow as she rifled through his pockets, pulling out his cell phone, wallet, keys, a wad of cash, and a glass vial.

She unlocked his phone and began going through his texts. She was looking for Paul or any signs of him. She muttered a steady stream of threats and curse words under her breath. Jamie Black was anything but a helpless vixen in distress, and it was becoming apparent to Joseph that Paul had inherited the backbone from her.

"I will get the car." She handed a pill bottle to Joseph. "These will numb the pain. Take one before you start popping them like candy; otherwise you will be useless the rest of the night, ok?"

"You will get the car? For what?" Joseph croaked at her.

"The body. He is going with us," she snapped.

Then she walked out the door.

Joseph looked at the bottle—no label—slid the gun underneath his belt, and twisted the top, opening it up. He looked inside and saw liquid gel caps—Tylenol maybe—shook one out, and popped it in his mouth, then swallowed.

They had a hell of a time getting the body in the trunk. Joseph all but useless. His head was swimming from the exertion and the pain.

"I need water," he said and leaned against the kitchen cabinet, wobbling a bit. Jamie found a large plastic cup and filled it up, then handed it over. She looked at Joseph then and went into the bathroom. When she came back, she had a cold compress and an ace bandage.

"The ice will help take the swelling down," she said and told him to lift his shirt. The bruise was immense and covered the left side of his ribcage up to his chest. It was swollen and several shades of purple with some green mixed in. His side had taken the brunt of the impact with the bumper.

"Sorry; that really looks bad," she said apologetically.

"Hurts as bad as it looks," he said and smiled weakly. "But hey, we are making progress now." He groaned when she pulled the bandage tight against the ice pack and began wrapping it around his body. He let go of his shirt and sat back in the chair with his eyes closed. She thought in another life, he'd be cute and charming, but in this one she was done with men. The one in the trunk seemed proof of that.

Joseph was floating. The last few days were surreal, and now he was planning to commit murder. He winced and thought about why he came in the first place. The no man in his soul. He needed a pyre to dance around naked with a head on a pike.

A reap fire.

Understanding flooded his body.

"I have to kill him. It's why I'm here," he said under his breath. Another piece of the puzzle fell into place, the steel in his voice resonating, the task at hand his to own. It had to be his if he wanted freedom from the no man.

His opportunity to right the wrong was here. It wasn't the Dick he knew, but it was another one and just as deserving, it seemed. He had never made it by the library, but that seemed moot now. The obvious became apparent as understanding fully dawned on him.

She didn't respond right away. "Thank you," she said quietly. "Thank you for helping us."

"I know where…to go," he said, and his eyes fluttered a little. She nodded, knowing it was going to have to be dealt with. Then she realized he might not be talking about disposing of the body.

She knew what was coming next as he made his way to the living room floor. He squatted gently and lay down on the carpet. She grabbed a pillow off the small sofa and threw it toward him. The narcotics would put him out for fifteen minutes or so if she were lucky, and when he came to, the pain would be mostly gone for a day or so. It was a blend that a chemist friend made for her when johns got rough. Jamie still wasn't sure where this man came from or who he really was, but she was glad to have the help. He was no friend of Eric's, and right now that was a good thing.

"Paul's atta mine…Republic," Joseph mumbled as the pictures shot through his mind. "It's a big…guard shack and gate. Fence." Then he stopped talking and was snoring softly. She desperately wanted to shake him awake but knew it would be useless. When she had to take the painkillers, she would often wake up feeling like she had been in a coma.

How he knew or how reliable it was didn't matter. She'd heard about a big mine recently and knew it closed last year. It was a big deal in such a tiny town, A lot of locals lost their jobs when the state forced it to shut down. It still resonated months later. They also didn't have anywhere else to start looking, and a closed down mine seemed right up Eric's alley. How many mines could be around here?

It also may not be a bad place to dump a body, and by the time they got there, Eric may be ready to talk if there was no sign of Paul. It was a start.

She called Mark Adams and watched the sleeping man. Mark seemed to like Jamie quite a bit, gave her his number a while back, said if she needed anything just call—likely for less than altruistic reasons, but a phone call never hurt.

"Hey, Mark, it's Jamie Black. How are you?" she said, and after several uh huhs, she spoke up again. "That sounds nice. Hey look, the boys said they were going up to check out an old mine. They said it was a big one with a gatehouse and a fence. Is that something you know about?" Mark Adams said he did. His company installed the fencing and built the guard shack back when it opened. Said it was a drive-in shaft mine, not a pit mine; told her boys will be boys, was happy to help, etc. She scribbled down directions and thanked him, then got off the phone.

21

REAP FIRE

The world spun and tilted sideways. Joseph opened his eyes, stared at the carpet fibers through a horizontal lens, then recognized where he was. The pain coming from his side was dull, and his body felt alive, buzzing, and bubbly.

The reap fire, Joseph. Get the keys.

The surprising thought came bounding in and captured his attention. He stood up and tested his abused body, then looked around for the woman, but she wasn't in the house. It crossed his mind to just take the car but he knew the gunslinger had uncanny speed, and he would end up with a bullet in him for the effort. Then he remembered the other keys Jamie took out of the man's pocket. He walked over to the counter, stretching out gingerly to find the sore spots, picked up the keys, and hit the alarm button on the clicker. He heard honking coming from the barn.

Jamie never checked then barn when they pulled up. She was frantic when she arrived at the house, and Eric was counting on that. He was counting on her to walk in the house, alone, as he hid in the closet waiting for her.

He hit the clicker again, the noise stopped, and he went outside in search of Jamie.

She was at the car when the truck started honking and ran down to the barn with her pistol drawn. She had her back to the wall under the carport and the gun in the ready position with both hands on it, elbows bent, barrel to the sky, then she made eye contact with Joseph as he walked out onto the front porch. She watched him raise the key fob, and the truck reported from inside the barn. She dropped her guard and the gun, slid it back into her jeans, then walked over to meet him.

"I know what we need to do," he said, getting to the point, then handed her Eric's phone and keys.

"You take the truck to the mine and get Paul. He is still there and hasn't left, far as I know. I didn't get the feeling he was in any danger either. As I was falling asleep, I got an incoming message, like the dreams we have been sharing."

Easier than explaining magic rocks, he thought.

"Do you happen to know where a place like that might be? There were a few mines around here when I was a kid, but I think most of them—" Joseph stopped talking as Jamie cut him off.

"I have directions, if it's the right one. I made a call while you were out," she said. "What about you?" She was grateful that Paulie seemed to be alive and not in danger but wasn't slowing down until she saw him with her own eyes.

"I will take your car. I will call one way or the other when it's over. We can meet back here if you're good with it. I will need a ride back to my truck since my bike is in pieces. If I don't make contact in the next twenty-four hours, you should assume something went really wrong." He was confident and in control now. She watched the man talk and wondered who he really was and if he could be trusted. So far, he seemed to be the only link to her son, though, and provided at least a starting point for her to get him back. He was willing to dispose of Eric alone, which made her nervous, but she had to make a choice. Or maybe not.

"If Paulie isn't at the mine or it's the wrong mine, then Eric is the only connection to finding him. What then? I think we should take both cars to the mine and get Paulie first," she said. She couldn't trust him completely and needed Eric alive until she heard from Paul herself.

A fleeting expression of frustration crossed his face. He was in a hurry to get to the reap fire. He dipped his hand into his pocket and started to fish out the rock from the cave.

She isn't going to believe this…

He was going to hand it to her when Eric's phone started to vibrate. She looked at it, then looked at Joseph. The eye contact lingered, then she handed it back to him. He put it on speaker and answered.

"Yeah?" he said gruffly.

"Mom?" the voice on the other end asked hopefully.

"Paul? Paul! Is that you?" she said, her face wrought with confusion.

"Yes! Yes! It's me! Listen: I am ok. I'm at a mine somewhere near Republic. I found a phone; I think it belonged to one of the guys that took me from the house. It had Eric's number on it. I felt like I should call. Was that you Joseph? Anyways, I'm ok. There isn't anyone else breathing here far as I can tell. The mine entrance feels like the cave but different. I can't really describe it, but I think it should be checked out. The only vehicle here is the white van I was brought in."

"Listen, Paulie, keep the phone on you. I will be in Eric's truck and am headed that way. Get into the woods and stay there. Find a spot where you can see the road. DO NOT go into the mine. You don't know who else could be down there. DO NOT go into the mine. Ok? Do you hear me? I am on the way. See you soon."

"Ten-four. I will be waiting. Love you, Mom." He paused, then added, "Good luck, Joseph," with remorse in his voice. Then the line went dead.

Jamie wasn't going to waste any more time sorting out details. She handed the car keys to Joseph and hugged him because it felt like she should. He told her where Paul was, and her son just confirmed it. Paul evidently trusted him, and they obviously had some kind of connection. She slid the lock on the barn door open and swung the bay door wide. Joseph heard the truck roar away as he walked up to the Subaru. He saw a gas can in the carport and picked it up on the way along with a shovel. He put the items in the back seat of the car, then climbed into the driver's seat.

An hour later, he turned onto the forest service road that led back to the Canadian border. He kept going another five miles, deeper into the woods and farther away from humans with every turn of the wheel.

The gravity of the situation became heavy in his mind, but his soul was dancing. The last year or so, he had been held hostage by some unseen force in his life, and it was giddy with joy at the coming retribution. He wrestled with the moral boundaries of it. He was a good man, and this wasn't something he wanted to do. This man wasn't Dick, and he was struggling to connect the dots. The paradox between the inner man and his thoughts created conflict.

Want to or not, it has to be done.

He questioned it again, not grasping why. Why did it have to be done? Why him? Who was he to the kid or his mom? Now that he wasn't physically disabled, at least for the time being, and his head was mostly clear, he began to question his previous motive for volunteering.

The no man: a power that seemed to have sway over the conflict in his soul—specifically, since he had started down a path to sober up.

Once he made the decision to do so, the devil's empire began crawling out of the woodwork.

The Cabalifornians, began to soften his mind. Real or not, they were the group of humans chasing Joseph through every step of sobriety in the world he lived in. Then the no man began thinning his reality, the dreams of the boy and his past started, opening the door to the phantasmal that still seemed to exist in the world.

All of that seemed like somebody else's life now. The howling fantods he lived in and out of each day while trying to break the cycle of addiction made it impossible to sort anything out, but now he was here—with a body in the trunk.

The reap fire. It's the only way, Joseph. The only path to freedom.

He sighed and thought of Memaw's God as he often did. He wondered if the no man was of his doing. All Joseph wanted in this life was freedom, and it didn't matter what he did or where he turned, he always ended up chained down, one situation after another. His childhood, then addiction, and then he was stuck living in California not long after, trapped by lies and duty. The life of a heavy heart.

He realized once again that hope was just a bridge of lies over the river of truth.

The cynical, bitter, and angry thoughts swirled as he got out of the car and slammed the door hard.

Anger and vengeance were boiling over. Now here he was, once again preparing a sacrifice, and there would be no ram in the bush.

It was your own flesh and blood that burned, and only you can right the wrong. Do it.

The intrusive thoughts darted through his mind.

He popped the trunk and faced his reality. The bug-eyed man was breathing hard and sweating profusely. His hands were still cuffed behind his back and his mouth gagged. He saw the venom in the eyes of his captor and tried to pull away, but there was nowhere to go. Joseph reached in and jerked the man out of the trunk hard, caring little of what tender meat may have been grabbed, cut, or bruised along the way. The man hit the ground with a thud and a groan. Joseph dropped the roadside kit on top of him, then slid the knife out of his pocket and cut the bindings away from his ankles. He pulled them off and threw them in the trunk, shutting it afterward. He grabbed the roadside kit, set it on the trunk of the car, and put the gas can beside it. He opened the back door and slid the shovel out then leaned it against the car. The prisoner was still lying on the ground when Joseph reached down and yanked him to his feet. They stood eye to eye.

"Cooperate, and die without much pain. Don't, and you will be holding your own guts while I pull them out an inch at a time." The menace in Joseph's eyes told the truth. He stuck the emergency kit in the man's hands, then put a boot on his butt and pushed him in the direction he wanted to go.

"Walk," Joseph said, teeming with anger.

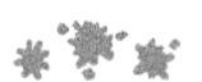

Sheriff Keating yawned as he waited for Jamie's Subaru. He just had a feeling he needed to keep an eye on that car. His intuition rarely ever let him down, and he could smell a good mystery a mile away. The limping fella with Jamie Black was all of that. He realized the man had been in the Gold Rush briefly, earlier in the day. Sara Abrams left, and then so did he, as quick as he walked in at that. The sheriff was still a bloodhound at heart, and that was one love that always drove him back to the job. It wasn't his love for people, locking up criminals, or the law itself. It was the hope of a good mystery among other things. It certainly wasn't prolific in this area, but he'd had some doozies over the years, and it kept him hungry year after year.

When Jamie pulled away in the truck, he thought twice about going down to the house for a little one-on-one time, but just a minute later, the Subaru was pulling out. He turned the opposite way of the truck.

Well, that's interesting, now isn't it? I have seen that fella before. I just know it.

The Impala pulled out slow but kept the Subaru in sight.

Jamie was turning onto Jasper Road in record time. According to the directions, it was another couple of miles to the mine. Peering at her scribbled directions had the truck drifting between the mustard and the mayonnaise stripes on the road more than once. Luckily, she made the turn onto the gravel road with only one near miss.

Paulie was in the woods, watching from the side of the road. He could see the glow from the mouth of the mine and the dim light from inside the trailer. He looked at the trailer and shuddered slightly, hoping his mom would show up soon.

The two corpses inside gave him the willies.

He managed to slip in earlier only to find his abductor lying face up, both eyes missing. The vacant stare scared the wits out of Paulie, and it took every ounce of courage he had to go back inside and grab the cell phone off the table. It was next to a half-drunk beer, where the man seemed to be sitting before his eyes were plucked out. The other man was further into the trailer, lying on his back, but Paul had no intention of checking it out any further. Eyes or no eyes didn't matter. Things had taken a very drastic turn, and the courage he seemed to never be in short supply of was used up. He snatched what he needed and ran back out the open door. Once outside he scrolled through the phone looking at contacts and text messages. He kept one eye on the trailer but after reading the text strings and finding several calls to and from EB, Paul was confident that was his EB. He tried to probe around in Joseph's head but had little success.

Call Eric.

The thought drifted into his mind ten minutes after he cleared the trailer.

A summer thunderhead was moving in, and the sky grew dark and ominous.

All 280 pounds of the sheriff stood stone still. Inches in front of Bill Keating's face was a large, silver semiautomatic with a wooden handle. The law dog had lost a few steps in his years behind a desk and should have left the footwork to one of the younger deputies. He should have called it in and let the team know what he was doing and his whereabouts. Unfortunately for him, he did not. Joseph heard the Impala long before he saw it and wasted no time. He clubbed Eric hard in the back of the head and dropped the man in his tracks. Joseph quickly opened the road side emergency kit and retaped the man's ankles then he headed back for the road and the sound of the coming vehicle. He made his way quietly through the woods, circling back to come up well behind the Subaru. He heard the engine from the coming vehicle shutoff up around the corner then heard the door open. Joseph squatted down in the woods and waited. He was hunting now, whoever and whatever was coming his way. He watched the fat sheriff try to quietly make his way down the road. Huffing and puffing with every step he was more like an elephant than a lion stalking a gazelle.

Joseph held the gun steady and waited. He watched the law dog pass him by without even a flicker of awareness that Joseph was only a few feet away. Joseph stepped out silently behind him.

"Bill Keating," Joseph said, the venom in his voice surprising to even himself. He was undone and deeply disturbed by the lawman's arrival. Long forgotten feelings moved, and he wasn't sure how long he could keep his finger off the trigger. This man was responsible in part for his childhood and the struggle that followed. He never stepped in when he should have. He never took Dick to jail, never charged him, never tried to protect Joseph or his aunt Jo. This man that swore an oath to protect the innocent and uphold the law, then, turned his back while the innocent were left to protect themselves. While the innocent died.

The extreme look of fear on Bill's face as he spun around, trying to draw his weapon told Joseph he didn't have a clue that he was there. The years of complacency made the law dog slow and obtuse. He fumbled with his gun then stopped as Joseph closed the distance, gun raised to eye level.

"No no, Bill, Hands up."

"You don't remember me, do you?" Joseph asked, then chortled, sharp and disgusted. Joseph lashed out, a primal reaction, and whipped the man across the face hard with the pistol. Bill barely managed to keep his feet, and the blood began to run. Joseph teethed with anger and stepped around Bill to his back side. He put the gun against the back of Bill's head.

"Drop your belt where you stand then take two steps forward. Any sudden movement and you die." The menace in Joseph's voice was all too clear. Bill complied. Joseph picked up the gun belt and slung it over his shoulder.

"Turn around," Joseph said, "and walk." He motioned down the road towards the out of sight Subaru with the gun barrel.

A few hours later, Joseph pinned the gun to Keating's head then pulled it away immediately as the urge to just kill the man consumed him. His insides were broiling with emotion. If anybody deserved to die, it was this man. He let out a scream in frustration, then put the gun back to the man's head and shackled his other hand behind the tree quickly before the bloodlust consumed him and the sheriff had a new hole in his head.

He walked back around to face the badge and cuffed him hard again across the temple with the butt of the gun this time. It may have been meant to kill him. Joseph raged and pulled the trigger on the weapon, discharging it nearby. The big man slumped down in an awkward heap and let out a low moan.

The soulless no man would never let him rest if he didn't finish the task. The hole was dug, the pyre was built and soon he would have a head on a pike.

"Little league," Bill finally said quietly after he came to his senses. His head was still tipped down, and the blood was dripping all over his uniform. The thunderhead was rolling in, and a cold, biting wind picked up. The clouds blew in under the moon, cutting off the light as they passed by. Bill's face took on a gaunt and sickly look, streaked with blood as he looked up at the sky and recalled a different life.

He knew he had an iron hand in shaping the man before him. He finally recognized who he was, and the feelings were delivered with the force of a hurricane. Bill was Joseph's little league coach.

"I was young and still trying to climb the ladder." He started out slowly, watching the clouds move against the backdrop of the sky. He knew the man had every right to kill him, if he wanted to, and he probably deserved it at that.

"Gladys and I had just married and bought our first home. Her mother was still living with us then. She was sick, and it wouldn't be long. Still a beat cop for the city before I transferred." Keating's voice was thick with guilt. He looked down and stared at the growing stains as the vivid memories began to play the highlight reel of his worst and most painful decisions. Tears started to roll down his cheek, and his chin quivered as he spoke. He remembered coaching the kid and remembered the night he should have taken Dick to jail but didn't. He should have taken Dick to jail a half dozen times but never did. Shortly after Bill joined the force, the mayor made sure William Keating was aware of who could and who could not be arrested. Business owners and certain other participants were off limits if Bill had any aspirations in his career.

Play the game right, Bill, and someday…

"Dick wasn't exactly influential, but the mayor's wife shared a habit or two with him. So did some of the other local business owners, and they all protected each other. Small-town politics, and I played the game." The sheriff hung his head in shame, sobbing quietly and concluding the story. They both knew what Keating saw in Joseph at the ball field. They both knew Keating had the power to change Joseph's life.

Keating volunteered to coach little league as a young officer, before he had his own son, because he aspired to be somebody.

All he had to do was his job and step in, but he never did.

The sheriff's well of suffering may have begun with turning his back on Joseph, but it didn't end there. His own flesh and blood, years later, paid the ultimate price because Keating did not want to upset the apple cart with the Colemans, who were some of his biggest supporters and one of the most powerful families in town, year in and year out. If he lost them, he might lose a reelection bid, and his name would be tarnished.

It cost him everything in the end. His son, Jerry, took his own life because of the bullying, primarily led by Bart Coleman, then his beautiful wife, Gladys, did the same. The sheriff moaned and wailed loudly. His sin had come full circle. The years of guilt tumbling out of every breath and tear. His sterling reputation paid for in blood, his blood, by his family. The last conversation he had with

Ryan Fedwick at the bar played loudly in his head, condemning him even further.

Joseph listened to the man weep as the pain of the past continued calling to them.

"Please, please just kill me. Just kill me. I'm begging you. Please just get it over with." He sobbed harder, losing all control. "I can't live with this anymore. It killed my wife and son. Please just kill me, Joe. I'm sorry, son. So, so sorry, but sorry will never do. It will never change anything." His belly quivered and shook from the sadness. He bellowed and continued, "It won't mend your life, it won't bring back my wife and son, but you can have your retribution. Take what I owe!" The big man bawled and heaved as the years and years of pain fell from within. Joseph watched the man with hatred in his heart.

He wanted nothing more than to open up the cowardly pig where he stood. Joseph, Jerry, and Gladys were all benefactors of William Keating's lust for power and status. The knife was in his hand, and he stepped forward to the sheriff, intent on gutting him alive, an inch at a time. The big man looked up, and lightning crashed into the forest behind them.

In a fleeting moment, Joseph saw the fragile human inside Keating's eyes as the sky flashed. He saw Memaw and her apple sauce cake and realized she either had a hand in guiding his values, or she did not, and to kill this man would mean turning his back on Memaw. Joseph was being forced to choose between Memaw and her teachings or the no man and his reap fire. Lightning hit again nearby, and the flash showed the chaos and pain of being human in the other man's eyes. Joseph suffered through much and had many of his own scars. Killing him would mean killing Memaw and everything she taught him. The booming thunder brought him back to the present.

The knife slid from his hand and fell to the forest floor.

Joseph felt peace.

For the first time in months, maybe years, his soul was surrendered and calm. The storm the no man, his past and his dreams brought were gone, vanished by the distance of a decision. It was a euphoric and overwhelming silence in his mind and time stood still.

Then lightning crashed again, directly into the treetops above. The sheriff's pleas to die were answered from the heavens above. Joseph dived to the side as a limb fell from the tree, then scrambled for the utility belt and the keys to the handcuffs.

He wasn't going to let the man burn. Joseph was wet and covered in mud. His hand slipped against the utility belt, and he struggled to loose the keys from the carabiner. He slipped and slid as the fire grew steadily. The mountains were getting dryer year after year, and the current rain did little to slow the burn as it came down the tree. The sheriff sobbed, his mumbling incoherent, but it may have been a steady stream of apologies to his dead wife and child. Joseph finally slid the key into the lock and popped a cuff open.

The sheriff ripped his hand away and spun around, an evil, bloody smile on his face, and for the second time in his life, Joseph was clubbed in the head with a shovel. The sheriff snatched it from the tree next to him as he spun. As Joseph fell into darkness, he could hear Memaw's kind and loving voice.

For God so loved the world, he gave his only begotten son...

William Keating took the raggedy, lifeless head of the man, stuck it on a pike, then took his clothes off and danced naked 'round the pyre, his body and face painted in blood just as imagined those many years ago. It was utilitarian as the chanting began, the words flowing steadily through him. His spirit was rife with lust for the growing darkness within, indifferent to the fire that blazed all around as he raised and lowered the head to the rhythm of the cadence while circling the burning body.

Jaka, the no man unearthed during Joseph's childhood, the one that drove him to the reap fire and haunted his soul, laughed with joy and elation as the ritual to bring him into the world finally began.

The truck rumbled up the road and rolled to the gate sputtering. He watched as his mom jumped out, then called to him in a shushed tone.

"Paulie? Paulie, it's me honey," she said, drawing her gun and peering into the darkness.

"Mom! Mom! I'm coming! Don't shoot; it's me!" His eagle eyes caught the glint of moonlight off the steel in her hand. He broke from his trance in the woods and ran to her.

She wrapped up her youngest son as tears of joy ran down their faces. A minute later they climbed into the truck.

"Look, Mom, the guy that helped us change the flat tire wasn't lying. The devil lives in this town, and we need to vamoose. Ok? This place isn't right. The two guys in the trailer are missing their eyes. The eyeballs are gone, Mom! Gone! Somebody or something took them out, and we need to get the hell out of here before whatever it is comes back. You hear what I am saying? Time to go. This place isn't right, and if we stay in this town, we are all going to die!" Paul said again, repeating himself. It was the last day of Prospectors. Saturday was officially here. Thirty-six hours until cleanup would begin. The rain was falling harder, and the thunder boomed from the thick clouds above. She swiveled in her seat toward Paulie.

"The eyeballs are gone?" she asked and shuddered.

Paul pointed to the trailer on the other side of the gatehouse.

"Right there! Go take a peek for yourself. Better yet, let's get the hell out of this town. Forever," he said.

Her head was spinning, and she was exhausted. The emotional toll of the day was setting in, and now they were surrounded by the eyeless dead.

"Ok, Paul. Give me a second," she said and cupped her head in her hands. She wanted her car, then to pick up Bryan and get as far away from here as she could. Paul was right. The devil was growing here and she could feel it in her bones. She looked up and turned over the ignition on the truck, planning to head for home. It turned over, and the motor whined but never fired. She cranked away again, but it didn't come to life.

"Dammit, c'mon, c'mon, c'mon," she said, hoping to influence the machine. Paul leaned over and looked at the instrument display.

The gas gauge needle was pointing at the E.

"We are out of gas! You have to be kidding me! Who does this happen to?" Paul was fuming. He let out a slew of cuss words under his breath as he looked out the window. Then he plucked the phone from his pocket, thinking to call the police.

No service. Damn. Calling the cops might not be a great idea anyways.

The storm was interfering with the already weak service in the area. It was moving in fast, the open trailer door slamming back and forth. The flickering light produced an eerie feeling. He stopped looking at the trailer and crawled in the back seat of the truck, digging around, looking under the seats and in the pockets, coming up with an inventory of items.

There was a large duffel bag filled with all the supplies needed to kidnap somebody. It wasn't much of a surprise considering what they both had just been through. Seems like Eric may have planned to nab Jamie and had everything to do it and then some if she wouldn't go willingly. There was also a small blanket on the floor, a full armored tac vest (which Paul handed to Jamie), a new tarp, a roll of contractor trash bags, a case of bottled water, and a brand-new headlamp still wrapped in plastic. Paul peeled it out of the packaging, popped the batteries in, and put it on. He found a beautiful black Ka-Bar combat knife in one of the backdoor cubbies and unhitched his belt, then slid it through the loop on the sheath. It felt like a small sword; it even had hand guards on it.

At least I am armed now.

He dropped a few of the water bottles into the bag, then climbed back into the front seat.

"Well?" he said and stared at his mom. He sure as hell wasn't spending the night with the dead. She picked up his attitude, tried the truck one last time to no avail, then flipped up the center console.

In it she found another holstered .45 and two full boxes of ammo. She knew the gun was there. Eric always carried one on him and the other in the truck. There was also a radio, a bottle of Jamie's paint pills, and a half-dozen glass vials of the stuff. She removed the top section of the console, and there was an old, leather crossover bag.

She pulled that out and set the console tray back in place, then stuffed the pills and ammo in the bag and started strapping on the leg rig with the .45. She learned to shoot when she was much younger, before life took a turn for the worse. The compact nine she carried in her purse was great for self-defense, but the .45 would punch holes in just about anything. She sat forward and slid the vest on over her clothes, it was much too large for Paul and whatever was out there wasn't going to get them without a fight.

"Keys to the van might be inside. I didn't look through pockets, just grabbed the phone and split, but I don't think I can go in there again," Paul said, looking at the trailer. He desperately wanted to get out of this place. He had honed, reliable survival instincts that saved their lives more than once, and he could feel trouble crawling up his backside.

Paul tried reaching out to Joseph again and felt nothing but the abyss. He wanted to find his friend.

"I will go. Stay in the truck so I know where you're at if I need to start shooting," Jamie said, looking at Paul. She couldn't think of a single time that Paul would opt out of something because he was afraid. His courage was callous and bold. It was something that defined him over the years; he held it in spades since he was a small child. He had never come face to face with dead bodies or been through a kidnapping, though. Her mother's intuition said that wasn't it;

this was different. Paul was changing before her eyes. He looked like he had grown and put on a few pounds. Almost like adolescence was skipped, she saw the man he was becoming. The hard look on his face and tight jawline said he was ready for a fight, that he was expecting one. Even when he knew he couldn't win, his ferocity and determination carried him forward, and it was usually evident. His blazing blue eyes that were always full of mischief, life, and lately anger, were filled with defeat and sadness. Jamie had never seen the look on his face before, and it shamed her. She tried a hint of a smile before getting out, but he looked back at the trailer door as a smacking sound drew his attention.

"Be right back," she said, then jumped out.

The wind slammed the door against the trailer again, and Jamie put her hand on the handle. She was soaked; the sky was shedding water by the bucketful. The torrent sheets blasted her again as she shut the door, closing herself in with the dead men. The lights flickered, and she saw the eyeless man staring at the ceiling; his vacant sockets were bloody and masked his face. His partner lay ten feet away, but his head was turned to one side. She took a breath and a moment, then steeled her nerve and set to task. The white plastic fold-up table was empty, and one end was pushed against the far wall of the trailer. Behind the table were two chairs that were pinned between the table and the back wall of the trailer. A third chair sat at the end of the table, the eyeless man on the ground in front of it. She stepped over to him and began patting him down. The office down at the other end of the trailer was closed, and it rattled in the doorframe. She looked up and realized it moved with the wind.

"Jamie." She heard the softest whisper of her name; it felt like it came from all around her. The uncanny speed the woman possessed was on full display. The .45 was in her hand, and she scanned the room in front of her. The closed trailer door was to her left. The table was behind her, off to the right, and the rest of the trailer was in front of her. The lights flickered again, and she kept her head up and gun in one hand while feeling around the man's pockets with the other hand. The rain pelted the sheet metal roof and sides of the trailer. The wind blew hard outside and made it rock slightly on the axle. She was fully aware of the fact that her mind could be playing tricks on her. The stress, lack of sleep, and situation were likely not going to let her out the door without some spine-chilling moments of terror. She braced herself and put her gun away, reminding herself to breathe through it and get back out to Paulie. She considered herself lucky that she had allergies and couldn't smell anything.

The pockets were empty. She moved onto the second man, quickly crossing the room and stepping around the bodies. The lights flickered again, and she knelt down next to the man, then started her search over. The keys were nowhere to be found. The office door, still closed, bumped back and forth again.

She looked at the door and wondered what to do. She did not want to go in there with the bodies out here. The creeping willies were moving up her spine, and the resolve she had begun with was deteriorating. The wind picked up, howling hard. A fresh torrent of rain broke through the sky, and the lights flickered and went out.

"Jamie." The soft whisper returned, coming from all around her. She stopped moving and put her back against a wall. Her heart began beating wildly, and the thumping in her ears, loud as dread, began rising. She could see the glow of the mine entrance through the window of the trailer. The gun in her hand gave little feeling of security as her mind started to spin. Then a whining came from the office, and the door rattled again in the doorjamb, this time violently, as the wind picked up again.

Her panic welled and climbed into her throat, then something brushed against her leg. The terror broke, and she bolted for the door. The eyeless man moved and tripped her up. She fell and rolled away into a defensive position.

"Jamie." This time it came from the man as he started crawling toward her. She was scrambling to get away with nowhere to go. She pushed away again with her feet and braced herself, then started pulling the trigger. The deafening roar of the .45 and the fire from the barrel were temporarily disabling. The man's head was shredded, but his reach continued. The second man began climbing to his feet. She panicked again and pushed hard against her back with all the strength she had in her legs. The dead man crawling toward her had his fingertips at her ankle.

Then the door burst open, and she rolled backward, down the metal steps into the mud, taking Paul with her.

"RUN!" she said, quickly gaining her footing and untangling from Paul.

He didn't need to hear it twice. He took off sprinting toward the truck with Jamie right behind him.

"THE MINE! GO TO THE MINE!" she yelled as he opened the door. He reached in and grabbed the bag, then threw her the leather one. They both took flight again and headed into the mine, away from the storm. The weather was raging, but once again here was another place where it couldn't be felt. Jamie made it twenty-five feet in, then stopped. The temporary lighting that gave it a glow was on and working. The shaft entrance was as wide as a three-bay garage, and the corridor went on for what looked like miles. She was breathing hard but could finally see again once her eyes adjusted. She turned to face the entrance and switched magazines, then began reloading the first one. Once complete she slid the .45 back into the leg holster and pulled out the .9, then handed it to Paul working hard to catch her breath.

"The men were alive! I shot one of them in the head, and he kept crawling toward me—I think anyways. The second man got up and started walking toward me. You opened the door just in time," she said, finally catching her breath as well as her wits.

"Thank you, son," she said and hugged him tight. The duo was soaked and covered in mud from the tumble. Paul watched his mom and her wild, panic-stricken eyes. She was in disbelief that any of this was real, but he knew better. He felt the world shift at the cave when Joseph showed up. He felt it shift again when the rocks actually worked and he absolutely knew a fight was coming; he just didn't know it was going to include the walking dead. His courage was slowly returning. He dropped the duffel bag and unzipped it, then rummaged around. He pulled out a sawed-off shotgun with a shoulder strap and shell holder on the stock. Then he removed a bandolier belt that went with it. He slid through the bandolier belt like it was a sash, then racked the shotgun to make sure it was loaded. He had been grouse hunting a dozen times, and the weapon had a familiar feel.

Just because there were rules didn't mean they had to be followed.

He handed the puny handgun back to his mother as backup.

After a few minutes, they crept back up toward the mouth of the mine. Paul adjusted the shotgun sling, allowing it to hang, with the barrel aiming down in front of him. He was gripping it with both hands, expecting to use it, though, and could pull it to his shoulder in a flash. Jamie was moving up on his left, the .45 drawn. The noises the storm brought were all they could hear outside the mine. The lightning illuminated the sky in strobes as it shot down. The thunder continued rolling across the mountains in ominous, distinct warnings. In the distance, small orange blossoms could be seen scattered throughout the wilderness as fires from the lightning started to grow.

Jamie could hear the trailer door slamming against the sheet metal siding. The doorway leading into the trailer was black and lifeless. Paul looked to the guard house and along the fence, but there was no one there. The dope light on the truck was still on, and the door was open, but it was empty, as far as he could tell.

"Jamie." The chilling whisper was loud enough for them both to hear. It came from everywhere. She spun and looked behind them, but the track down into the mine was empty.

"Jamie." The whisper was louder this time. Paul's eyes were fixed on the trailer. He knew where it was it coming from even if Jamie didn't. He could feel the evil. He stared hard, waiting, and raised the shotgun in expectation. Red eye shine appeared in the trailer entry. It was deep in the trailer and low, much closer to the ground than a man would be. Paul squinted, then blinked, and the shine was gone as abruptly as it appeared.

He stood frozen, not wanting to move.

"Shoot it," he said quietly, trying not to move his lips. "Shoot the tanks, Mom. Shoot it before that thing gets out."

He looked at her, then motioned with his eyes to the big white tanks at the front of the trailer. The shotgun likely wouldn't reach them, but the .45 would.

"Mom! Hurry up and shoot them! Do it now!" Paul said through clenched teeth.

Jamie, not knowing what Paul saw, aimed and fired in one fluid motion. The ting of the bullet hitting metal was all Paul heard as he dove for cover back into the mine. The explosion shot fire across the entrance to the mine and engulfed the trailer. The inferno was instant, and the noise that followed was a mind-piercing wail. Paul covered his ears as the shriek grew louder. He could see his mom doing the same as tears grew in her eyes. The noise was a searing, relentless high-pitched scream that began carving its way into their heads. Paul's nose started to bleed, and Jamie had a trickle running from an ear. They both were on the ground still. Through blurry vision, Paul saw a cart on tracks that headed down into the mine. He forced himself up and stumbled, then grabbed the duffel along the way and threw it in the cart as he fell in. Jamie was following close behind. She staggered her way to the cart, hands over her ears, and fell against Paul, shrinking down inside the cart, trying to hide from the wretched sound that was killing them. As Paul started to black out, he fell forward onto the joystick at the instrument panel. His unconscious body pressed it forward, and the electric cart began to quietly speed away.

Paul was stretched out in the front passenger seat of the trolly with the blanket from the truck over him. The cart would seat five people side by side, one row at a time, and had several more rows behind him that remained empty. Jamie had managed to pull him over the conductor's seat so he could rest, and she could drive. He briefly woke up after the wailing siren faded, then fell into the deep sleep of exhaustion. His light snoring said he would live.

She figured out how to operate the trolly and, shortly after, realized it was fully automated. It had a functional touchscreen in the dash with a virtual assistant who acted as a guide and conductor. According to Jay, the AI, the mine had at least two other entrances. One was not in service at this time and had been brought down because of safety concerns. The tunnel they were in was an old road through the mountain. It ran twenty-plus miles end to end; the skip and main shaft were in the center, the belly of the mountain. The other exit was another ten miles past that. Jay had tracks that ran end to end. His sole duties were transport of all types, to and from the headframe. Charging docks were at each entrance and the main shaft. All were still functional due to EPA testing, which was required before the mine would be cleared for shutdown completion. Jay was friendly and a welcome addition to Jamie's frazzled mind. He said his battery was low, and he would need a recharge at the headframe to continue the trip to the west entrance. It would be thirty-eight minutes before they arrived at the charging station, and Jay would need two hours charge time before he could ferry them to their destination. Jamie crawled into the row of seats behind Paul and lay down. The men in the trailer were blown to bits and wouldn't be a problem anymore. Paul was safe and sleeping. His snoring echoed off the cavern walls. The light whirr of the electric motor and the wheels rolling on the tracks were the only other noise. She lay down hoping to rest, then shifted around, feeling a pinch against her hip. She slipped her hand into her pocket and pulled out the brass knuckles she picked up off the counter of her house. She inspected them in the dim light and could just make out the inscription.

Praeparet bellum.

She ran her thumb across the engraving unsure of what it meant then slid them into a different pocket and got comfortable.

Three hours until we can walk out of here. Hopefully we will have service, then we can call the cops.

She thought of how kind Sheriff Bill Keating had been to her and Paul since moving to Republic and began looking forward to telling him the story. Eric showed up at her house with his goons, snatched her son, then she showed up, and they took her too—Paul in the van, her in the truck. No idea where Eric was. They were tied up in the mine when they heard the explosion.

The sheriff would look the other way; she was certain of that. If not, she only needed to make him think it spelled trouble for his legacy, and Paulie had already set up those dominos. Waitresses learned everything about everybody; it was one of the reasons she took the job. Small-town politics. It was how the game was played. The thoughts comforted her as exhaustion set in, and she drifted away.

"Joseph," Paul said in dismay and woke up briefly, disoriented and confused. He could feel his friend in the beyond no more. He quickly fell back into a grieving and uncomfortable sleep.

Joseph who? Jamie thought right before she fell asleep, picking up on her son's discomfort.

AFTERWORD

Paul and Joseph were grown from events and times in my life. They are different parts of me, but I am not exactly them, if that can be understood. From what I gather, they are not each other either, but that truth has yet to be revealed, even to me. It became paramount over time to free them, so to speak, that I may live in peace. They brought a world of chaos with them, which required a necessary turn and direction was eventually driven by the no man and his narrative. His power over even me became evident as the story unfolded. Writing the dark horror, was therapeutic, I suppose, as well as intentional. It was over the top intentional at that, but the divergent paths creating the story was critical albeit confusing at times, even to myself. I don't doubt the story is lacking, ugly, incomplete and questionable but such is life. Please forgive my current lack.

Republic, Washington, on the other hand, is a beautiful and real place that has little to do with evil. There is no one represented in the story who is an actual person living in that town, nor did I live there long. While many of the earlier chapter events are drawn directly from my own life and times, Republic just happened to make a magnificent setting for this story to grow from.

Cabalifornians II (not sure of an exact title yet) is underway and will pick up with Paul and Jamie in the mine. Where it goes from there, well, your guess is as good as mine. This is the first attempt to bridge our worlds, and it certainly has come with challenges and more questions than answers. Foundations are not the prettiest parts of the house, but you have to start somewhere. Consider this along those lines.

I hope to see Paul and Jamie survive what's coming. Who knows, maybe the Fedwicks and some others can give a hand, but Keating made his plans clear the other night, and they are disturbing at the least. Joseph cracked a rotten egg in that one. Or maybe it was the no man's plan all along, and Joseph was just a much-needed vessel. In any case, our friends will certainly need all the help they can get. The next story will move further from the sharp edge of reality, a fundamental ingredient in the recipe of escapism.

In the world we currently live in, people need somewhere safe to turn—something to escape to that isn't toxic, deadly, or destructive. I believe our imaginations exist, among many other reasons, to produce a peace that can help heal a suffering mind. More than once, I needed that and still find solace every time I pick up a good book. I can retreat from the world, as many of us often do, and I want to thank the writers of such out there.

You cast a beacon of hope on the shores of the storm. At times it was just a dot, a speck of light in the distance. Other moments, it was a safe haven of warmth and comfort, a fire that burned brightly, on the beach of surrender. In the end, though, it was always a light in the dark, and for that, many blessings to you and yours.

Should you still be in question of the perils of addiction, or a fan of real-life train wrecks, watch for the upcoming prequel to *Cabalifornians, Cabal U.*

It details the truth about reality, the world we live in, the chains and horrors of addiction, and one with the power to break them.

To the real life Cabalifornians- You meant it for evil but God made it for good, and that is the genesis of Joseph's legacy.

Thank you Lord for your everlasting mercy and grace.

CABAL U

(EXCERPT)

Two weeks into the new job, he said, "You've got a lot of hate coming your way."

I watched the words drop from my new supervisor's mouth, like a bomb falling from the sky.

I was out of my element and out of my craft. I once heard that those who can, do. Those who can't, teach. Truth or not, I certainly fit the bill of one who couldn't, and after a year of a recycled life teaching at a trade school in which I spent more time inebriated than anything else, somehow I landed a gig at a state institution, taking a step back toward the stock, standard, and exceedingly average life I had worked so incredibly hard to build for myself and my family.

Or so I thought.

Then my mind zeroed in and carved those words into reality. I lost contrast and definition at that moment, and my universe spun toward insanity, with the gates of hell opening wide.

"You've got a lot of hate coming your way."

It was a voodoo curse spoken directly to my soul. The wellspring all of the chaos in my life began to spawn from.

Witchcraft certainly, forcing the dark side into a living, breathing entity that took over seasons of my life once again. As I was lifetime aficionado of fantasy, science fiction, and such, it opened my imagination to the exploitation of the weaknesses in my reality. I became a living character trapped in a horror story.

The distrust I already harbored toward others became absolutely crippling, and that comment rolled the rock that started an avalanche, leaving me no choice but to run down the side of a mountain daily or be swallowed up and choked out by the madness.

Was it a warning? A real flag waving? Was it the empty cup of addiction or a checkered past coming back to haunt me?

Or could it be, above all else, the one who gave spirit to the dust reaching into the land of blood and bone, clamping his hand on my broken, incomplete life, telling me to bear down, that the time for a cutting had come.

Memaw would say, "Shore enough, das wat it is, chile. For whom he loveth, he chasten."

No doubt I spent years as the prodigal son wasting my inheritance.

It was all too much to take. That was all I knew for sure. After another week of skirting madness and delusions, the weekend brought much-needed relief.

At first.

I heard the car pull up in our driveway, at home, and went outside to help with the groceries. I picked my daughter up, out of her car seat, and walked around the front yard, holding her and talking her out of the confusion of life. She had no interest in our conversation and continued to unleash terror on the neighborhood, screaming at the world for green grass and blue skies. The shopping trip with Momma was apparently agonizing.

As she continued to loose her demons, a grown man from around the corner came running onto our street in jeans and T-shirt at a dead run with his phone held up in front of him, aiming directly at my daughter and me. It was a surreal moment, and I was completely caught off guard. When he saw me staring him down, calmly holding my little girl, he stopped running, put his arm down, and then stared at his phone like he was out for an innocent stroll.

Yet his chest heaved in and out, his need to breathe showing the lie he was caught in.

Is he just another social media whore looking for likes, trying to capture anything he could, or was he a minion of the Cabalifornians?

The latter seemed likely, but the question lingered momentarily.

I watched him intently and shot a sharp whistle out, then waited for him to melt down, or look back up, or do something.

The queer little man continued to walk swiftly to his car, keeping his head down, ignoring the incident and the other humans nearby altogether.

He climbed in his car and drove away quickly, never looking my way.

I felt a long-lost and familiar growl of anger, but that life died at fifteen. I had children that needed me, and it wasn't coming back.

Though Memaw was never really mine, her values lived down deep like an anchor, and it was becoming all I had to keep and guide my course.

The Cabalifornians were working a variety of angles to build a rap sheet, to manufacture a report somebody could sink their teeth into. It seemed likely it was all tied to the state institution somehow, but they certainly were trying to cast a web around my life. I wasn't incubated by the empire and had no issue making enemies, so I was certain there were at least a handful of adversaries cheering on my demise. Show me the man, and I will show you the crime. It was the world we all lived in now.

He who stands for nothing falls for everything, and I developed my convictions over the years.

It was hard march of a life from behind enemy lines in the beginning, and real conviction is often grown through pain, blood, and tears.

The situation brought me back to my roots, and I could feel the tension of a complicated life rising.

ABOUT THE AUTHOR

Born in a land of shadows and sunshine, PJ will always call the mountains in the western United States home, his beloved mastiff his eternal companion, and his little humans the best of friends. He is an avid outdoorsman, is proud to be an American, loves his family, and believes in a God that will still split seas today. *Cabalifornians* is the first book in a series, derived from "bones of truth" in the author's life. The prequel, *Cabal U*, details a journey of despair, hope, and everything in between. Less fiction and more memoir, it drops the reader into a living nightmare. *Cabalifornians II*, (title TBD) picks up with Paul and Jamie in the mine, and Keating setting out to finish a task that Joseph never could.